ONYX

BOOKS BY TIM FRANKOVICH

Heart of Fire
Until All Curses Are Lifted
Until All Bonds Are Broken
Until All the Gods Return
Until All the Stars Fall

Dragontek Lore
Viridia
Incarnadine
Auric
Onyx

ONYX

DRAGONTEK LORE, BOOK 4

by Tim Frankovich

To everyone who inspired my love of reading:
Starting with my parents
And the library
And that bookmobile I barely remember

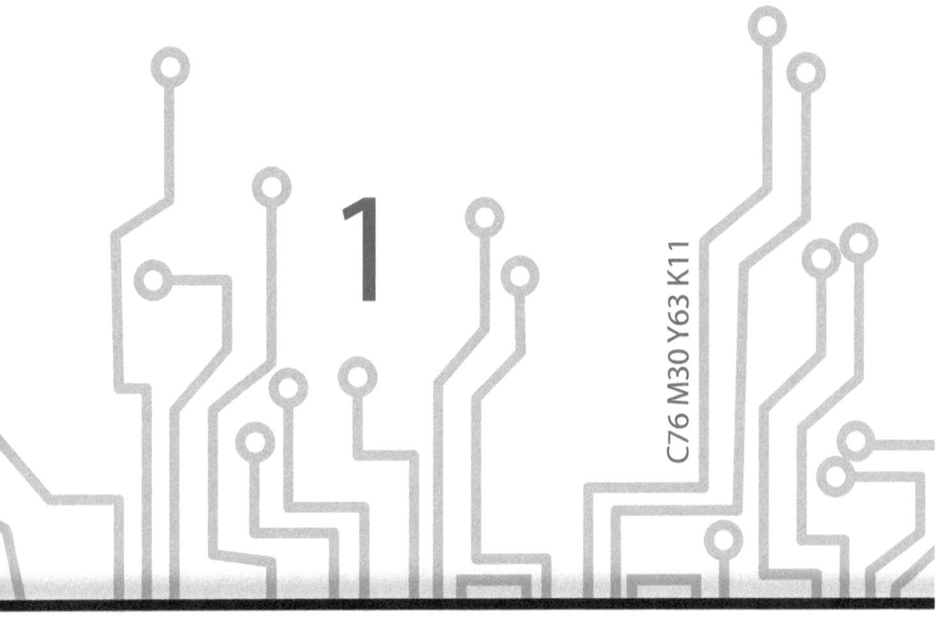

Everything had changed for the city of Viridia. And yet, I couldn't see any differences as I looked out over the streets and buildings I knew so well. Concrete everywhere. Maybe over time, that would change, especially now that we knew why everything was concrete. And more importantly: now that the dragon was dead.

I flicked the switch to activate my talker. "Stacy, are you ready?"

An exaggerated sigh answered me. "Yes, Beryl. Lovat and I are in position, as we've been for the past thirty minutes."

"Good. Mason?"

Some static answered me. For a tech guy, Mason still had trouble grasping how to use the talkers. "Mason!"

"Oh, uh, yeah. I'm… uh, about to head down to the doors." Some more static. "Did I mention how much I'm opposed to this whole thing?"

"Yes. Eight times."

"Make it nine."

"Fine. We're doing it anyway."

"I don't even know this girl you're looking for. I—"

"You're the backup only. We'll let you know if we need you."

"Okay, but—"

I turned the talker off. We only had three talkers now, so I couldn't contact Lainey. But I trusted her more than the others. She would be where she was supposed to be.

From my perch on top of a two-story building's roof, I had a clear line of sight to the front doors of the Emerald Ascendancy. A quick zoom with my cybernetic eyes let me see everything happening anywhere near them. Two Viridian Guard stood right at the doors, extended shockspears at ready. I watched their body language for a few moments: the shuffling feet, the glances in every direction… they were nervous. As they should be.

"The truck is approaching," Stacy reported. "We're moving in now."

I watched Stacy and Lovat cross the street and climb up the stairs toward the doors. Stacy held Lovat's hand and waved expressively with her other hand. To anyone else, she was a young mother or big sister showing off the Ascendancy to a youngster. They approached the guards, one of which stiffened, while the other relaxed. That confused me for a moment until I saw the relaxed one remove his helmet and pull a notepad or something from his pocket. Ah, a fan of Stacy Moss, wanting an autograph.

His partner gave him a shove and pointed at the black truck which pulled up at the base of the stairs. I re-focused on the vehicle. Once it came to a complete stop, the first people to exit were two members of the Sable Legion. Not unexpected, but it did add a bit of complexity to our mission. Four scientists climbed down next, two men and two women. I tried focus on them, but none of them turned in my direction. Our target would be among them, if our intel was accurate.

I couldn't tell from their backs, but one of the females looked to be the right size and shape. The scientists and their escorts advanced up the stairs. The Viridian Guard who'd been talking with Stacy yanked his helmet back on and stood at attention. Stacy and Lovat moved to one side, still acting the part of guests. And then Lovat played his role. He pulled away from Stacy and ran right in front of the scientists. He made an abrupt halt, pointed at the female scientist I'd picked out and began to yell something. I could hear him from my position, though I couldn't make out the words. I knew what he was saying, though. Something about her being an agent of Onyx, and being there when the great Viridia died, and any other accusations Stacy had come up with.

Now came the moment of truth. Would the guards take Lovat seriously? Stacy caught up to him and put a hand over her mouth, staring in shock at the scientist. Her actions confirmed Lovat's words better than anything she could have said. The two Viridian Guard moved forward, shouting and waving their shockspears. One of the Sable Legion stepped up to meet them, holding up a hand. His companion turned to look back at the truck, maybe to call for more help.

That's when the "scientist" made a break for it. She knew Lovat, of course, and recognized her danger. With all the confusion between the Guard and the Legion, she got down the stairs and halfway across the street before they could start the pursuit. Good. She would need a bit of a head start. Wouldn't want her caught out in the open.

I flicked the talker back on. "Mason."

A loud crackle answered me, followed by: "Are you trying to get me killed? I'm in the lobby, for Viridia's sake!"

"Just keep an eye out. If they catch her and bring her back, you're up. I'll let you know when it's clear."

"Good, because I—"

I turned it off again.

Hm. The fleeing scientist bypassed the alley beside my building and ran on. No problem. I ran, boosting my legs, and leaped from one roof to the next. She turned down the next alley. Her closest pursuer, one of the Sable Legion, turned right behind her. He yelled at her to stop, but he wouldn't be able to catch her very well in that bulky armor they wore. Even so, I needed to put a stop to it.

I timed it out, and vaulted over the edge of the roof. A strong boost into my legs protected me as I smashed into the black-clad soldier's back. His helmeted head bounced off the concrete ground, and he lay still. I turned slowly and stared at the two Viridian Guard who'd entered the alley in time to see me.

They came to a stop. I couldn't see through their helmets, but I imagined them staring. My face made an impression these days.

"It's him," one of them said.

"It can't be. He's just a myth," the other one answered. He lifted his shockspear. When I made no move in response, he threw it straight at me.

I'd been practicing this trick. Boosts to my mental acuity, my eyes, my hand, and my nervous system. Loden, I'm still amazed at your genius.

My hand shot up and caught the shockspear in mid-air before it hit me. The electricity crackled around my hand, but I showed no signs of collapsing in pain (though I did grit my teeth a little). With an extra boosts to my arms, I calmly snapped the shockspear in half and tossed the pieces aside.

"The girl is mine," I told them, then turned and ran down the alley. I heard no sounds of pursuit. Smart guys, after all.

Lovat waited for me at the end of the alley and pointed to the right. I nodded and turned. Sure enough, I saw our target ducking into another alley two blocks away. Perfect. Viridia had been built with so much concrete and so many buildings so close together, it made it easy for people to get lost if they wanted to. Unless we were the ones doing the chasing, of course.

I dashed to the new alley and watched her run toward the end. Where did she think she was going, anyway? Her master was bold, but he wouldn't show his face here. He might have more agents in the city than we knew about, I reminded myself. Fortunately, the scientist wouldn't get far.

Even I jerked at the roar that brought her to a sudden halt. She tried to backpedal and almost fell. I zoomed in a bit so I could see. A white cat-like creature almost the size of an adult human stood at the end of the alley. Muscles rippled across its back and legs. It opened its mouth, showing a pair of elongated fangs, and growled. Glacier scared me sometimes, and she wasn't even done growing yet.

Lainey stepped into view, holding her rifle in one hand. She put her other hand on the cat, warning it not to pursue just yet, though the target didn't know that.

I returned my eyes to normal and watched the scientist scramble back and run toward me, keeping her eyes back at Glacier and Lainey. I stepped to the side and waited in the shadows until she almost passed me. I reached out with lightning speed and caught her arm. She gasped, and spun to see me, her black hair flying. Her glasses almost came off, but she caught them with her other hand.

"Hello, Dusk," I said.

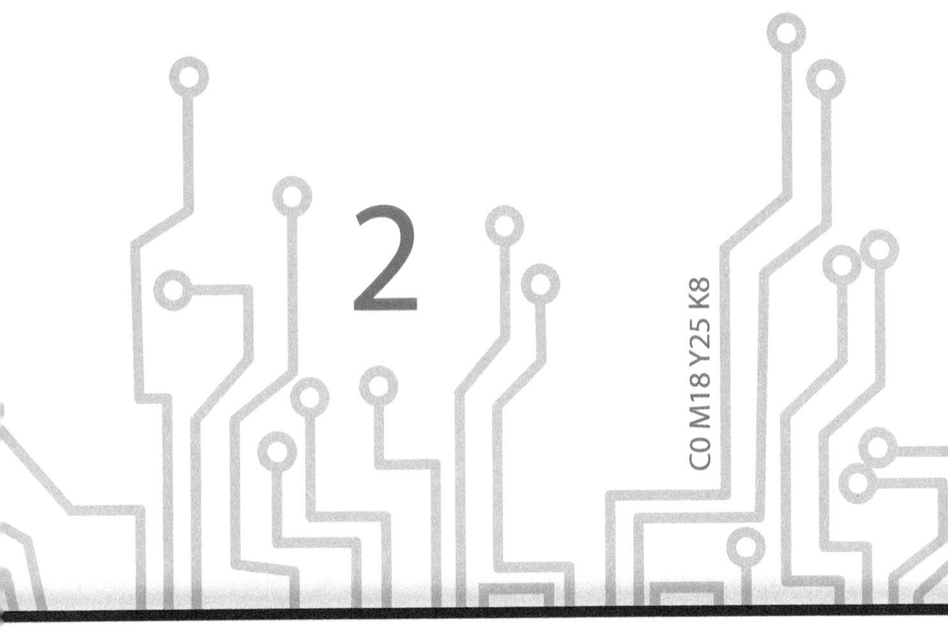

I'll give her this: Dusk regained her stoic composure faster than I would have expected. "Beryl," she said. "I like the new mark."

I tilted my head so she could get the full effect. "I thought it appropriate. Jaden did a good job." Where once my face bore the standard green chromark of all citizens of Viridia, now it included lines in gold, black, blue, and red. I saw it as a symbol of embracing my role to serve all the people of The Circle.

She looked back at Lainey and the cat. "The last time I saw that thing, it was the size of a house cat. What happened?"

"It grew." I took a step closer. "Where's Onyx, Dusk?" My former best friend, after revealing himself as the lost dragon Onyx, destroying our home, and kidnapping my friends, had disappeared. No one had seen him since then.

The tech girl straightened her glasses. "He's preparing for his reign. How did you know I'd be here today?"

I knew she was trying to distract me, to keep from answering my questions, but I still answered: "Onyx wants the cyb tech breakthrough he helped create. He can't come in himself and ask for it, so I figured he'd send someone in with the scientists from Atramentous. You were the logical choice. Now where is he? Where are the rest of my friends?"

Dusk wrinkled her brow. "Your friends? I don't know anything about your friends."

I walked right up to her. She took one step back, but stopped at a growl from Glacier. "Kelly. Bice. Don. Where are they?"

"Oh, the broodmare? She's being kept safe, of course."

My hand flew out, but I stopped, just short of slapping her. She flinched only a little, and her glasses slipped down her nose. "I don't know anything about the other two," she added.

"Then where is Kelly?"

"Safe, I told you."

"I'm done with patience, Dusk. You will answer my questions."

"Or what?" She straightened her glasses again. "I know you. Without Onyx to goad you, you're a simple man, too soft for what needs to be done. You won't hurt me. Your conscience won't allow it."

I channeled a boost into my left hand and punched a hole in the brick wall beside us. Maybe not the smartest thing to do. That would hurt once my adrenaline wore off. "You don't know me any more," I said in a low tone. "Your boss betrayed me and took everything away from me. You two destroyed my home and took my closest friend. I have nothing to lose any more. What makes you think I won't hurt you now?"

"Come on, Beryl," Stacy's voice came from behind me. "You can bluster all you want, but she's right." The actress walked up beside me. "You're not going to hurt her."

Dusk smiled a bit. "You must be Stacy Moss," she said. "I'm—"

Stacy punched her in the face, sending the glasses flying across the alley. "I know who you are. You're one of the dragon droppings that kidnapped a good friend of mine." She pointed at me. "He may not hurt you, but I bleaking will. And then I'll feed what's left of you to the cat."

"Eh, she doesn't have enough meat on her bones," Lainey said. "Glacier wouldn't care for her much."

"I don't know," Lovat said from his position atop a garbage bin. "I've seen her gnaw on an empty bone for hours."

When did these three become so bloodthirsty? I shook my head. "You heard them, girl. We're not the same group you betrayed three months ago. Tell us."

Dusk's eyes darted from one face to the next. "You're bluffing."

Stacy looked at Lovat and put out her hand. "My knife, please, Lovat." The boy produced a thin dagger from inside his baggy clothes and handed it to her. Stacy held it up and looked at the tip. "You learn a lot of interesting things as a stage actor," she said. "You never know what you'll need to know to play a part to perfection. In this one play four years ago—it was really dark—I learned about a killer who would keep his victims alive for as long as possible." She turned to look at Dusk. "By cutting them in places that would cause great pain, but not incapacitation. Would you like me to show you where some of those places are?"

"Y-you can't. The Viridian Guard will—"

"The Viridian Guard is a shell of its former self," I interrupted. "We've made sure of that. Almost half the force quit, either out of fear or because we persuaded them. The remaining draconics have been in hiding since the dragon's death. We've been able to do almost whatever we want in this city."

"The Sable Legion, then," she argued. "Atramentous is sending more of them here to maintain order."

"Maybe so, but unless they're arriving right this minute, they're not going to help you."

Stacy took a step and pointed the dagger to the right of Dusk's belly. "I think I'll start here."

"Gods, you people are insane. You can't hope to stand against the might of Onyx!"

"Spare us the religious speech," Stacy said. She grabbed Dusk's shoulder with her left hand and brought the dagger in close. "And stop stalling. Answer Beryl's questions or I start cutting."

"Where's Kelly?" I demanded.

"I don't know!" Dusk exclaimed, looking down at the dagger. "I swear I don't know!"

"You're one of his top two people. How could you not know?"

"He took her away, along with the high priest! He sent me to Atramentous to wait for his orders. I don't know where they went!"

"How does he communicate with you, then?"

"In my dreams."

I blinked. I didn't expect that answer. "What?"

"He, he comes to me in my dreams." A shy smile spread across her face. "They're very… erotic."

Ew. "He tells you things in these dreams?"

"Yes, sometimes. He told me he'd arranged for me to be on this trip, and told me where to find the data I needed." She sighed. "If I please him, perhaps one day I'll be allowed to bear one of his children as well."

"That's sick," Stacy said.

"The women who give birth to draconics die!" I told her. "Is that what you want?"

She looked at me. "You wouldn't understand. You don't know what it's like to have a god like him."

No, I didn't. And I didn't want to. I looked around at the others. "Do the rest of you think she's telling the truth?"

"I've never heard of dragons communicating through dreams," Stacy said with narrowed eyebrows. "Maybe I should cut her just once to see if she changes her story."

"I've told the truth!" Dusk insisted.

"I've heard of it," Lainey said. I looked toward her in surprise. She didn't look back, busy scratching Glacier's head.

"But even out—"

"Beryl." Now she looked at me. She was reminding me of our agreement. She and her father had told me many things about the world outside The Circle, some of which I had a hard time believing. But I couldn't tell the rest of the team, at least not yet. Frustrating, but I had agreed to it.

"All right." Stacy lifted the dagger, but kept her eyes on Dusk. "Let's say she's telling the truth, for the sake of argument. Where does that leave us?"

"Do you know of any place where Onyx would go?" I asked. "Places you went before you came to us? Places he talked about?"

"I've spent my whole life in Atramentous," she answered. "I worked with Mister Onyx briefly when he lived there, but I didn't know his true glory. He didn't reveal that to me until he recruited me again to join your team. He never said anything about other locations, other than the cities."

"None of the cities would harbor him, and we'd have heard about it, anyway," I muttered, mostly to myself. This whole operation hinged on Dusk knowing more than she was telling. Well, the first part of the operation, anyway.

"Guess it's time to move to phase two," I said. I pulled the talker from my belt and activated it. "Mason, are you still there?"

"Ack! Yes, yes. I'm here. What's happening?"

"Stand by." I flicked it back off.

Dusk bent and picked up her glasses. "What's going on?" she asked. She wiped the glasses off with the tail of her shirt and held them up to look for dirt or damage.

"You know that data you're supposed to get for Onyx?" I stepped back next to her, and took the glasses from her hand. I carefully placed them back on her face. "You're going to get it. For me."

She laughed in my face. "What makes you think I'll do that?"

"Here's how it's going to work," I explained, ignoring the question. "You'll go back to the Ascendancy, explaining how you managed to escape from your pursuers after a long and difficult chase. You'll reassure them you're all right and able to continue the job you came for. Then you'll hook up with our man on the inside and give him a copy of all the data you obtain."

"Again: why would I do that?"

I gestured to Lovat, and he tossed me a backpack. I held it up. "Recognize this? Rick left it with me, so I could find the explosives in it to destroy the green dragon's power source."

"It's a backpack. So?"

I opened the pack and withdrew some heavy-duty tape, a small rectangle of a putty-like substance, and a device with a single switch and a button on it. "Except he left more equipment in here that he might not have intended me to keep." I handed the switch device to Stacy, and turned back to Dusk. "I'll need to see your ankle."

Her skin was already pretty white, but I think it paled a little more. "What for?"

"You asked a question. I'm giving you the answer." I knelt down at her feet. "You're wearing loose pants. That helps." I started to lift one of her pant legs.

She yanked her foot away. "What do you think you're doing?"

"I need to guarantee that you'll do what I ask."

"There's no need for that. I'll do it."

I looked up at her. "Well, that's a fast change." I sighed. "Unfortunately, I just can't trust you. You've betrayed me once already."

She glanced at Stacy, who toyed with the switch. "I don't... that is..."

I ripped off a piece of tape and stuck it onto the rectangle. "I'll just tape this to your ankle. Stacy will hold the activator. As long as you do what I say, you can take it off when it's all over."

"No, I... I promise I'll get the data for you."

I shook my head. "Not good enough."

Dusk dropped to her knees and spread her arms out wide. "I swear on the gods of Onyx and Amaranth to do what you ask. May I be banished to the Chromatic Hells if I break my oath."

Okay, I didn't expect that. I looked at Stacy. She pursed her lips and nodded.

"Well... maybe we can leave this off after all." I put the tape and rectangle back into the backpack. I got to my feet. "You do know my capabilities, right? If you do break your oath, I will come after you. And Onyx is not around to protect you."

She nodded, her breath coming in short, quick gasps. "I'll do it."

I gave her a few more instructions, then pointed to the end of the alley. "Go." She ran.

Stacy stepped up beside me. "What is that thing you were going to tape to her leg, anyway?"

I pulled it back out of the backpack. "It's just some colored clay. But it looks like the explosives that Rick used. I wouldn't really blow a girl's leg off." I chuckled. "Maybe she's not as smart as she thinks."

Lainey joined us. "Did you hear her oath? Onyx and Amaranth."

"Yeah... kind of odd for a girl from Atramentous." I pulled out the talker. "Gotta check on our guy real quick." I toggled the switch. "Mason, she's on her way back. You remember what to do, right?"

"Oh, uh, yeah." His voice came across in a whisper. "I help her out, and tell her I'm with you."

"Once she's got the information she came for, she's going to give you a copy," I told him. "Hold on to it, and I'll get it from you when you get off work today."

"Got it. Oh, I think she's coming."

"Sign off." I put the talker on my belt, but left it on.

"I saw one problem in your strategy, though," Stacy observed, handing me the useless switch device.

"What's that?"

"You told her to give you a copy, not the real thing. She can still give that to Onyx."

I nodded, flipping the switch on and off. "I know. That's why Lovat is going to follow her when she leaves."

The orphan jumped down from the garbage bin with a big grin.

"Wait, wait, wait," Stacy objected. "Lovat's going to follow her back to Atramentous? Isn't that dangerous?"

"I can do it!" Lovat protested.

"He's grown up a lot in the last few months, Stacy," I said. "We all have. I think he can handle it." I put the switch back in the backpack, then laughed a little. "This isn't even Rick's backpack, you know."

"Very funny." Stacy folded her arms. "Is my part in this mission over now?"

"Sure. You can go back to your real job. We'll wait for Mason, and then head back to our new hideout."

"You're really staying in the city now?" She shook her head. "I know we've built you up as some kind of legendary revolutionary, Beryl, but it's still dangerous to be here."

I pointed my thumb toward the end of the alley. "Didn't I just have this conversation with her? The Viridian Guard isn't going to stop me, unless they all come after me at once."

Stacy's sigh came across as more sad than exasperated. "You've really changed. I don't know if Bice or Loden would like this arrogance."

"Yeah, well, one's dead and the other's missing. Right now, I have one goal: rescuing Kelly."

"And that's why I'm helping you." She stepped forward and gave me a quick hug. She pointed at the others. "Lovat, always a pleasure. Lainey, good to see you again."

The cat actually growled a little. Stacy laughed. "And Glacier. Can't ever forget you!" She patted it on the head and sauntered out of the alley.

"Now what?" Lainey asked.

"Lovat, you may as well go get into position," I told him. "Remember: keep an eye on her until she's getting that information to Onyx. Then let us know how it's happening."

"You got it, Beryl!" He waved at Lainey and took off.

"And now we wait." I turned back to Lainey. "I think this building here is empty. Maybe we can find a more comfortable spot."

"At least out of sight," she agreed.

I broke open the side door and we entered what looked to have once been some kind of business. We found a desk and chair in one small office and settled in to wait for Mason. I gave Lainey the chair, and stretched out on the desktop myself. Glacier sniffed around a bit, then settled on the floor near the door.

"Did you think that was going to work that well?" Lainey asked.

"I didn't see any reason for it not to work," I answered, staring up at the ceiling. Some of the tiles were cracked, and three were missing.

"Stacy's right. You are getting arrogant."

I turned my head to look at her. "I'm stronger, faster and tougher than any other human in The Circle. I've been practicing for three months with these powers and learning more about myself. Once we get Loden's notes back, I'll learn even more."

"You're not invincible."

"I know." I looked back up at the ceiling. "But I'm the closest thing to it, outside of a dragon. I'm sorry, Lainey. I just don't care about holding back any more. I'm going to do whatever it takes to find my friends and stop Onyx."

"What will—" she began.

The talker squawked. "Beryl. Beryl!" Mason hissed. "It's not good. It's not good at all!"

I flipped my own switch. "What's going on, Mason?"

"He's here. I think he knows who she is!"

"Who's there?" I sat up and looked at Lainey.

"Oh gods. I thought… I didn't know, Beryl. I didn't know they did it."

"Did what? Mason, you aren't making any sense."

"Holy Viridia! He's seen me! He—" The talker stopped.

I flipped my legs around over the side of the desk. "Mason? Mason?"

A different voice answered me. A voice I knew, but never thought I'd hear again. A deep voice, with just a bit of a rasp.

"I believe Mason doesn't want to talk any more."

I hesitated, then asked, anyway: "Who is this?"

A low chuckle answered me. "I recognize your voice just as well as you recognize mine, I believe. Welcome back to Viridia, Beryl. It's been a long time."

"Who is that?" Lainey asked, her face scrunched up.

I dropped the talker onto the desk, jumped off, and backed away several steps, staring at it.

"It's Troilus Green."

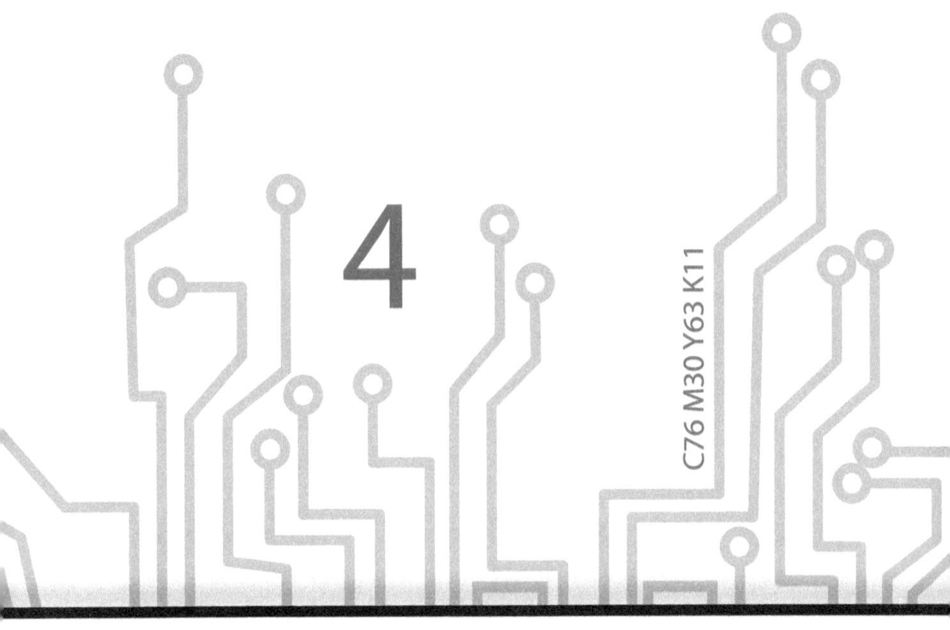

"Isn't he the dead one?" Lainey asked.

I nodded, too shaken to do anything else. She didn't know. She hadn't been with us when that draconic hunted us down throughout the city, threatened my friends at every turn, and killed Loden on the train... before I killed it. Or so I thought. Mason told me it lived, but I didn't believe him. Until now.

"Come, Beryl. Let us reason together," the voice of the dead offered.

"What about Mason and Dusk?" Lainey hissed.

Reluctantly, I picked the talker back up and flicked the switch. "What do you want, draconic?"

"Ah, there you are. I only wish to get reacquainted."

"I'm here." I took a deep breath. I could handle this. One more enemy wouldn't make that much of a difference to our mission.

"Now I understand where our breakthrough came from," Troilus Green said. "The notes are about you. It's truly fascinating what that scientist did to you. Quite a shame that I had to kill him. He could have done much more for us."

"His whole purpose was opposing you!" I snapped. "He would never have helped you."

"Now, now. You know I can be persuasive. I look forward to... persuading these two friends of yours here."

I shot a look at Lainey. That answered the question. Fortunately for us, Dusk knew next to nothing, and Mason knew even less. We'd only recruited him again for this job. Even so, I felt sorry for him.

"Two?" I asked. "I know one person that I 'persuaded' to work for me. Other than that, I have no friends in that building."

"As you say. I will uncover the truth." The draconic chuckled. "I've been hoping to hear from you again, ever since I woke up. I've heard a lot about you in the last few weeks."

"How did it feel to wake up and discover your god was dead?"

"Hmm, yes. You were there, I saw. As you were there when Caesious died. How long have you been working for Onyx, anyway?"

"What? I don't work for Onyx!"

"Really? We now know he's the one behind all of our troubles of the past few months. Once we are able to fully explain this to the other cities, this war will be over and we can unite in tracking him down."

I stomped around the desk in frustration. It galled me to think Onyx would get the credit for all we'd done so far, but what good would it do me to deny it? To claim it was actually a group of humans behind it all? I suppose in some ways, it was better for Troilus Green to follow this theory. Sure, maybe the war would end, but the dragons would still be trying to kill one of their own number, and he'd be trying to kill them. Same kind of chaos. But I couldn't just drop the topic.

"Do you think the other cities will listen to someone who let his god die?"

I smiled at the growl I got in response. Glacier lifted her head and growled back.

"I am coming for you, Beryl. You tried to kill me once, but I will not underestimate you again."

"I'll do a more thorough job next time," I promised. "I mean, I thought jamming a sword down your throat and then crashing your train would do the trick, but... I'll do better."

"As will I." The draconic's voice deepened. "I don't need you alive to yank the final tech secrets from your brain now. With what we have, your body will be enough to complete the process. And then we—I will live forever. All thanks to you."

"Good luck with that." I flicked the switch off and turned to Lainey. "We may as well find Lovat and head back to base."

"There is one more thing I want you to hear, Beryl," came the voice from the talker.

I rolled my eyes. "That thing won't shut up," I grumbled. I flicked the switch again. "What is it?"

I heard someone say "Hey, wait—" followed by an abrupt crack. My eyes met Lainey's. I'm sure mine were as wide as hers.

"I'm sure you can figure out what that sound meant," Troilus Green said. "Until we meet again." The talker went silent.

"W-was that Mason?" Lainey asked.

I didn't know. It sounded like it might have been his voice, but... I didn't want to think about it. "Let's get out of here."

It took about twenty minutes to find Lovat and inform him that his mission wouldn't be happening. Naturally, he was annoyed, since it was the first time I'd trusted him with something so big. Together, the three of us returned to our current base of operations.

I took a twisted sense of pride in my choice for our headquarters: the former shrine of dragon god worship where Bice had once served. With the death of the dragon, many of the priests had abandoned their work. Kind of hard to encourage people to worship and sacrifice to a dead god. Some of the temples and shrines still remained open in various odd ways, but this one had been left empty until we came back and took it.

Bice would have been proud of how Lainey and Lovat took care of the plants he'd left behind. I suspected that with the dragon's power source destroyed, it might be a little harder to grow things in and around the city, but they were doing pretty well, from what I could understand.

Of course, I'd cleansed the place of anything related to the dragon worship: statues, documents, anything at all that even hinted at the dragon. I took delight in destroying it all.

We used the sacellum as our primary "home," the spot where we ate, slept, and planned our next moves. Its best quality might be the most mundane: it had a working bathroom. We hadn't had one of those since Don fixed the one in our warehouse hideout.

We also made good use of Bice's old gardener's cabin. Lainey's father stayed there with his equipment, much of which I didn't understand at all. He met us outside when we returned, his lanky frame recognizable the moment we entered the gates. "You're back earlier than I expected."

"It didn't go well," Lainey reported, giving him a quick hug.

Carl Roberts acknowledged Lovat, then turned to me. "What happened?"

I explained how we captured Dusk and sent her back in. "Everything appeared to be going right, and then Troilus Green showed up."

"A draconic?"

"The draconic." I snapped a twig off a tree beside the path. "The one who killed Loden, and caused us so much trouble the last time we lived here. I thought I killed it."

"Are we in danger here?" Carl asked. "I never should have let you talk me into coming down from the mountain. I knew this was a mistake!"

"Relax. It doesn't know where we are, and doesn't have the resources it needs to truly track us down." Then again, Troilus Green had fought us here once before. At that time, Bice used the power to stop it. At least with the dragon's source gone, no one could use the mysterious power any more. I started to feel better about the situation. What could it do to us, anyway?

"But you lost our one asset inside the Ascendancy, and our one connection to Onyx."

"I'm sorry that I didn't account for resurrections from the dead!" I threw up my arms. "How was I to know?"

"How did he know, anyway?" Lainey asked.

"What?"

"How did the draconic even know something was happening? That Mason and Dusk were working for you?"

For a moment, I trembled a bit, considering the possibility of betrayal once again. I suspected my mind would always jump to that conclusion now. But no, not this time. I shook my head. "Mason was an idiot. They probably noticed him using the talker out in the open, and then waited for him to speak to Dusk before moving in."

"I hope you're right." She didn't look convinced.

"Look, Onyx didn't get the data either," I pointed out. "We succeeded in that much, at least."

"But Atramentous is getting it, right?" Carl asked. "He might be able to get it from them easier than here."

"I don't think so. It's the same reason why it wouldn't be easier for us." I broke the twig into multiple pieces, letting them fall onto the path.

"Atramentous still has a dragon, all of his draconics, and a full army. Onyx won't find it easy to get past all of them. We're safer here, and have a better chance of getting what we want from here."

"Then how will we get it?"

"I guess I'm going to have to break into the Emerald Ascendancy again."

Three months ago, after my best friend betrayed me, I thought it was all over. Then Lainey stepped in. She saved everything.

I mean, it couldn't have been much worse. Onyx destroyed our home. We know he took Kelly with him. We don't know what happened to Bice and Don. Protogonus Blue died. Not long before that, Peri also died, saving his city. And Caedan left us. Lainey, Lovat, and I were left alone with new recruit Jaden. We had no home, no tech, no food, and no hope.

The first thing she did was go hunting, while I buried Protogonus Blue as best as I could. He was already halfway buried beneath the rocks in the caved-in tunnel leading to Loden's old workshop. I covered the rest of him with rocks and filled it in with some dirt. It would be awkward to have him there if I ever managed to get the workshop un-blocked, but I didn't know what else to do. Lovat helped as he could, while Jaden waited outside. His bad leg wouldn't allow him to climb into the tunnel.

Lainey returned with meat. I don't even remember what it was, but I remember eating around a fire with the others. I don't think I tasted anything. While we ate, Lainey outlined her plan to return to her father. Jaden wasn't thrilled with the idea of walking halfway across The Circle and climbing a mountain. The discussion stalled until I pulled myself out of my depression long enough to suggest taking him to Stacy. Lovat could handle that once we got near the city of Viridia. We stashed the remaining four-wheeler in the remains of the tunnel and set out on foot.

Stacy, of course, was shocked and horrified when we told her all that had happened. She took Jaden in, and promised to keep him safe. I still remember what she said to me while no one else was listening.

"Beryl, I've seen you cope with things that would break an ordinary man. And I'm not talking physically. This may be the worst ever, but you can get through it." She glanced back at the others. "You still have friends, even if some of them aren't here right now. Take some time. Recover. And then come back." She looked me in the eyes. "You hear me, Beryl? You come back. Viridia isn't done with you. And I don't think you're done with it."

I mumbled something lame in reply, but her words stuck with me. Lainey, Lovat, and I made the trek back to her father's hiding place in the mountains. He was pleased to see us, but not so pleased to hear all of our news.

"You promised to keep my daughter safe!" he accused me. "Being around three different dragons is not safe!"

"She kept me safe!" I answered. I looked at her. "She's… amazing."

"Every time I was in danger, I overruled Beryl to be there," Lainey said. "He did his best, Father." She spread her arms out. "And here I am. Safe and sound."

He grumbled a bit more, but then got around to asking why we'd returned, anyway.

Lainey pointed at me. "Beryl's broken. He needs to see more of the bigger picture, to convince him to get back into the fight."

A little part of me surged up inside, wanting to insist that I wasn't broken. But I was. Rick's betrayal destroyed me. Losing Kelly and Bice ripped away my heart and soul. I felt completely empty inside.

Mister Roberts studied me. "There is a much bigger world outside your Circle," he said at last. "And your struggle may have repercussions far beyond what you can see within these mountains."

My heartsick brain tried to parse his words. How could what I did here have any impact on a world beyond the mountains, a world none of us knew anything about? I couldn't grasp it.

"I'm going to tell you some things," he went on. He glanced at Lovat. "And only you. All I ask in return is that you tell no one else anything that I tell you, unless Lainey or I give you permission."

"Who am I going to tell? I have no one left."

"That's not true," Lainey said. "You still have friends, and more will come. You're a lightning rod for change, Beryl, and it will happen, if you don't give up."

"Fine. I won't tell anyone."

"Walk with me," Roberts offered.

We left his cave hideout and stepped out into the cold air of the mountainside. There, looking down toward the city of Caesious, he told me of the outside world, of the people who lived there. He described technology beyond anything I knew in some ways, yet way behind The Circle in others. And then he told me about another battle for freedom. At first, I struggled to believe it. Then, I felt even greater despair, for what he described made our struggle here seem completely pointless. But he carefully redirected my thoughts, and I finally saw it: the big picture. What we did here could make an impact. Not only could we change the lives of the million or so people who lived within The Circle, but eventually, we could changes the lives of even more outside it. At the time, I didn't think we would have any chance at all, but I agreed to keep fighting. For now.

Nothing Carl said took away the unbelievable pain of Rick's betrayal, or the grief and despair I felt over Kelly, Bice, and Don. But he gave me something to fight for, a reason to move on.

I kept his secrets. Though Lovat pestered me about it, and then later Stacy asked a lot of questions, I held to my word. Would it make a difference to the others to know what I knew? Maybe. Maybe not. Over the next few days, as we stayed in the mountain cave, I felt a tiny spark of hope begin to grow within. The others refused to let me mope or wallow in my sorrow. Every time I tried to be alone, one of them dragged me back into the company of the others.

I also grew closer to Lainey. It was inevitable, I suppose. She was the only person my age left. Lovat and Carl seemed to hit it off pretty well, and the two of us were often left alone together. She had already pulled much of my own life story from me, but I found myself telling her even more: about my parents, their death, Loden, Bice… And now that I knew more of the outside world, she told me more of her own life, including the loss of her mother a few years ago. I could certainly sympathize.

I would like to say we fell in love. And maybe we did. I could tell her feelings toward me were growing, or at least I thought I could. And I felt…

strongly about her. But every time we got close, every time I thought I might kiss her or something, Kelly's face filled my mind. Stupid, I know. But wherever she was, Kelly was in deadly danger, and I felt guilty entertaining a relationship under those circumstances. It wasn't that I had a wild idea that Kelly would fall back in love with me once I rescued her from Onyx. Or maybe it was. I don't know. How did I even tell the difference between the love between friends, and the love between… lovers? A line would be crossed somewhere, but I didn't know where or when.

Kelly once told me I didn't know what love meant. And then she told me my problem was that I hadn't had anyone show me how to love. She implied a lot of it had to do with the physical side of things, but I think it's more than that. Bice called Peri's sacrifice of himself the "greatest love." And I think he was right. Love is being willing to sacrifice part or all of yourself—your needs, your desires—for someone else.

In that sense, I loved all my friends. I would do anything for Kelly, Bice, Lovat, Caedan, and Lainey—and to a lesser extent, Don and Stacy. But who would I be willing to sacrifice the most for? I couldn't answer that. And so, I didn't pursue the romantic side of things with Lainey… much. I think it disappointed her, but she was always hard to read.

After three weeks in the mountains, I stood outside one day, watching The Circle. I looked toward the city of Caesious. All of those people lived today because of Peri. Could I do less than he? Hiding in the mountains accomplished nothing. If I were going to do anything for my missing friends, it would not be from there. A movement in the sky above the city caught my attention. I zoomed in with my cyb eyes and made out the shape of a red dragon flying lazily over the city. From here, I couldn't tell if it were Incarnadine or Amaranth, not that it mattered. The dragons still lived, still ruled, even though two of them were dead. My job wasn't over.

Stacy's words came back to me, and I told the others I would return to Viridia. From there, I argued, we could reach out to our other allies, and begin our work anew. We could search for Onyx and our missing friends. At first, Carl wanted to stay in his mountain, but Lainey and I persuaded him to join us. I didn't say it at the time, but his medical skills might be needed when we found Kelly.

And so, carrying a lot of equipment I still didn't understand, we returned to the city of Viridia.

"Will you be breaking into the Ascendancy before or after your usual trip to the Asylum?" Lainey asked.

I hesitated. Once a week or so, ever since we arrived in Viridia, I took a trip back to the ruins of our former base, the Achromatic Asylum. I spent a few hours moving rocks in the tunnel. I figured in a couple more months, I might break through to Loden's workshop. I could work faster, but one fear kept me from it: that I would find Bice and Don's bodies inside.

"This is more important for the present," I decided. "We need to act fast, before Troilus Green understands what we were after."

"You mean before he tortures it out of the girl," Carl said.

Ouch. I had been trying not to think about that possibility.

"Do you even know what you'll be looking for?" he asked. "Or what it will look like when you find it?"

"Loden's notes. I mean… I know his handwriting…"

Carl rolled his eyes. "How you've managed to stay alive through all of this is beyond me."

"Then what do you suggest?" Annoyance colored my words. I'd been doing "all of this" for the better part of a year now. I think I deserved some credit.

"Obviously, I'll have to come with you. It'll give me a chance to see this city's tech development up close and personal."

I blinked. I did not expect that. "Um, it's going to be dangerous in there. We might run into one or more draconics."

"Then it's a good thing I'll have you, isn't it? When do we leave?"

I looked at Lainey, who shrugged. I couldn't really argue with her father, but I didn't want to take him into the Ascendancy either. I knew him to be brilliant, but he wasn't a warrior in any way. I would have to protect him. I just… I didn't know if I was up to the task. Things hadn't gone so well with people I wanted to keep safe.

"I, uh, I guess it would make sense to go at night," I said at last.

"And you have a way in, correct?"

"I think so. It's the way Rick—Onyx—and I were going to take the last time." I looked away. I hated thinking about that day, but it shaped everything.

He nodded. "Fine. I'll gather a few things. Flashlights and such. You don't have night vision in those eyes, do you?"

"No." At least, not as far as I knew. I'd tried different things with my eyes, but all I'd been able to accomplish was zooming. "Oh, maybe we should go by Stacy's and have her give you a fake chromark, just in case."

"I'm not wearing one of those." He shook his head. "Besides, I'm less conspicuous than you."

That much was true. My facial tattoo, much larger than anyone else's, would never be mistaken for anything else. I'd done that on purpose. Once back in Viridia, we engaged in multiple missions, from destroying a Viridian Guard station to gathering food for out-of-work laborers. In every instance, I made sure to be seen. Over time, I built a reputation. People didn't know what to call me, but they knew the man with the multi-colored chromark, and they knew he fought for them.

After Carl disappeared back in the cabin, I turned to Lainey. "I'm not sure about this. I don't know if I can protect him."

She stepped up and patted my arm. "I have confidence in you." She gave me a wry smile. "But if you're worried, maybe you should take Glacier with you."

I glanced at the cat, stretched out in the sun now, ignoring us. "That thing never listens to me."

"She's a cat. They don't listen to anyone."

"Except you."

She giggled. "Sometimes."

I sighed. "Let's find something to eat. Tonight is going to be stressful."

Inside the sacellum's inner circle, with the sun shining down on us, we made a meager meal of various dried foods. We didn't have much, most of the time. And when we got meat, it usually went to Glacier. Lovat and I were annoyed by it, but I couldn't deny the advantages of having a growing saber-toothed cat on our side.

"You were really freaked out by that draconic," Lainey said after a while.

"It's supposed to be dead," I answered, taking a drink of water. Maybe inside the Ascendancy, I could snag some good food somewhere.

"It's more than that." Lainey studied my face. "You've stood before a dragon and showed more courage. But when this Troilus Green spoke, you… you were afraid."

I didn't want to discuss it, but I'd told her everything else. "It's hard to explain. I'm… connected to that thing in strange ways. And for the first weeks of our rebellion, I kept running into it everywhere we went. And then it killed Loden. And I killed it. Or thought I did."

"What do you mean by 'connected'?" She got to her feet and dusted crumbs off her shorts.

"Loden fixed both of us," I explained. "The accident—the one that killed my parents—almost killed me and the draconic. Loden used his work on Troilus Green to explain away his work on me." I scratched the back of my neck. "But I got the best of it, apparently."

"So he's got a cybernetic implant too?" Lainey stretched her arms above her head. Fewmets, she was attractive when she did that. I thought about looking away, but I didn't.

"No, uh… I mean, it has, um, some cybernetic parts. Two of its claws, and part of its, uh, chest. I'm not sure how much inside might be cyb." Did she know how much she was distracting me? "Oh, and it has a plate on its face where Rick—Onyx—stabbed it."

Lainey sat back down. "So you were at the same place at the same time. That makes you connected?"

"I don't know. It's weird. Maybe there's more to it, somehow."

"Like what? Did Loden mix your parts up?" Her green eyes twinkled.

"Don't even suggest that!" Images of the operation I'd seen in the Flame in Incarnadine flashed in my head: the doctor removing a heart from a human to place into a draconic. Loden would never have considered anything like that!

"Then he's just another draconic," Lainey pointed out. "You've fought and killed how many of them now?"

I thought for a moment. "Technically, I think the other green one a few months ago was the only other one I've killed. But I did a lot of damage to a couple of red ones, and a gold one. I could have killed them."

"Then this one is no different. You don't need to be scared of him."

"I'm not scared," I said aloud. But I wasn't sure. Troilus Green gave me an odd feeling inside. Besides, I hated it almost as much as I'd hated the green dragon. Viridians wouldn't be free as long as that thing remained in power.

"All right." Lainey got up again. "Where has Lovat gotten off to, anyway?"

"Up here," his voice called. We looked up and saw his shaggy head peeking over the inner ring of the sacellum's roof. He and I had been up there before, when we'd come here to save Bice, and…

"We fought Troilus Green right here," I recalled. "Bice trapped it with his magic. I could have killed it then, but we had to get away." I'd also killed a man for the first time, but I didn't like to think about that. "It almost killed Kelly." That moment started a chain of events which led to us fleeing the city, and eventually killing the blue dragon and Troilus Green. Or so I thought.

A horrid thought struck me. If Troilus Green hadn't been dead, what about the dragon? We'd killed it, hadn't we? For sure? No, no. Rick had made sure. And apparently, he knew what he was doing. Ugh. Just like he'd made sure in killing the green dragon.

"I'd better take a nap," I said, getting up and moving out of the direct sunlight. "Won't get any sleep tonight."

"Sure." Lainey frowned a little, disappointed in something, but I didn't know what. Girls still confused me.

I moved into my own little room, what had once been some kind of storage for priestly junk. I tossed and turned for a while, my mind sorting through all that the day had brought so far, but eventually I managed to doze off.

It felt like only a few minutes before Carl shook me awake. "It's time," he said.

I got up and followed him out. Yeah, it was time. Time to visit the dragon's old lair.

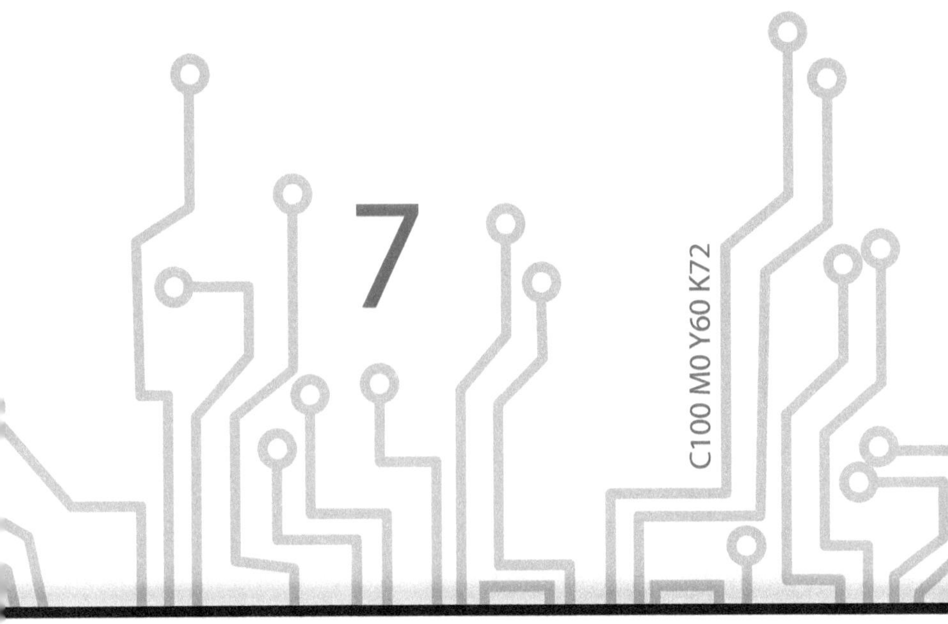

7

With a little extra guidance from Lovat, we made our way to the edge of the city nearest to the dragon's former source of power. Carl carried a satchel with flashlights and some other tools. I took only my sword.

Not far away, I saw a great mound of earth and lights from people moving about it. The burial place of a god. Were the visitors there to mourn? To hope he might come back? Since Onyx tore the green dragon's head off, that didn't seem very likely. I knew some priests still refused to give up their worship, but how did you worship something that was dead? In life, the dragon never did much for them; how much less could he do in death?

In the dark, we reached the former source. I hadn't visited this spot since I blew it up. None of the enormous trees, and very little of the rest of the greenery survived the explosion. The spring still flowed, but its course was erratic throughout the devastation caused by the explosion.

"You said there's a tunnel?" Carl asked.

"Yeah, as long as it didn't get buried." I shone my flashlight around briefly. We couldn't use them too much out here without attracting attention.

To get to where the tunnel entrance had been, we had to cross the enormous crater caused by the source's explosion. Once we stepped down into it, I turned my flashlight back on. To my surprise, I saw sprouts of grass popping up throughout the crater. I guess some of the dragon's power source effects remained in force, strengthening life in this area. Who knows? Given time, it might grow back similar to the beauty it had before.

My light shone across an area of greater darkness. I scrambled over the uneven ground and got a closer look. "Over here," I called. Carl joined me and we looked down into the darkness of a huge tunnel. Only a small entrance remained.

"Looks like a bit of a drop," I said. "I'll go first." Without waiting for an answer, I jumped off the edge. I sent a boost to my legs and bent my knees. I landed several feet down without difficulty. Carl sat on the edge of the hole and then slid down without difficulty. Sure, I guess you could do it that way, if you wanted to be boring.

We both turned on our flashlights and looked around. "You came this way before, right?" Carl asked.

"I wasn't very conscious at the time, but I crawled my way out." I peered as far as I could down the tunnel, and sniffed. "I should warn you, though. This is where the dragon used to live. Some of his poison may still linger in the air."

"I'll take my chances."

I nodded and started walking. The ground, worn down from hundreds of years of the dragon's movements, was smooth and almost completely barren of any debris once we'd traveled a hundred feet or so past the entrance. It sloped down at first, then leveled out after a while.

"How long does this go on?" Carl wondered.

"I don't know, exactly. How far was it to the Ascendancy?"

"I don't suppose you ever bothered to calculate that."

"No, why would I?"

He snorted. He confused me sometimes. He seemed to be amazed at some of what we did, but annoyed when we failed to meet some expectation I never would have thought about.

We walked on in silence for some time, before he broke it again: "Have you even kissed my daughter yet?"

I tripped. I don't think anything on the ground caught my feet, but the question took me so off guard that I lost the rhythm of walking. I stumbled for a few feet, then managed to catch myself against the tunnel wall to keep from falling. "Uh, I, uh… no, sir."

He snorted again. "I don't know what to think of you sometimes, boy."

He didn't know what to think of me?

"I know she's falling for you, so you'd better treat her right."

"Yes, sir."

"I mean it. If you hurt her, emotionally or physically, then I will hunt you down, cyborg or not."

"I will not hurt her, sir."

"Good. Glad we got that settled."

The silence of the tunnel remained unbroken for a long time. I didn't keep track of the time, but I suspect Carl did. Eventually, the tunnel started to slope up again.

"Better turn the lights off," I warned. We flicked off the flashlights and let our eyes adjust to the darkness. Up ahead, we could see the glow of lights again.

I'd told Carl about the interior of the dragon's lair, but we had no way of knowing if anyone would be there. Would the draconics hang out in their former father's sleeping place? Would there be anything they could gain from the site? I couldn't think of anything, but I was smart enough to know there were many things I still didn't understand when it came to the dragons and draconics.

We moved slower now, both because we had to move uphill, and because we walked mostly in the dark. The light ahead grew stronger the higher we climbed, eventually becoming bright enough to see all around us. And then we reached the entrance to the dragon's lair.

It looked almost precisely how I remembered it. The underground chamber stretched to an immense size. Dozens of giant electric lights shone from the ceiling, reflecting off numerous mirrors mounted on the chamber walls. When the dragon had been here, the lights and mirrors reflected off its green scales in a myriad of ways. Now… they were just bright lights. One other large opening lay off to our right, leading into the central grounds of the Emerald Ascendancy itself. We couldn't go that way. From what I remembered, there weren't any doors into the building that way. And it led into an enormous pile of dragon droppings.

No, our target was the doorway across the chamber and a little to the left. I knew the draconics used that door when they came to visit the dragon, so it must lead into the Ascendancy somewhere. We just had to get through it.

Carl and I walked across the chamber, our footsteps echoing through its vastness. Even though I knew the dragon was dead and gone, I almost expected him to emerge from one of the passageways, furious at our invasion of his home.

"This is disconcerting," Carl muttered.

"Yeah." I didn't know what else to say.

Eventually, we reached the steel door, a foot taller and wider than doors designed for puny humans. As I remembered, it was set into the rock itself, with no visible handle. I felt around the edge, seeing if I could get a grip on anything. When Rick and I were planning to come this way, we'd discussed using his cybernetic hand to help tear this door open. Without that option, I wasn't sure about the best method of gaining entrance. Maybe I could use my sword as a pry bar… but I'd probably end up with a bent or broken sword. Not worth it.

"Any ideas?" I asked.

"I thought you knew how to get in."

"I know it's through this door! I just… don't know how to get the door open." I tapped the door with my knuckle. "I could try hitting it as hard as I can, to see if it pops loose or something."

"You could…" Carl examined the outside frame of the door. "Or you could smash through the rock right… here,"—He pointed to a spot midway up the side of the door.—"and break through to the locking mechanism, I believe."

I lowered my eyebrows. "Hit the rock? I guess I could… I'm not sure if my finger bones will like that…"

"Not with your fist, idiot." He reached into his satchel and pulled out a hammer. "With this."

Oh.

I took the hammer and looked it over. "Well, as long as it doesn't break…" I aimed it at the spot indicated. "Right here?" He nodded. I took a firm stance, sent a strong boost into my arm, then brought the hammer around as hard as I could. Sparks flew and a few shards of rock broke off. The sound of the impact echoed through the cavern. Even though no one was around to hear, it made me self-conscious. I glanced around, half expecting to see Viridian Guard soldiers charging us.

"Angle it a bit more from the right," Carl suggested. I did as he said, and this time, a much larger piece of rock broke off. It narrowly missed my foot before ricocheting off the floor and bouncing away. Carl stepped further back.

I hit it again and again. Under Carl's direction, I changed the angle of attack multiple times, chipping away at the rock. After six or seven such hits, I could also see the hammer taking damage. "It's not going to last much longer," I pointed out.

"It doesn't have to. You're almost there."

One more hit exposed some kind of mechanism, showing a number of wires. Carl opened his mouth to say something, but I was in a rhythm and hit it again.

The lights went out, plunging the entire cavern into darkness.

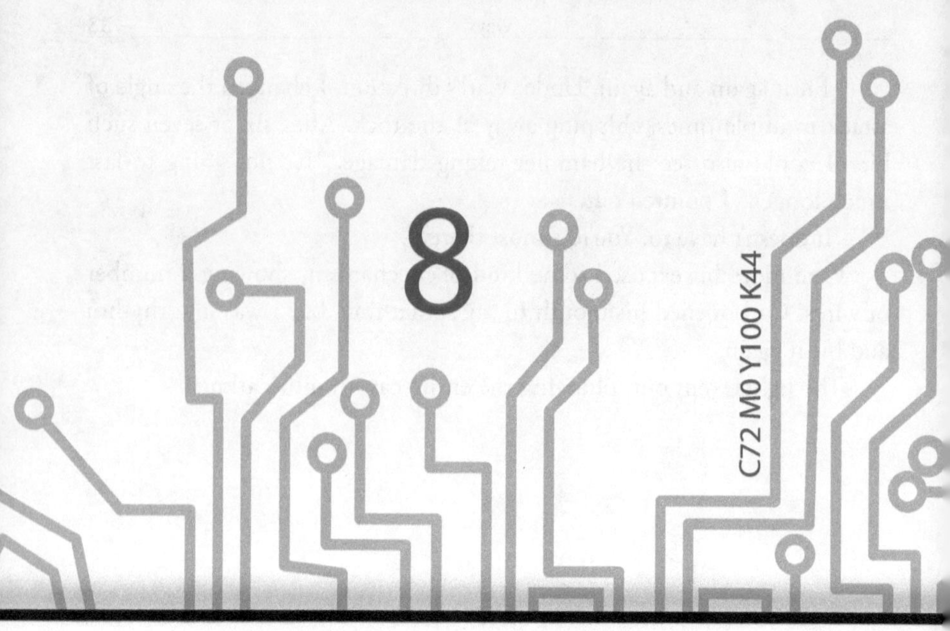

8

Carl flicked his flashlight back on. "Well, that's not helpful," he grumbled, pushing past me to look at the door lock's mechanism.

"That doesn't make sense," I complained. "Why would the door be connected to the lights for the whole place?"

He studied the exposed wires and smashed parts. "Maybe it's not. Maybe someone heard us. Or maybe the lights just go off at a set time… in the middle of the night…"

I drew my sword. Better to be prepared for danger.

"Just give me a minute… Here, hold the flashlight for me." Carl handed me the flashlight, took the hammer and knocked a few more pieces loose. He reached inside to do something I couldn't see. A few seconds later, a loud click echoed almost as much as the hammer blows. The door popped inward and swung a few inches to the right.

I pushed it open the rest of the way with the tip of my sword. A hallway stretched ahead of us, dimly lit by a row of lights near the floor. At the end of the hall, I saw the unmistakeable shape of an elevator door. Great. A single button decorated the wall beside the door, slightly higher than I would have expected. Carl put the hammer back in his bag and walked down the hall. I sheathed my sword and followed.

"How do you feel about elevators?" he asked, finger hovering over the button.

"Not so good. Could be anyone waiting when the doors open." I tried to pull on them myself, but couldn't get a grip. "In the Flame, Rick pried these open and I climbed the shaft."

"Well, I'm not doing that." He pushed the button. I waved for him to stand back, while I waited, sword at the ready again.

Only a few seconds later, the doors slid open without a sound, revealing an empty elevator car, decorated in garish green shades. As I stepped into it, I realized that everything about the elevator was sized a little bit taller and larger than normal. The operating panel was a few inches higher than normal, the ceiling a foot or more higher, and so on. They'd designed everything for the draconics' exclusive use.

I studied the buttons on the panel, recalling what little I knew of the interior of the Ascendancy. A lot of tech work took place on the third floor, the very first button on the panel. That's where Mason worked… or had worked. But the floors above that interested me more. Those were the more restricted levels. The numbers ranged from four to fifteen. If I remembered correctly, anything about twelve wasn't on the map for the Ascendancy's human workers.

"Pick a number," I suggested.

"Fifteen. Start at the top and work our way down."

"Fifteen it is." I pushed the button and watched the doors slide closed. We were committed now.

The elevator vibrated as it ascended. Carl moved to one side, so he wouldn't be visible when the doors opened. I chose to make a stand and be ready. I gripped the sword with both hands in front of me, facing the doors. If someone were waiting for us, I'd be ready to charge.

The elevator stopped. The doors slid open. I stared down another dimly-lit empty hall, but this one looked more like the hallways in the lower parts of the building, complete with doors to either side. Carl followed me out, aiming his flashlight around.

"At least it's not the draconic living quarters," I said, turning on my own light. "I kind of figured they'd be at the top."

"Impractical," Carl said. "It would be a long trek down to the dragon's lair, or to anywhere else important. They probably live somewhere in the middle."

Huh. I wouldn't have thought about it that way. "It wasn't like that in the Flame." I hadn't actually seen the draconic living quarters there, but I was pretty sure they were in the restricted levels near the top of the building in Incarnadine.

"Viridia strikes me as much more practical," he answered. "Look at the way the city is laid out. Look at these signs on the doors. Everything is organized."

I shone my own light on the door signs. The numbers confused me. They all started with fifteen, but included multiple decimal places. The words weren't much better. "Genetics Laboratory One," I read aloud. "What's that?"

"Dark stuff," Carl answered. "But not what we're looking for." He walked down the hall, checking the other doors. "This floor seems dedicated to the life sciences. Cybernetics is a close relative, but it won't be here. Let's go down a floor."

I agreed. Since no one had shown up yet, we used the elevator again. The fourteenth floor proved a disappointment as well, appearing to be nothing more than storage for old experiments. Any other time, I would have been curious about exploring, but we had to watch our time.

"We're doing this wrong," I realized. "They need humans to do their work, right? The draconics can't handle the delicate jobs involving wiring and stuff."

"So?"

"So humans aren't allowed above the twelfth floor. That's where we should be."

Carl nodded. "Can't argue. Maybe the draconics live on thirteen, then."

On the twelfth floor, I felt a surge of elation when I read the first sign: Cybernetics Laboratory Three. The door was locked, but I opened it in seconds. I stepped inside and used my flashlight to examine my surroundings. Carl stepped in behind me and flipped on the overhead lights.

"Hey!"

"Why not? No one seems to be around."

"Yeah, but…" I looked to the other side of the room. No windows. The light wouldn't be seen from outside.

Carl walked around the room, examining different devices, opening drawers, and thumbing through papers. He'd been right, of course. I wouldn't have any idea what to look for. Where in all this mess, organized though it might be, would we find the notes I wanted?

"This room seems focused on artificial internal organs," Carl reported. "Kidneys and such." He raised an eyebrow at me. "You got any of those?"

"How would I know?"

We moved on to the next room, a more practical-seeming design with numerous cybernetic hands and feet in various stages of construction. Most were human-sized, but a few appeared designed for draconics.

In Cybernetics Laboratory One, we finally struck gold. As soon as we flipped on the light, we were faced with an enormous model of a brain suspended over a circular table. Numerous wires hung from it, and a large area at the very back looked like some kind of mechanism grafted onto the model.

"We'd better search thoroughly in here," Carl observed.

Once again, I let him take the lead. I examined the model. Was this what my brain looked like? It didn't look like something Loden would do; his work always had a more… stylish look to it. The train, the four-wheelers, the *Sky Claimer*, even my artificial eyes: they all had a certain elegance to the design. This looked like someone just slapped some metal and wires onto a brain.

I poked the brain with a finger. It felt like some kind of rubber material. I tried to remember what I'd learned about brains in the Learning Years. The front portion had to do with decision-making, I think. The implant here was at the back, so… I'm not sure what that meant.

"Most of this is worthless," Carl announced. He tossed a huge sheaf of papers onto the floor. I started to say something, then stopped. I guess it didn't matter if they knew we had been here.

Carl moved to an elevated desk. "Now this looks promising." He opened a binder and flipped through a couple of pages.

I tugged on one of the wires connected to the brain. Maybe this design intended the wires to run down the spinal column. What difference would that make?

"Beryl. Come look at this."

I joined Carl and checked out the binder. Each of the pages inside were hand-written, but placed inside clear plastic sleeves to protect them. It took me only a quick perusal to know: "That's Loden's handwriting."

"I thought it might be." Carl glanced up at the brain model. "This is far beyond what they have modeled there. And there are references to his two patients."

"Two?" I frowned. I was the patient he'd worked on, except... Oh. Right.

"I would be patient number two, apparently," said the voice from the door.

The voice of Troilus Green.

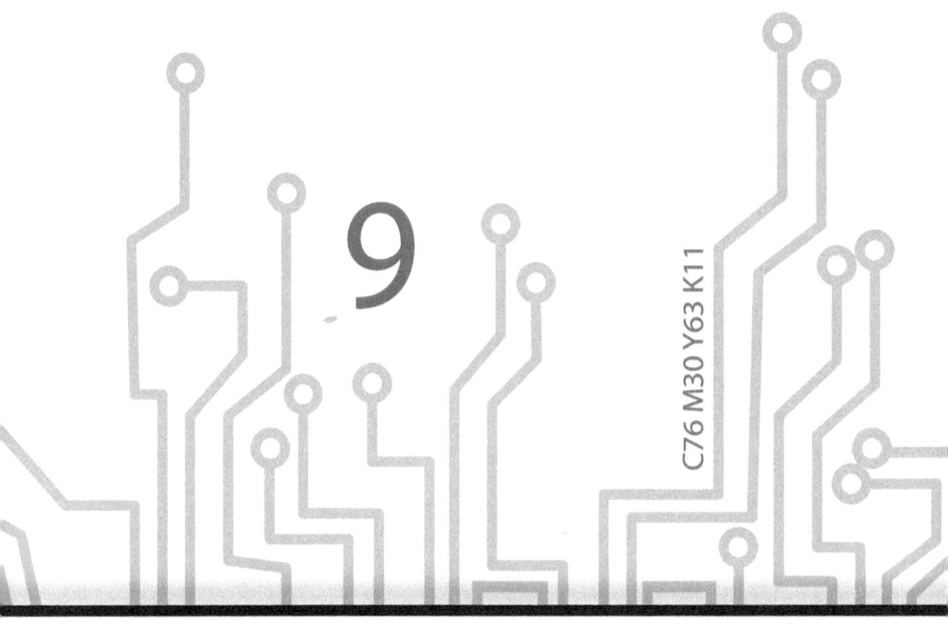

9

I drew my sword and turned to face the door. The green draconic filled the exit, watching us with an amused air. Or maybe anger; I still couldn't read draconic expressions much.

Troilus Green looked much the same as the last time I saw it, when I plunged my sword down its throat. Its jade scales glinted from the lights not far above its head. As usual, it wore a dark green robe with purple edging. The hood was thrown back, and the robe gaped at the front, showing the chest criss-crossed with strips of gleaming metal pulsing with an electric green glow. Loden had done that work, I knew, but not the metal plate on the left side of its head where Rick had stabbed it.

The sickly-sweet odor drifted across the room toward us. Carl sniffed behind me. I channeled slow boosts into all my limbs, preparing for action.

"The girl told me you were after the scientist's notes," the draconic said. "I've been expecting you to come for them, though I must admit you arrived sooner than anticipated."

"I enjoy surprising you," I answered, taking a step to get into better position for charging him. I actually said it too; I didn't have to think of it later. Maybe it wasn't the best taunt, but… progress. Sort of.

"It does seem so." It waved a claw in the air. "Charging me would not be a surprise, by the way. Far too predictable. I do hope you have something more interesting in mind."

I didn't, but my eyes darted about the room, trying to come up with something.

"And you always come with a different friend! This one has no mark. Fascinating. Tell me, friend of Beryl, how are things outside The Circle? Are you a slave for—"

"Just shut up, draconic," I interrupted. "I'm taking back these notes that were stolen from my friend, the friend you killed, and we're leaving. You can try to stop us, but it won't end well for you."

"I do regret killing the scientist," Troilus Green said, with a short bow of its head. "At the time, I did not realize his true abilities. He could have helped us so much. As it is, his notes have given us a significant breakthrough on the problem of brain implantation."

"He would hate to hear that."

"Yes, well, I would have had to re-educate him, I suppose. Once he understood his duty to his one true god, he would have come around."

I pointed out the door. "Have you checked outside lately? Your one true god is dead!"

The draconic laughed, a deep, guttural sound, different from other times I'd heard it laugh. For reasons I didn't understand, a chill swept over me. I suddenly felt as if I stood on the brink of an enormous precipice, teetering, about to fall into its depths, and if I did, I would never see light again. I took a step back and gasped, breaking the imagery in my head.

"You understand so little, both you and Onyx," Troilus Green said. "A god cannot be killed, not forever. Caesious, for example, never did reach true godhood. Not like… me."

"You?" I choked back a laugh. "You're going to take Viridia's place? Get the people to worship you?"

"Their worship will not change. They will worship as they have always worshipped. The word is even now spreading to the priests, who are repenting of their doubt."

I didn't like the sound of this. I still wanted to charge right at it, but my mind explored a couple of variations on the idea. Maybe I could still take it by surprise.

"The death of the physical body is one thing, but it is not the end."

"Oh, so you're going to pretend that Viridia is here in spirit now, is that it?" I wanted to sneer, but that feeling of teetering on the edge kept trying to overtake me again. What was happening?

"I don't have to pretend anything. Viridia is here, in every way that matters."

"Except for his body missing a head."

Troilus Green lifted a finger and slowly turned it to point at its own head. "Viridia is here," it repeated.

"Inside of you? What? You think I—" I broke off as the feeling came back, and I knew the cause. Words came back to my memory, the words of Protogonus Blue, describing a mystical bond between a dragon and draconic, a literal sharing of minds. "Viridia may be seeking to perform a similar ritual, to connect with his fallen child…"

Viridia might have been engaged in that very ritual when we destroyed his power source. I swallowed. The connection between the two creatures might have remained, even to the point when Onyx killed the green dragon.

"Ah, you begin to understand, I think," Troilus Green said. "If not, let me make it completely clear: I am Viridia. I am Troilus Green. I am the father and the son. We are one, now and forever. And you, human wastrel, have outlived your usefulness."

The draconic charged me. Really? After saying it would be too predictable for me to do the same? Fortunately, I'd been preparing for my own attack. I launched myself into the air with boosted legs, and slashed at the wires holding the giant brain in the air. It came crashing down onto the table and rolled off in the path of the charging draconic.

I landed on top of the table as Troilus Green slashed out and ripped the brain model in half with a ferocity and strength that seemed greater than what I'd seen from it before. Maybe it really was inhabited by the green dragon's mind or spirit or whatever. Either way, it meant I got to kill it again… both of them.

The draconic slammed its fists down on the table, splitting it. I jumped free and landed in a crouch. I figured it would be better to let the monster rage for a bit, and watch for any mistakes, rather than charging in myself.

Troilus Green spit at me. Venom struck the ground where I would have been if I hadn't lunged away, almost falling. Had it ever used that trick before? I couldn't remember. Regardless, I didn't want to see what happened if that stuff hit my bare skin.

I stumbled, trying to recover my balance. The draconic came at me much faster than I expected. I slashed with my sword to keep it back.

Sparks flew as the sword connected with the metal chest strips. Its claws tore my shirt sleeve, narrowly missing my flesh.

I sent boosts everywhere, including my brain. I needed a faster reaction time or I wouldn't make it through this fight. In previous battles, this trick let me see my opponents moving almost in slow motion. This time, I saw Troilus Green moving at normal speed. The draconic had always been fast, but not like this. The precipice feeling returned, followed by an even sicker feeling in my gut. I backed away, keeping the sword in front. "What are you doing to me?"

"Question not the powers of a god," Troilus Green answered. It rushed me again, trying to pin me into a corner of the room. I darted to the right, escaping the intent.

I spared a glance for Carl. Wisely, he'd worked his way around the opposite side of the room while the draconic chased me. He stood near the door now, watching our conflict. I considered yelling at him to leave, but if he ran into any other trouble without me, he'd be defenseless.

"Though you have been in proximity to almighty Viridia, never once has he turned his full attention on you," the draconic said. "A dragon's powers go beyond what you can see."

Its eyes began to glow. The sick feeling in my gut roiled within, threatening to push its way up my throat. At the same time, all of my muscles seemed to pull down on me, dragging me toward the floor.

What was happening? I'd stood in the presence of multiple dragons as they spoke to me. Never once did I experience anything like this. Even if Viridia himself was now a part of Troilus Green, this made no sense. I stared up at the draconic's jet-black eyes with the glowing flecks of green, and fear took hold of me. I wanted to run, to hide, to scream. But I couldn't do any of them.

"Kneel." The command echoed in my head, sounding far stronger, deeper and greater than the draconic's usual voice. A part of my brain screamed against the command, but my body moved to obey. My sword clattered to the floor. My knees hit it next, followed by my palms.

A god commanded. And I obeyed.

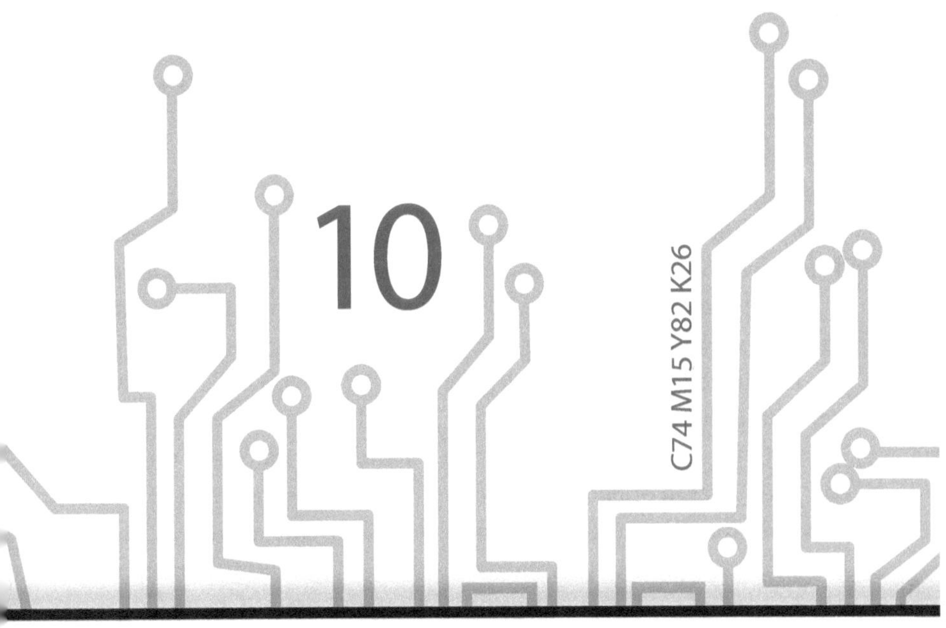

10

Troilus Green stepped forward. A warm rush of air and the smell of decay swept over me. "Oh, Beryl." A hand rested on top of my head. Five claws wrapped around it. The thumb claw tickled the skin on my temple. I had no doubt the hand could crush my head, or twist it and snap my neck. I was completely at its mercy.

But only that still conscious part of my brain acknowledged these facts. The rest of my mind and body struggled with the sensations of nausea and fear. I felt frozen, unable to react in any way.

The hand shifted on my head, two claws probing the very back, where my neck began. "Here is where he would have cut you open, implanting that wondrous device into your head," Troilus Green murmured. "If only we'd known. Our other body could have been modified. Onyx would have stood no chance against us.

"Now… what will she think of us? If we modify this body, we will become even more powerful than the others."

"Good luck with that." The voice, Carl's, intruded on my consciousness in a confusing way. His wasn't the voice of command. He—

A light almost as bright as the explosion that killed Peri erupted around us, along with a cacophonous boom. I fell from my knees onto the floor, shaking and working my jaw open and closed. Like the previous explosion, my vision cleared rapidly, though the room appeared washed-out and muted. Small fires dotted the room, consuming the papers Carl had tossed about earlier.

Troilus Green staggered near me, holding its hands over its ears and blinking over and over. Its mouth stood open, maybe roaring something, but I couldn't hear a thing. The strange hold it held over me vanished with the explosion. Aside from my vision and hearing, I returned to normal.

I grabbed my sword off the floor and stabbed it through the draconic's ankle. It jerked away, spewing blood.

Carl grabbed my arm and pulled me to my feet. His mouth yelled something, but I heard nothing. He pointed at the door and started that direction. I looked at the draconic and hesitated. How many times before had I run instead of fighting this thing? How many opportunities to kill it once and for all? And yet, these new abilities frightened me. If I couldn't kill it fast enough and it regained control of itself, I didn't stand a chance.

I followed Carl. But just before leaving the room, I stopped, boosted my arms, and picked up half the giant brain model. I threw it at the staggering draconic, then ran through the door. I'm not sure why I did it, but it felt right.

Carl held open the elevator door, and I raced inside. He stabbed the button for the lowest level. The doors slid closed. As the elevator descended, I massaged my ears and tried popping my jaw. Carl took my face in his hands and spoke in what must have been a loud voice, but came to me as barely a whisper: "Give it time!"

When we reached the base level, I was shocked to find it still empty. I'd fully expected to meet at least a squad of Viridian Guard, if not another draconic or two. Had Troilus Green truly been that arrogant to think it didn't need any other help or precautions? Maybe the dragon really was within; he'd always been arrogant enough.

Behind me, the elevator doors shut and it began to rise again. Someone would be after us shortly, it seemed. We raced out across the former dragon's lair and into the passageway, flashlights waving with our movements.

By the time we reached the more level part of the tunnel, my hearing began to return. "Hello? Hello! Hey!" I popped my jaw again. "What was that?"

"Just something I had for emergencies," Carl answered, though his voice still sounded faint. "It's all sound and light, but effective when needed."

"Did you bring the notes?" I asked, suddenly remembering our purpose.

He held up the binder. At least we'd accomplished that much.

As we continued on, Carl commented that he could hear voices in the distance behind us. I still had trouble just hearing him. We picked up our pace and made it to the exit without being caught. From there, we disappeared into the darkness surrounding the city's outskirts. Within another hour, we'd made it back to our home at the shrine. I wanted to examine the notes right away, but queasiness and other sensations fought within my body, warning me against further activity. I collapsed into my bed and slept the rest of the night away.

In the late morning, I stumbled out to find something to eat. Glacier, stretched out in the sun, gave a low growl as I passed.

"What did I ever do to you, cat?" I grumbled. It wasn't that I didn't like cats; I just never had any experience with them until now.

After satisfying my hunger from our eclectic collection of foodstuffs, I made my way to the cabin where I found everyone else. I guess I was the only one who needed sleep. Jaden, the former Viridian Guardsman, had dropped in for a visit as well.

"There you are," Lainey said, coming toward me. "Get your rest?"

"I'm fine," I claimed, though I still felt a little groggy. "What's everyone doing in here?"

"Reading about you," Carl announced from his seat at Bice's old desk. Part of me didn't like someone else sitting there. I missed Bice more than I would admit to anyone else. His calm wisdom annoyed me sometimes, but it always guided me to a better place.

"It's some crazy stuff," Jaden said from a seat on the arm of Bice's couch.

I approached the desk and looked down at the binder we'd taken from the Ascendancy. "Tell me."

"You remember how this is only half of the notes, right?"

I nodded. "And he gave the other half to Incarnadine. We're going to have to go after those at some point too."

"There's still a dragon in that city," Lainey pointed out. "Plus you've already broken into it once. Won't they have increased their security?"

"Yeah, I'm sure they have. But Onyx is going to have to go after it too. So we either get it first, or be there when he tries."

"Didn't work out so well here," Carl observed.

"We still got the notes. So tell me what they say."

Carl flipped back to the beginning. "He writes here about his patients, the human and the draconic. He first lists some of the injuries they—you—sustained in the accident. What was that, anyway?"

"What was what?"

"The accident that started all of this."

"Some kind of explosion in one of the factories. A wall fell on my parents and me."

"An explosion. A wall. That's pretty vague."

"I never asked for more details. My parents were dead, and I was in the hospital." I didn't like to think about that time.

"Hmm. I was just curious." He pointed at the page. "We know, of course, that you lost both eyes. Your skull was fractured. In fact, it looks like most of the bones in your body were broken in some way or other. And that includes your spine, of course. Without some kind of radical intervention, you weren't going to live, and if you did, it wouldn't be much of a life: blind, crippled, in constant pain, worthless to Viridian society."

I vaguely knew all these things, but hearing them listed reminded me of how lucky I really was. Bice wouldn't have called it luck, though. Maybe some god was looking out for me. Lainey put her hand on my shoulder in sympathy. Like most of my friends, she'd had no idea of what happened to me.

"So Loden describes his goal of full-scale cybernetic operations. The brain implant was the key to all of it, of course, and it's documented here in some detail, but he did much more than that."

"What do you mean?"

Carl flipped a couple of pages. "If I'm reading this right, there's not a single part of your body that is not connected to the brain implant, or reinforced or even rebuilt cybernetically."

"There are parts of me, other than my eyes, that are fully cybernetic?"

"Maybe not fully. Here, look at this sketch of your arm." He looked up. "I mean, I'm assuming all of this is about you. Unless he had another human patient?"

"None that I ever heard of." I bent down and looked at the drawing.

"And the draconic patient was Troilus Green."

"Yes, and… you may not want to hear this."

"What?" I studied all of the squiggly lines running through the sketch of an arm, but didn't understand what they meant.

"Loden may have used some of the draconic's… parts… to save your life."

I froze. "What did you say?"

Carl took the binder and flipped the last page. "Right here, before the notes are cut off, he writes about how some human organs may not be strong enough to handle what he's doing. He theorizes that since draconic bodies are much stronger, then maybe…"

"Maybe what?"

He shrugged. "I don't know. It must be in the rest of the notes. But he seems to be implying that he was going to use draconic physiology somehow."

I shook my head. "No. No, I can't accept that." I pointed outward. "If he'd taken anything from Troilus Green, why is it still walking about?" Loden wouldn't have done that to me, anyway. Would he? The idea that something inside me might be draconic in nature… I wanted to gag.

"That's a fair point," Carl admitted. "I'm just telling you what I read. We'd have to get the other notes to find out the rest."

"Go back to the arm," I instructed. "What does that part mean, exactly?"

He turned back to the sketch. "Do you know how your boosts work?"

"Not really," I admitted. "I think it, and it happens."

"So when you want that arm"—he pointed at my right—"to be stronger or faster, you just think it?"

"I have to trigger it. Give it a mental command, I guess."

"And then you... what?"

"I feel it happen. I call them boosts because it's like I can feel energy rushing in, I guess."

"But where does that energy come from, and where does it go, exactly? Have you never thought about this?"

"Of course I've thought about it." I scowled. This was irritating. "But I have no way of knowing any of these things."

Carl pointed to the sketch again. "If this is right, if this is really what he did... it's almost like he built an entirely new system into your body."

"What's a system?" Lovat asked from his perch on the back of the couch. I'd forgotten he was there.

"The human body has multiple systems inside it," Carl explained, turning to him. "You have the respiratory system, which is how we breathe. You have the circulatory system, which is how your heart pumps blood throughout all of your veins. You have the digestive system, which is how your body takes food and breaks it down into energy, and gets rid of what it doesn't need. The nervous system. The reproductive system."

"What's that one do?" Lovat held one knee and rocked back and forth.

"Ask Beryl to explain it later. The point is"—he pointed at me again—"he has another system in there. It's like Loden ran a series of wires or tiny tubes or something throughout all of your muscles. Like your veins, only... artificial. So when Beryl triggers a boost, as he says, the brain implant sends the energy through these... cyber veins... and stimulates the muscles. At least, that's the best way I can describe it."

Lainey took my forearm and looked at it. If it had been one of the guys, I might have objected. "I can't see any differences," she said. "His veins and muscles look just like anyone else's."

"It's inside," Carl said. "You probably can't see it, even when he's using it."

"Put a boost into this arm," Lainey suggested.

I obliged. I could feel the difference immediately, of course, but she saw nothing. "Did you really do it?"

"Grab hold of my arm," I told her. When she did, I lifted. She held on tight, and I picked her up with just the one boost. I let her back down and she relaxed her grip. "I couldn't see or feel anything different," she said, "except maybe your muscles getting tighter."

"That's normal for anyone," Carl said. "You can stop touching his muscles now."

Lainey released me and turned to her father. "But where does the energy come from?"

He lifted his hands. "That's the part I don't get yet. I sort of understand how the energy stimulates the muscles… theoretically, anyway. But where does it come from?"

"Where does any other energy come from?" I asked.

Carl chuckled. "That's a long discussion. But let's assume it's a kind of electrical energy for now."

"We have electrical power everywhere," I pointed out.

"Yes, because of power plants that generate it. You don't have a power plant inside of you."

Lainey plopped down on the couch. "I don't remember the details, but doesn't the brain use some kind of electrical power?"

"You're correct," Carl answered, smiling at her. "The brain's neurons communicate with electrochemical charges. But it's a long way from that to powering anything. The human brain is not a battery."

"But we do generate power of our own," Jaden pointed out. "The body creates heat, and that's a form of energy."

"Yes, yes. All of these things are true, but none of them answer the questions. We need the rest of the notes." He paused and touched the open page. "There's one part I especially don't understand."

"What's that?" I asked.

He looked up at my face. "How could you possibly survive the operations necessary for this?" He tapped the pages. "They would have had to cut open virtually every muscle in your body, one at at time, and implant all of this, not to mention the parts of you that had to be rebuilt. I just don't see how it's possible."

I considered his words while I walked to Bice's kitchen to get something to drink. None of what Loden had done to me made any sense to me, even with these explanations. But still…

"Wait." I turned around. "You said 'they.'"

Carl shrugged. "I'm assuming. One person couldn't have done all of this by himself. I don't care how much of a genius your friend Loden was. He didn't have six hands."

"You're saying he had help." I took a step closer. "An assistant or two."

He nodded. "Of course."

I smacked my forehead. "Why didn't we think of this before? If we could find Loden's assistants, maybe they could help us understand more!"

"Makes you wonder why the dragon's people didn't do that first," Jaden said.

"Troilus Green admitted they didn't know how important Loden was," I recalled. "But… they might be dead, for the same reason. They got rid of Kelly's parents, so there's a good chance they did the same to anyone associated with Loden." I returned to getting my drink. "How would we find out, though?"

"There would be records somewhere, right?" Lainey asked.

I found a brown liquid in the refrigerator. Tea? I sniffed it. Smelled like lemon. "Maybe," I said over my shoulder. "But we don't even know who to look for. No names. It's not like the records would say they were Loden's assistants."

"There's one mentioned in the notes here," Carl said. "But it's only a single name: Hunter."

I poured some of the tea into a plastic cup. "Not much to go on. And the dragon's people have had these notes for months. I'm sure they thought of looking for someone with that name." I took a sip. Hm. It had a strong flavor, but a little too bitter for my tastes. "Jaden, where do the Viridian Guard take their prisoners?"

"Uh, well, there are holding cells at each one of the stations, you know." He seemed hesitant in answering. "And, um, they get transferred sometimes."

I turned around to see Lainey bending over her father looking at the notes. "You said parts of him had to be rebuilt," she said. "What parts?" She glanced up at me. "Um, if you don't mind us talking about it."

I shrugged. "What difference does it make? I know I'm a freak. Everyone here knows it. May as well know the details."

Lainey frowned at me. She didn't like it when I cut myself down. Kelly never liked that either, come to think of it.

"I've been trying to make a list of that," Carl told her without looking up. "We knew about the eyes. The skull needed to be seriously reinforced too… which probably explains some of his survivals. Most of the bone was reinforced with steel or something similar. Loden is vague on the materials here."

I tapped my head in a couple of different places, wondering if it would be possible to tell which parts were bone and which were steel.

"Most of his spinal column was rebuilt, both because of damage, but also to facilitate the boosting system."

That made sense.

"Both shoulder blades were significantly altered, I guess for strength."

I moved my shoulders around. That hadn't stopped me from dislocating one of them. Twice.

"Also his left thigh…"

Uhhh… what?

"Apparently, that bone was shattered so much in the accident, it had to be almost completely replaced." Carl looked up. "You're fortunate you were finished growing when all this happened. Needless to say, these artificial parts wouldn't keep growing with you."

That was not a pleasant thought.

"And then there's the hand."

"What?"

"Your left hand. It's almost entirely cybernetic. You didn't know?"

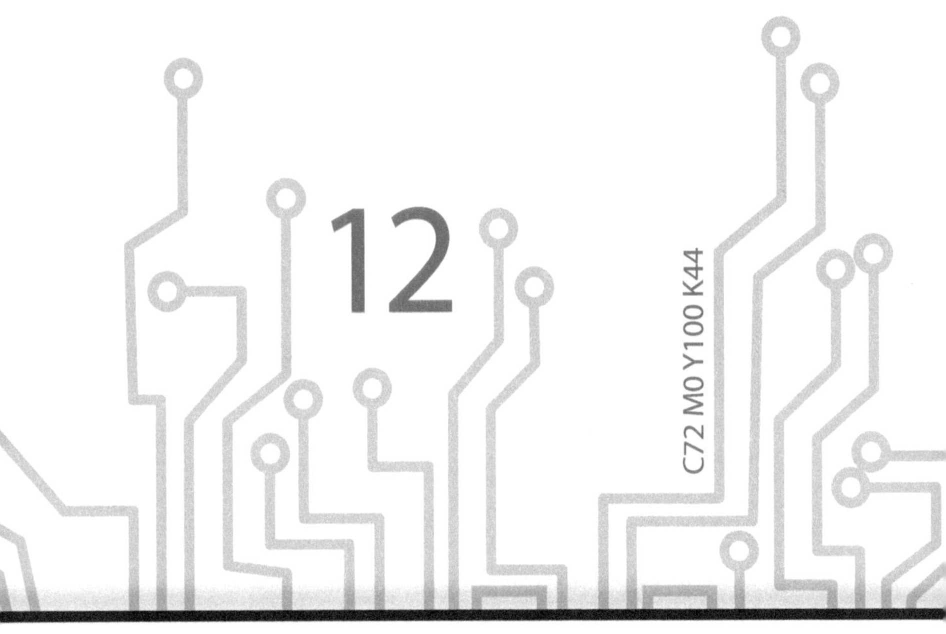

12

"What?" I repeated myself. I couldn't think of anything else to say.

"I've known this since we first met," Carl said. "How could you not know?"

"How could I know?" I held up my left hand and stared at it. "It looks and feels completely normal to me!"

"When we found you after the crash, some of the flesh was torn open," he went on, "and I got a look at the inside."

"But… but I've hurt it. Multiple times! It's gotten burned and, and it bleeds!" I set my cup of tea down and poked at my palm with the other hand.

"That's because the exterior is still flesh and blood. It's only the interior that's cybernetic."

"You mean just the bones?" I flexed my hand over and over.

"Maybe a little more than that," he hedged.

"But it's nothing like Rick's cybernetic hand. I can't do the things he does! Did."

"Probably not. His is entirely cybernetic. He has no skin or nerve endings on the outside."

"But…" I couldn't think of another objection.

"Why?" Jaden asked. "If he was replacing so much, wouldn't it have been easier to give him an entire hand, instead of keeping the outer, uh, flesh?"

"Easier, yes," Carl said. "But harder to disguise. Remember, Loden was trying to hide what he did from the dragon and his followers. He couldn't have Beryl walking around with an obvious cybernetic part."

"Rick did it and we never noticed," I mumbled. I gripped my two hands together, trying to tell the difference. "You had to splint my wrist," I pointed out.

Carl nodded. "Yes, because I wasn't sure at the time how much was artificial. It seemed to have gotten twisted, but it snapped back into place with little effort. Still, I assumed it must hurt."

"It did." I thought back to the other times I'd injured my hands, like when I'd gotten Troilus Green's venom all over them and burned all the skin. Except… soon after, I'd hung on to the top of Loden's speed train. My right hand gave out, but my left hand never did. Wow.

"I'm not left handed," I grumbled.

"And that's probably the main reason you've never noticed any difference," Carl observed. "You don't try to do as many things with it."

I wondered what my limits might be. Clearly, I could hold on to things longer. But beyond that? I'd have to experiment.

Lainey gave a little gasp. "You punched a hole in a wall with it yesterday!" she exclaimed. "I wondered at the time how your boosts could help with that, but then forgot."

Oh. I did do that. Hmm.

Jaden got to his feet and stretched. "Well, as interesting as all this is, I'd better get back to my work at the theater."

Officially, Jaden was missing in action, so he couldn't go back to his old life with the Viridian Guard. Stacy gave him work at one of the theaters, and he lived in an unused storage room backstage. I'd offered to let him join us at the shrine, but he preferred his current arrangements.

After he left, I turned back to Carl. "Any other shocking surprises about myself in there?"

"I don't think so." He closed the binder. "But like I said: we don't know what's in the rest of the notes, and they might answer some more questions."

"I'll think about that, and also get in touch with Marcus and Cerise. They may be able to help again." I headed toward the door.

"Where are you going?" Lainey asked.

"I need time to think about all this." I lifted my left hand and flexed it.

"So I'm going to head out to the Asylum and dig for a while."

"A-all right." She took a step toward me. "Be careful. Onyx could still show up there. Or, or anything."

I smiled. "You just heard a list of all my advantages, and you're still worried about me?"

"Of course I worry! You've almost died several times. You're not immortal, no matter how much metal and stuff you have inside!"

"I know, I know. And… I'll be careful. I promise."

"Want me to come?" Lovat asked.

"Nah, buddy. I need you to watch out for these two, okay?"

He nodded.

"I'll be back in a couple of days." I left the cabin, returned to my sleeping space in the sacellum, and assembled a backpack with the supplies I'd need. Then I headed out of the city.

Walking through Viridia was different now. Everyone used to keep their faces down, walking around in constant fear, or at least intentional solitude. I still saw some of that, but more and more people walked with their heads up, greeting one another. The Viridian Guard still existed, of course, and now some of the Sable Legion were assisting them, but the dragon was dead. It changed things. Even though I risked being spotted by the wrong eyes, I walked with my head up, unique chromark proudly displayed. The right people would see me more than the wrong people. And the story would continue to spread.

When the trains were running, I could have hitched a ride and been there in a couple of hours at most. But… trains didn't run during a war. For an ordinary person, a walk from Viridia to the Asylum would take at least a full day. But as we'd just established, I wasn't ordinary. Once outside the city limits, I boosted my legs and increased my pace. I didn't run, at least not right away, but I kept up a steady jog. Not only did it speed up my trip, it gave me some of the exercise my body needed on a regular basis. Rick had pointed that out; it didn't matter how much I could boost my muscles, if the muscles themselves didn't exist.

As I walked, my mind wandered through all we'd just learned. At least now I knew how much of my body was rebuilt or modified. I'll admit I'd been worried during the conversation that Carl would announce something really embarrassing, like my butt was fake, or other parts even worse. Ever since the revelation about my eyes, I'd been nervous about what else about myself might not be real. I guess organic is the right word, as opposed to technological. As it turned out, it was less than I thought.

The hand thing did weird me out a bit. I flexed both hands, still trying to tell the difference. Both felt the same.

I remembered how I'd believed I had a scar at the base of my spine from the implant, but it turned out I didn't. That seemed even stranger now. Based on all that Carl described, I shouldn't have a single scar... I should be covered in scars! How did Loden do it? I knew he was an absolute genius technologically. But in this case, he would have needed another genius, a medical genius. Carl said he would have needed an assistant or two, but it was more than that. He would have needed a partner.

Could that person still be alive? And if so, where? Hunter, I reminded myself. If he (or she) had been taken by the Guard, where should we look? Finding out should be added to the ever-growing list of things to do, a list existing only in my head for now.

My feet jogged along at a steady pace, keeping parallel with the train tracks. The tracks used to connect all of The Circle in ways most of the population didn't think about, and we'd disrupted all of that. I suppose you could argue that Auric disrupted it even more with his takeover of the Hub and his subsequent threats.

Huh. Whatever happened with that, anyway? We stopped the destruction of Caesious, but last I heard, Auric still had bombs aimed at the other four cities. He threatened to destroy any of them that didn't agree to end the war. But the war was still going... wasn't it? Come to think of it, I hadn't heard of any actual fighting happening in the past few weeks. Had the dragons made peace and just not told anyone about it? Or had something else happened at the Hub? Maybe once I arrived at the Asylum, I should dig out the four-wheeler and scout out the Hub.

As I considered this idea, I heard a noise I hadn't heard in months. It had been so long, it took me a moment to realize what I heard:

A train whistle.

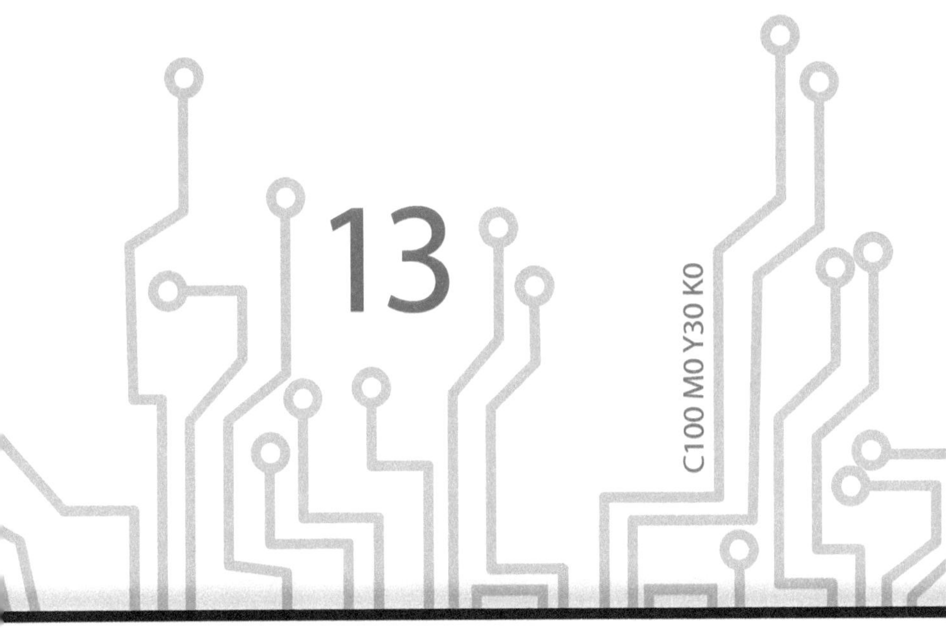

13

The train whistle blew again. I looked about and found a small collection of bushes and shrubs a dozen yards away. I had no sooner managed to crawl in to hide than I heard the sound of wheels on tracks. A train approached from the direction of Viridia!

I waited and watched. Sure enough, a few moments later, a train engine came into view. It was followed by two flatcars, each of which held a truck and several armed members of the Viridian Guard. The train chugged on past my hiding place at a rate that would have been considered slow for trains before all of this.

Once it moved out of sight, I emerged and considered the situation. Where would the Viridian Guard be going along these tracks? All the way to the Hub? Not knowing bothered me. I determined to investigate as soon as I could.

In the meantime, I needed to get moving again. I channeled new boosts into my legs and set out jogging.

Twilight approached when I reached the remains of the Asylum. Natural vegetation growth now concealed most of the destruction that had taken place here. I almost couldn't even tell where our headquarters had been. The entrance to the cave remained hidden and difficult to enter. I climbed inside and decided I'd had enough for one day. After a good night's sleep on the cave floor, I could do some more digging and then head out to the Hub.

Despite my intent, I didn't fall asleep for a very long time. Too many thoughts kept chasing through my head, and very few of them were positive. When I finally did sleep, I tossed and turned throughout the night, troubled by mixed-up dreams.

In the morning, after taking care of my personal needs and hiking down to the stream to clean up, I returned to the collapsed portion of the tunnel. I crawled past the resting place of Protogonus Blue. As always, I considered the miracle of a repentant draconic, one I could almost call friend. He'd died trying to preserve this place for me. It gave me hope that somewhere, somehow, we might be able to convert other draconics to our cause.

Yet as I paused there, one hand resting on the stones that covered the "good" draconic, it reminded me of all I'd lost that terrible day. I sat down beside the cairn (I think that's the right word), and brooded.

We'd been a family here, of sorts. Bice, Rick, Kelly, Caedan, Don, Lovat, and me. Then along came Mazarine, Peri, and Protogonus Blue. In some ways, those were the best days of my life. To live together with so many friends, so many people I cared about and that cared about me...

I still had Lovat, and I knew Lainey cared for me. Carl might too, if he wasn't too worried about a relationship between myself and Lainey.

But I missed my other friends.

Yes, even Rick. He'd been my best friend. I'd never had one of those. But he'd betrayed me, and I didn't think I'd ever truly get over it.

I missed Kelly. She'd been betrayed by Rick even more than I had, and would die if we didn't find her in time.

I missed Caedan. He'd gone back to Caesious after Peri's death. Did he even know what had happened?

I missed Don: quiet, dependable Don. He wouldn't know what to do now, but if we needed help in any way, he stood ready to offer it.

Most of all, I missed Bice. He'd been my sage, my mentor, my advisor. If I didn't know what to do, I could always talk with him about it. I needed his wisdom now. Where did we go from here? I didn't know what to do. Carl provided some of the same kind of wisdom, I supposed, but it wasn't the same. I still didn't know him very well.

I came out here to be alone, but if I were honest with myself... I hated alone. I wanted my friends, my family back. Without them, did I have any reason to go on? What if I never found Kelly? What if I couldn't find Bice and Don because they were dead?

I looked at the collapsed tunnel. Beyond several tons of rock lay Loden's workshop. My workshop. I wanted to get into it, but I was terrified of what I might find. If I found Bice's body, I might just lie down next to it and die myself.

I picked up a large rock and threw it across the tunnel. It smashed against the wall, broke in half, and clattered across the floor.

"Who's there?" came a voice from the darkness.

I froze. No one else knew about this place, except… it couldn't be. I hadn't recognized the voice, but in this cave, it could be anyone.

A flashlight beam burst into the darkness and waved around near me. What was the worst that could happen? If it was an enemy, I would have to fight my way out, no matter what. If it was a friend… I stood up and waited for the light to strike my face. I blinked.

"Beryl? Is that you?"

I knew the voice now. My hands trembled.

"Caedan!"

I scrambled over the rocks. He dropped the flashlight and leaped forward to meet me. We slammed into each other and wrapped our arms around each other. Caedan pounded me on the back while I just held on to him, overcome. I'm not ashamed to say tears filled my eyes.

"I thought you were dead again! Stop doing this to me!"

I couldn't answer him. It was Caedan. He was here. He was all right. And for the first time in a very long time, so was I.

He pulled away from me at last and looked me in the face. The glow from the fallen flashlight gave us just enough light to see each other. "What did you do to your face?" he asked. "I almost didn't recognize you!"

"I…" I swallowed. "It seemed like a good idea." My voice broke on the last word, and I sank to the ground, letting the tears fall.

"Aw, man. I should have thought…" He grabbed up the flashlight and took a step back toward the cave entrance. "Turq! Bring me some water!" he yelled, then turned back to me. "I have no idea what you've been through, but I know it's not good."

I perked up at his yell. "Someone else is here?"

"Friends from Caesious," he said. "What about you? Are you alone?"

I nodded. I pulled up the bottom of my shirt to wipe my eyes.

Caedan sat down on a large rock opposite me. "What happened here,

Beryl? Where is everyone? I came back a few weeks ago and found it like this." He waved. "No sign of anyone. I thought you were all dead."

I swallowed again and rubbed at my eyes. "Give me a second." I took a deep breath. I think I managed to compose myself. Some.

A muscular young man with a blue chromark scrambled over the rocks, holding a bottle of water. He froze on seeing me. "Holy Caesious. Is that...?"

"Yeah, it is," Caedan said, taking the bottle. "Tell the others to wait until I come back out."

He nodded and disappeared from view. Caedan offered me the bottle.

I took a swallow of water, closed my eyes, and took another deep breath. Okay.

"Have you heard about the black dragon?" I asked.

"Atramentous? Did he do this too?"

I shook my head. "No, not Atramentous. Onyx. The other one."

"The dragon that died? He's back? I've heard stories about a black dragon, but I thought it was Atramentous."

"It's worse." I raised my head to look at him. "It's Rick."

"What?"

In halting words, with lots of interruptions, I told him about the day it all went wrong: the day my best friend revealed himself to be my worst enemy. I talked about death, and missing friends, and our lost home. When I finished, Caedan sat back against the cave wall and shook his head.

"I heard about the black dragon killing Viridia, and attacking the Hub, but I never thought... wow..."

"The Hub? What happened at the Hub?"

"Oh, apparently the dragon—Onyx—attacked it the day after killing Viridia. There's hardly anything left now of it or Auric's forces. I guess he didn't want the threat of those explosives any more."

Yeah, that wouldn't serve Onyx's purposes. No wonder I hadn't head anything more about that. "And you've heard nothing since then? About the black dragon, or any of our friends?"

He shook his head. "No, no. I thought you all were dead. And you've heard nothing from Bice or Don? No hint at all?"

I took another swig of water and pointed down the tunnel. "I've been coming here every so often and digging a little. But I'm afraid... I think they might have been trapped in the workshop."

"Then let's find out for sure." He got to his feet. "Come on. Let me show you something."

Caedan led the way out of the tunnel. I stood blinking in the bright morning light, confused. Four young men and a woman stood in a semi-circle, staring at us.

"Beryl, I want you to meet my team," Caedan said, gesturing. "Team, this is Beryl, the one I've been telling you about."

One by one, Caedan called them forward and introduced them. Turq, Saxe, Royal, Cobalt, and Sapphire, who he identified as Peri's sister. "When I told her what happened, she wanted to help," he explained. "And together, we found these other guys. The movement's growing, Beryl. We're growing."

"That's great," I said. "But what are you all doing out here? This isn't a good place to hide, not any more."

"We came to dig," Saxe said, picking up a shovel.

"We're here to get into that workshop," Caedan said. "You can't do it all on your own, you know." He clapped his hands. "All right, team. Let's get busy. We don't know how far we have to go, and I want us through it by the end of the day!"

I almost cried again, watching the team gather up their equipment: shovels, pickaxes, and lanterns. It was beautiful.

"You gonna be all right?" Caedan asked, putting a hand on my shoulder. "We could use your cyb strength in there."

"You'd better believe it!" I laughed. It felt good. Then I remembered. "But there's something we need to do first."

Fortunately, the team had brought along some old blankets and tarps. Together, we dug up the body of Protogonus Blue and wrapped it. I tried not to look at the body; I had no desire to see how much it might have decayed in three months. We dragged it back out and found a good place to bury it. Even with all of us working, it took a couple of hours to get him buried again. Once done, the newcomers headed back into the tunnel while Caedan and I remained.

"Kind of crazy that we're taking all this trouble for a draconic," he observed.

"Yeah," I agreed. "But he wasn't just another draconic. Protogonus Blue was... almost human." I smiled. "I guess that's the highest praise I can give him."

"Not sure he'd take it that way, but you're right. The more he hung around the place, the more I got used to him."

I nodded, looking down at the mound of dirt. "He died trying to save our friends and home." I paused. "I don't know what else to say."

"Then let's get back to work."

We returned to the cave and set to it. With the seven of us, we set up a rotating system. Those who weren't working held the lights and fetched water for those who were. I took it on myself to work longer and harder than any of them. Any time a stone proved too heavy or awkward for anyone else, I moved in. I guess I felt a little proud of myself, showing off my cybernetic strength. I enjoyed their exclamations of amazement. Caedan only laughed.

None of us had experience at anything like this, so we made it up as we went along. Royal, at least, had some engineering understanding, and had an eye for how the rocks supported each other. He would warn us against moving certain stones before taking care of others. Even so, we managed to cause a couple of small cave-ins as the afternoon wore on. Saxe sprained his wrist during one of them and had to sit out the rest of the time.

Our progress seemed minuscule at first, but after a few hours, I could see we'd made significant inroads into the debris. I couldn't tell how far the blockage stretched, or remember exactly how much further we needed to dig until we reached the workshop itself. It still seemed like we had a long way to go.

Sapphire, sitting on top of the pile, pulled out a head-sized chunk of rock and rolled it down to me. As I caught it and set it aside, she reached into the gap it left behind. "I think we've broken through!" she cried. "I don't feel anything. Caedan, throw me a flashlight!"

He tossed one up to her. She caught it and shined the light into the gap. I climbed up beside her. "See anything?"

"It… I see a rock wall at an angle, but… I think there's open space before that."

I stepped back a few paces and surveyed the angle of the tunnel walls. "If I remember right, the tunnel curves just a bit here before it reaches the workshop," I said. "Does that seem right to you, Caedan?"

He shrugged. "I never paid attention, but sure."

"Let me up there."

Sapphire obligingly slid down, and I climbed to the top. I pulled rock after rock out of the way. The new possibility gave me a burst of adrenaline. In a few minutes, I was flat on my stomach, pushing rock and dirt back around me as I inched forward. And then I was through, my head extending out into open air.

I wiggled my hips and pushed forward. I tumbled through onto more rocks, but didn't fall far. I ignored the minor bruises and scrambled back to my feet.

"I need a light!" I called.

Sapphire, the smallest of the team, pushed through the hole I'd made and handed me an electric lantern. I held it up and looked around. As I'd guessed, the tunnel made a slight turn to the left before it reached the workshop. Except the workshop wasn't there; a solid wall of rock met my eyes.

Someone had closed the workshop door. From the inside. My hand shook, making the light vibrate in an odd pattern.

"Is everything all right, Mister Beryl?" Sapphire asked.

"Tell Caedan I need him."

I set the lantern down and tried to compose myself while I waited. Maybe it didn't mean what I thought it meant. Maybe the door shut on its own in response to the cave-in. Maybe something else went wrong. It could be anything. But my rational mind wouldn't accept the excuses. The logical explanation said someone closed the workshop from the inside. And if so… that someone was still inside, three months later. I would find one or more dead bodies when I opened it.

Caedan grumbled behind me. I turned to watch him struggle through the hole. A little wider than me, he had to shove some more dirt and rocks out of the way before he could fit. I stepped up and grabbed his hand to help pull him through. Finally, he stood beside me, dusting off his clothes. I pointed to the wall. "Someone closed it from inside."

"Oh." He stood still for a moment. "Well, at least Rick, or Onyx, didn't get in there, right?"

"Dusk was working for him. She probably took out everything worthwhile before all this happened."

He grunted. "You can open it, right?"

I nodded. I stepped up to the wall and took a deep breath. I placed a finger against the rock surface and channeled a quick boost into it. Somehow, Loden had programmed this to react to my boost power and nothing else. I stepped back as the familiar metallic hum began. The wall vibrated, and shifted with a loud crack. Then it slid to the left. Light spilled out, making both of us blink. A horrible smell struck my nostrils.

Caedan stepped in without hesitation. I waited, unable to bear what we would find. I'd rather face one of the dragons than step into that room.

"Beryl, come in," he called. "There's no one here."

A wave of relief swept over me. I didn't know how it could be possible, but I knew Caedan wouldn't lie. I stepped into the workshop.

It looked exactly the same as it always had… for the most part. I did see a few empty shelves, though I couldn't remember how many of them we'd emptied ourselves in re-arranging everything. But that smell! I saw a bucket in the far left corner, and knew at once what it meant. Someone had been here, for some time. Then where were they now?

"Over here," Caedan said. "You need to see this."

I walked around behind one of the tables and stopped. Caedan stood by the far wall, most of which wasn't visible from the doorway. A ton of dirt lay scattered on the floor. A hole had been torn in the wall, and a hand-dug tunnel stretched away.

Someone had escaped. They were alive.

15

Caedan shined a flashlight into the tunnel. "Wow. Someone worked really hard."

"Don," I said. "It had to be. And if he was in here, maybe Bice was too."

Caedan looked back at the workshop. "I can see signs of someone being in here, besides the obvious bucket toilet, but I can't tell if it was one or two."

"It had to be two," I said. "I've got to believe it. They're alive."

"Let's see where they went," Caedan said. He bent down, about to crawl into the tunnel.

"Uh, we should tell your team what's going on."

"Oh, right. Sorry. I'm just not the leader type. Like you." Caedan trotted back to the door and called back, "Keep widening that hole! We're going to check something out."

"Is everything all right back there?" someone asked. "Something stinks!"

"It's streak," Caedan answered. "Keep working."

He rejoined me at the hand-dug tunnel. "Maybe you'd better go first," he admitted.

I nodded and bent down. If we ran into trouble in this enclosed space, I had a better chance of surviving.

The tunnel started out large, about three feet in all directions, but grew narrower as I crawled further. I could only imagine the difficulty involved in digging such a thing, all while starvation threatened.

The further I went, the less I could see. My own body blocked out the light behind me. Soon I had to move only by feel. What if they hadn't made it? What if I ran into a pair of feet? I gritted my teeth and mentally ordered myself to stop being so negative. Someone got out. It was a miracle.

"Oof," Caedan said behind me. "You're pushing dirt back on me. I'll hang back a bit."

"Okay." I kept crawling. A minute crept by. And then the tunnel ended. I felt around to see if it changed directions, but no… it just ended.

"Caedan! I can't go any further! It just ends!"

"Maybe the last bit caved in after they got out," he suggested. "Try pushing through."

I took a deep breath and held it. I gave a boost to my arms and legs and shoved forward. Dirt rained down on top of me and for one terrifying moment, I thought I would be buried alive. Then my hands burst through into open air. I pushed to the side and dragged myself out into the suddenly bright sunlight. I tumbled out, covered in dirt. Behind me, I heard Caedan yell something about the light.

"I made it!" I called back into the tunnel. I wiped dirt from my face and arms, and spit out what had gotten in my mouth.

I got to my feet and looked around. Of course I wasn't far from the Asylum, but it was easy to tell why I hadn't noticed this exit hole before. For that matter, I doubt anyone would have noticed unless they were looking for it. The exit hole came out on the side of a small hill facing to the north. A cluster of trees stood at the base of the hill, obscuring the hole from most directions. I walked around a little, while I waited for Caedan to join me. He pushed his way out a few moments later.

"Wow." He wiped dirt from his forearms and joined me in climbing to the top of the hill. From here, we could see the ruined Asylum not far away.

"They made it out," I said. "They really did."

Caedan spit dirt out of his mouth. "And then where did they go?"

I shook more dirt off my shirt. "Good question. If it were you, where would you go?"

"I'd have gone back to Caesious myself, but Bice and Don wouldn't.

Shouldn't they have gone back to Viridia?" He ran his hands through his hair, trying to get still more dirt out.

I frowned. "Yeah, they should have gone to see Stacy right away. Why didn't they?" I looked back at the hole. "How long do you think it took them to dig that?"

"Don's a tough worker," he pointed out. "He would have kept at it until Bice made him stop to rest. I'd guess they were out in around a week's time, if that." He paused. "Of course, we're assuming it was two of them. It could still have just been Don."

"I'm going to believe it was both." I started walking back toward the Asylum. "But where are they now? That's what I don't get." I stopped and looked to the south. "If they went toward Viridia, and were captured… maybe the Guard has had them all this time."

"Does that make sense?"

"I don't know." I started walking again. "Okay, I have three priorities right now. First, I need to find out where the Viridian Guard takes prisoners, and maybe do something about that. Second, we're going to have to infiltrate the Flame in Incarnadine again to find the rest of Loden's notes. And third… we have to find Onyx."

"Where could a dragon hide?" Caedan wondered.

I spread my arms and turned in a circle as we walked. "I have no idea. He wouldn't be in any of the cities, right? What does that leave?"

Caedan gestured. "Out here somewhere? Maybe a bigger cave?"

"Eh. It seems like… I don't know. Anything big enough to hide a dragon would be easy for the other dragons to find. Wouldn't it?"

"Maybe in the mountains? Or even on the other side?"

I shook my head. "No. He wouldn't go over. Trust me. Lainey's dad has told me enough to know that."

"There aren't that many places left, Beryl. He's not hiding in the Blasted Lands, you know."

I stopped short. "No… he's not. But…"

"Nooo," Caedan let it draw out. "You're not thinking about that tower?"

"Why not? Until I spotted it, no one had ever heard of it."

Caedan stared off in the direction of the Blasted Lands. "But it wasn't that big of a tower, was it? Big enough for a dragon?"

"I don't know. I only saw it from a distance with zoomed vision." I walked in a circle. "We need to check it out."

"Hey, that's something my team can handle!" Caedan jumped in front of me. "We can't help you in Viridia or Incarnadine, but scouting a tower on the mountains? That we can do!"

"You'll have to circle all the way around the Blasted Lands," I pointed out.

"We can do it. Your other missions are going to take a while, anyway. Trust me on this."

I smiled. "I do trust you." I closed my eyes and leaned my head back. "Wow, it feels good to say that. To have someone to say that to!"

"You don't trust Lainey?"

"I do, but… she's not part of our first team, you know. And she didn't grow up here." I opened my eyes and looked at him. "Gods, I missed you, Caedan."

"You too, buddy."

We resumed walking. Caedan suggested his team first finish up clearing out the way into the workshop, and establish their base camp inside. Cobalt had some tech knowledge and could look over some of the workshop's remaining equipment. After that, they could scout the tower. "And maybe check out the Hub too."

"I'd stay away from there." I told him about the Viridian Guard on the train.

"Now I'm really curious."

"Caedan…" I stopped just before we reached the cave entrance. "This team you have. They seem like good kids. Don't put them into more danger than you have to."

His shoulders fell. "Yeah, you're right. It's not easy trying to think about other people. I'm used to running off and getting in trouble." He grinned. "Usually with you."

I laughed. "We both need to watch out for others more. Part of being leaders."

"I'm not a leader."

Royal exited the cave with a load of rocks and dropped them at the sight of us.

"Yeah, you are." I laughed again.

"How did you guys get out here?" Royal demanded.

Caedan walked forward and clapped him on the shoulder. "Go bring the others out here," he said. "We've got some things to discuss."

As the young man headed back into the cave, Caedan scratched the back of his neck. "Things sure would be easier if we still had the four-wheelers."

"Oh, we have one left," I said. "I hid it over that way." I pointed.

"What? Where?"

I swear Caedan showed more excitement over finding a four-wheeler again than he had over finding me. But that was part of his character. Even as he matured into a leader, I don't think he'd ever lose that action addiction. I don't think I'd want him to.

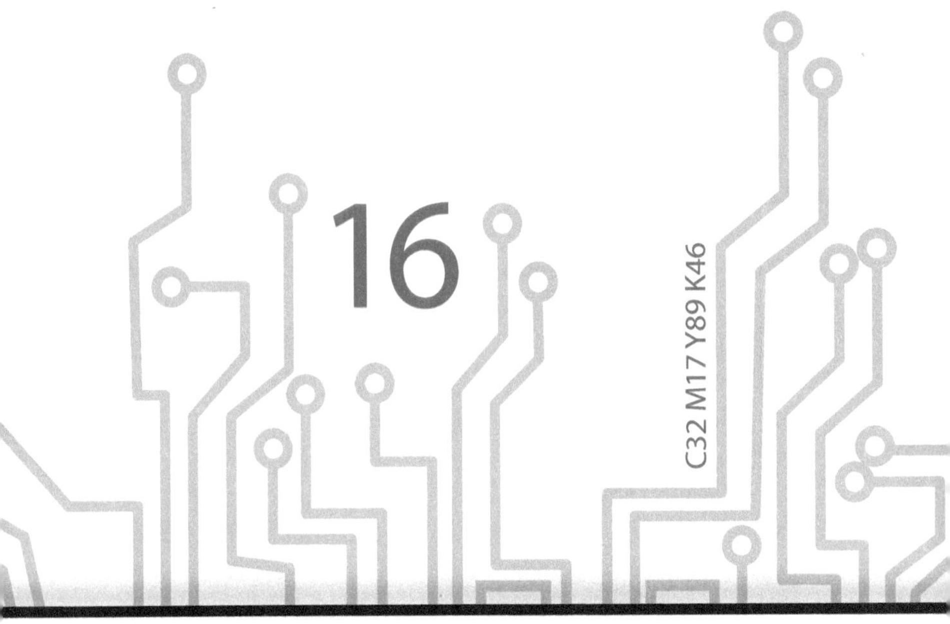

Saying goodbye to Caedan and his team was difficult, but I left with a much lighter heart than I arrived. Caedan was back. The Asylum was open again, sort of. And I had new hope for finding Bice and Don.

All the way back to Viridia, I considered the possibilities. I decided my first stop would be to see Jaden. He'd been vague in the previous conversation, and I hadn't pressed him. But I needed to find out what he knew about Viridian Guard prisoners. After that, I should probably check in with Stacy before heading back to the shrine. Didn't want to worry Lainey too much.

I slept out under the stars, feeling thankful for the first time in a very long time. In the morning, I entered the city and made my way to the Greenhawk Park, the theater where Jaden lived and worked for now.

In moments like these, I regretted my new chromark. But maybe the stage hand who gave me directions thought it was makeup for one of the shows. His wide eyes implied otherwise, though. I found the backstage storage room where Jaden lived, and was about to knock when I heard voices inside. I stopped and listened.

"Really?" That was a female voice.

"Yeah, I gave him his new chromark. He wanted to represent everyone, you know." That was Jaden. Was he talking about me?

"That is so hue," the female voice gushed. Wait. I knew that voice.

"I'm kind of important in the resistance," Jaden said. "Oh, uh, but don't tell anyone."

"The resistance is all the rage right now," she answered. "But you can trust me. I won't tell a soul."

I knew it. Olive.

"I knew a Beryl," she went on. "But he's dead. And he worked for the Viridian Guard. Not like this Beryl."

"It's a common name," Jaden said. "So… you like resistance fighters, huh?"

"Oh, I don't know. Depends on how cute they are."

"Do I count?"

"Well… you do have some nice muscles in these arms…"

Wow. I'll admit it: part of me was annoyed to hear her flirting with another guy. But I really shouldn't be. She was far too flighty and flirtatious to take seriously, even if I did recruit her for that one mission. It's kind of funny that she didn't connect me with me… I mean, the me she thought was dead with the resistance leader me. Argh. I was getting my thoughts mixed up. She had that effect on me, and it wasn't even me she was flirting with!

I couldn't hear any more voices for a few moments. Huh. I lifted my hand to knock, but stopped myself. If she saw my face, she would know me. Fewmets. I needed to talk with Jaden, but I didn't want to sit around while he and Olive… did whatever they were doing in there.

Something clattered. "Holy Viridia, is that the time?" Olive exclaimed. "I have an audition in five minutes!"

I ducked back into a darkened area of the hallway. The door burst open and Olive ran out, tucking in her shirt. Jaden appeared in the doorway a moment later, looking downcast.

"You can do better," I said.

"I don't know about that," he answered without looking. "She's hotter than a red dragon."

"Seriously, Jaden?"

He jumped and spun around. "Beryl! What are you—I mean, when did you get here?"

"A few minutes ago." I walked past him into his room, a small space decorated with numerous posters for stage performances of the past few years. "By the way, the dead Beryl she knew?" I pointed at myself.

"Oh. Ohhh." He glanced back in the direction Olive had gone. "She thinks you're dead?"

"That's what I just said. And I'd like to keep it that way for now, if you don't mind. So don't tell her any of our secrets." I paused. "For that matter, don't tell her anything about us at all."

Jaden shut the door and winced. "Yeah, okay. Sorry. I just… it gets lonely, you know?"

"Yeah, I know." I nodded. "I really do."

"So, um, what brings you here?" Jaden pushed past me in the narrow room and shoved some junk off a chair. "Have a seat?" He sat down on his bed and faced me.

"I just got back," I said, sitting down. I paused, distracted by the poster nearest me. It featured a scantily-clad Stacy Moss pointing at the sky and screaming something. And there might have been a performance title somewhere. I didn't notice. "Oh, we might have a new mission. First of all, I need more information. The other day, you said the Viridian Guard sometimes transferred prisoners away from the stations. Where do they go?"

"I, um, I don't know exactly, but…" He glanced at the door. "I always heard stories about a prison. One of the guys called it a pit. A place where they would send undesirables. You know, people whose crimes were bad enough."

"Like what?"

He shrugged. "The big stuff, of course. Murder. Rape. Child abuse. And anything that made the dragon look bad, I guess."

"Is that where they would send us if they caught us?"

"Me? For sure. You? I don't know. You're too big for that. Plus, there's the whole cyb thing." He tapped his head.

"Yeah, besides that." I frowned. "You mean they don't kill anyone?"

"People don't come back from that prison." He kind of shivered with a shrug. "I don't know if they put people to death, or they just die there. Either way, they're gone and not coming back."

We all knew of people who had "disappeared" under the dragon's rule. But no one knew where. And as he said, none of them ever came back. I thought of Kelly's parents, who'd been taken after she'd been identified with our group.

"They may have taken Bice and Don." I went on to explain what

Caedan and I'd found at the Asylum.

Jaden cocked his head and narrowed his eyes. "I don't know, Beryl. I don't think they'd whisk Bice away like that. He's kind of important to them, remember?"

Oh, right. "The heretic."

Jaden nodded. "If they'd captured him, I think they'd make a big deal out of it."

"Even with the dragon dead? He's sort of been proven right."

"That's a good point." He considered for a moment. "I guess it's possible, but I still don't think it's likely."

"Okay, but we also want to try to find Loden's assistant. And for that matter, anyone else that might help us out. Where do we find this 'pit'?"

He held up his palms. "That's the thing. I never heard. I don't know."

I started to get up, but realized I would have no room to pace about. "We need to find it. Do you have anyone left in the Viridian Guard you could talk to?"

Jaden's eyes bulged. "I can't do that! They all think I'm dead! If I show up to talk to anyone, I'd get shipped off to the pit myself!"

I rubbed my chin. "You know…"

If possible, his eyes got even bigger. "No. No! I am not going to prison for you! I don't care what you say!"

"We'd break you out," I said.

"I don't care! You can't guarantee how soon that would be. No. No way."

I sighed. "I'd do it myself, but… Troilus Green would just have me torn apart to find my implant." I thought for a moment. "And there's no one else that could do it. I won't risk Lovat or Lainey. And Carl's knowledge is too valuable."

"They'd probably torture me first," Jaden argued. "And I might tell them everything. I'm not good with pain."

"I thought you were Viridian Guard! A big, tough guy!"

He pointed at himself with both hands. "I got in when they were desperate for new recruits. I'd have never made it otherwise." He shook his head. "I'm sorry, Beryl. But you're going to need a different plan."

"All right. You give me a name, and I'll go visit him. I'll get the information myself."

"Okay, okay. Now that I can do. Let me think…" He punched one hand into the other palm repeatedly, while he stared off into the distance. "I can remember several names, but the one most likely to have the information would be the highest ranked... Got it! You need to find Captain Lime."

"Lime?" I repeated.

"Yeah. Captain Rodney Lime. He was the highest officer I encountered. If anyone would know the prison's location, it's him."

"And where do I find him?"

Jaden thought for a few more moments. "There's the station three blocks over. He shows up there sometimes. But you probably don't want to assault the whole station to find him."

"Been there. Done that. Sounds like we're going to have to watch for him then." I got to my feet. "I assume you can help with that?"

"Yeah, sure. When I'm not working, of course. And—"

The door burst open, and Olive sauntered in. "The audition got postponed," she announced. "Why don't we—oh!"

Her eyes met mine.

Oh. Fewmets.

"Hello, Olive," I said before she could react.

"But you, you're, you can't, you…" she spluttered.

"I, um, I'm not dead."

She screamed. Literally, she screamed. Right there in Jaden's room. He jumped to his feet, but before he could do anything, she ran into me. Her whole body slammed into mine. I started to fall, but threw a quick boost into my legs and stabilized myself just in time. Olive wrapped her arms around me and squeezed. "Holy Viridia! Holy Viridia! Holy Viridia!" she repeated over and over into my chest.

Jaden took a quick look outside to check for reactions to the scream, then closed the door. He looked at me over the top of Olive's head and gave an exaggerated sigh. I couldn't blame him.

I gently disengaged Olive, though there wasn't enough room to push her very far from me. "Hey, it's, uh, good to see you too."

She pushed against my chest. "They said you were dead! That Incarnadine ate you! How are you alive?" She looked at my face. "And your mark!" She gasped. "You're the resistance leader! But, but, you worked for the Viridian Guard! How?" All of this poured out of her mouth before I could say anything.

"All right, all right." I held both my palms up, then pulled them back right away before she accidentally (or purposely) pressed her body against them. "I'll try to explain. I see you know my friend Jaden here."

She didn't even turn to look at him. "Yes, we've met. Now tell me! How are you here? How are you… you?"

"I've always been me," I joked. When she didn't react, I kept going: "Yeah, um, the red dragon didn't get me, obviously. I managed to escape, but I was badly hurt. It took a long time for me to recover."

"Why didn't Stacy tell me?" Olive demanded. She crossed her arms. "I cried and cried over you!"

"Really? I mean, we didn't know each other that long…"

"Time doesn't matter! I thought we had something special!" She leaned in toward me again, and I took hold of her upper arms to keep her from getting closer. "Remember the night in the orchard?"

I glanced at Jaden and wished I could hide. "Nothing happened," I reminded her.

"But it almost did. If the dragon hadn't gone after you, then on the way back…" She smiled the way she always did, and I swallowed. I had imagined what could have happened. Of course I had. But now…

"Yes, well. Stacy thought I was dead too, for a very long time. And since I came back, I've been keeping it a secret."

Her eyes widened. "Ohhh, because you're fighting against the Guard now! That's so hue!"

"Something like that." How did I get out of this? I couldn't tell her everything. Could I? She'd managed to keep our mission to Incarnadine and her part in it a secret, I suppose.

"I want to help you!" she announced. "Without the dragon, we can get rid of that annoying Guard and be free, right?"

"Uh, yeah. Freedom. That's what we're doing. Yes."

"Beryl is looking for someone to get arrested and thrown in prison," Jaden said with an edge to his voice.

"Ooo, I could do that!" Olive held up her hands. "I would look fantastic in handcuffs."

"I, uh, wouldn't want to put you in that kind of danger."

"But you'd rescue me, right? That would be so exciting!"

"Let me put it this way." I finally let go of her arms and crossed my own. "Imagine you're dragged in before a seven-foot-tall draconic." I leaned toward her. "And he leans in, with his mouth open and teeth dripping venom, and demands you tell him everything about the resistance… Would you be able to look up into those jaws and say you didn't know anything?"

"I, I think I could."

I leaned back and uncrossed my arms. "Maybe you could. I don't know. But I'd hate to put you in that situation. Besides, we came up with a new plan. I don't need anyone to get arrested now. Right, Jaden?"

"Yeah, I guess so."

"Good. I'll get back with you on that. Olive, it's been great to see you, but I have to get back to my, uh, secret headquarters." I started to move toward the door.

Olive made it difficult for me to get past her. "Aw, I want to see your headquarters."

"Maybe some other time." I pointed at Jaden. "If you come across anything you think might help us, let Jaden know. He's one of my top men, you know."

"He is?" Olive glanced his way and I took advantage of the moment to push past her to the door.

"Yep, so check in with him. Jaden, see you later!" I hurried out and almost ran down the back hallway to the exit. Yikes. Talk about awkward.

I made it back to the shrine, our "secret headquarters," without any difficulty. Lainey and Lovat greeted me enthusiastically, and both were excited to hear about Caedan. After some other talk, we gathered with Carl Roberts to discuss the possibilities for finding and getting into the secret prison.

"So what are you thinking?" he asked after hearing all of my information. "You want to break into this prison and see if your friends are there?"

"For starters, sure. We can also try to find Loden's assistant, like you talked about."

"You don't even have a name. How's that going to work?"

I shrugged. "I guess we'll just have to free everyone there. Think Troilus Green will mind?"

"But won't there be some bad people there too?" Lainey asked.

"Look, we don't even know if we can find the prison," I said, "let alone who's actually there and how they're being guarded. Let's save the details for when we have more information." I paused. "I guess, if it comes down to it, I'd rather release some bad people in order to free the good people."

The information came sooner than I expected. Jaden showed up at the shrine three days later with the home address of the Viridian Guard captain he'd talked about. We'd only just set up observation on the station one day earlier. Turns out, the captain worked there every day now. Jaden and Lovat followed him home, made sure he left from the same spot again the next morning, and then brought us the address.

"I guess we'll pay him a visit tonight," I suggested when the whole group had gathered again.

"And then what?" Carl asked.

"Get him to tell me where the prison is."

"After which, he'll go tell the draconics about your visit, and they'll be ready for you. You've got to think things through, Beryl."

Ugh. He was right.

"Fine. Anyone else got any good ideas?" I looked around the tiny cabin. If Rick were still a part of this, his first suggestion would be to kill the captain. I wanted a different option.

"Maybe we could keep him a prisoner!" Lovat suggested.

"Like I did with Caedan?" That had worked out well.

"You're not going to convert this guy to your side." Jaden shook his head. "He's one of the die-hard dragon lovers."

"Maybe..." Lainey said. She scratched Glacier's head without looking up. "Maybe if you asked a bunch of different questions, and didn't make it obvious which one you were really interested in."

"Huh. What questions could I ask?"

"You're the infamous resistance leader now," Carl pointed out. "You could be planning a devious attack against the power grid."

"The power what?"

He closed his eyes and shook his head. "The electrical power for the city, or something like that."

"All right. I think I can come up with something like that."

"You're going to have to fight him," Jaden said. "And threaten him a lot. If you're going to get anything out of him. Remember, this is not some scared scientist you can bully into telling you stuff. This is a captain in the Viridian Guard. He's been serving the dragon for decades."

"I've fought draconics. I think I can handle him."

Carl cleared his throat. Right, right. Think things through.

"But... just in case, Lainey, why don't you and Glacier come along? And Lovat can guide us, as usual."

"Sure." Lainey looked up and smiled.

"Anything else?"

Lovat dug into his pocket. "Oh, Stacy gave me a note for you."

He'd been to see her yesterday. I hoped it wasn't urgent. I took the note and spread out the wrinkles. "She got word from Marcus and Cerise," I said. "They don't know anything about a cybernetic breakthrough with their scientists, but they'll keep an ear out."

"Will we go back to see them again?" Lovat asked. "I liked that city better than this one."

"Sometime soon," I promised. "First, I need to go intimidate a soldier and find a prison."

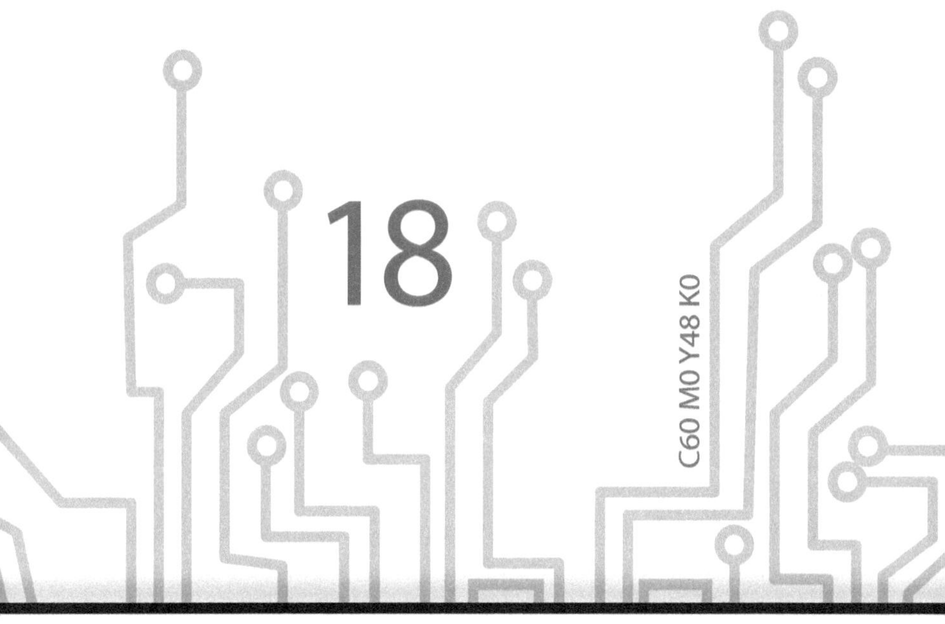

I wasn't surprised to discover that the Guard captain lived in a house. An actual house, not an apartment. Only the most loyal servants of the dragon were allowed such luxuries. Still, it wouldn't be much different from the usual apartment break-ins we'd done before… just larger. The captain lived all alone. If he'd had family, it would have complicated things. I didn't want to threaten women and children… Dusk being a notable exception.

We arrived about an hour before he was scheduled to return home, assuming he kept to his routine. We avoided the front and soon found the back door. After I broke the lock, we walked into a kitchen. I looked around at the excess and shook my head.

"This kitchen is bigger than Bice's cabin," I said. "It's half the size of the entire apartment I used to live in. And only one guy lives here."

Lainey didn't answer. She opened the refrigerator and poked around. She wore a hoodie to obscure her unmarked face. No need to announce that particular twist to our enemies. She found a steak and tossed it to Glacier, who pounced on it appreciatively.

"How about you two stay in here, far from the front door," I suggested. "I'll move to a closer room and wait. We don't know where he'll go once he enters the house."

"I should at least see how it's laid out," Lainey said.

"Right. Of course."

We checked out the rest of the house: large living area, dining space, a nice bathroom, and two bedrooms. Why did he need a second bedroom? Lainey returned to the kitchen, and I sat down in a corner of the living room. When the captain came through the front door, he would be just on the opposite side of a narrow wall from me. I took survey of the living room: couch, two end tables with lamps, a coffee table in the middle, and a recliner over near the fireplace. Besides the large entry from the front door, one other opening led into the dining space.

I heard movement from the kitchen, and Lainey scolding Glacier. Hopefully, the cat would settle down before our prey arrived.

We'd come too soon. Sitting around and waiting was always the hard part. Maybe we should have arrived after him, and burst in. No, that would have given him more of a chance to escape or grab a weapon or something. At least this way, we could surprise him.

As time ticked by, I tried not to think about everything that could go wrong. At last, I heard a sound at the door. I gathered myself, ready to jump up. The door opened. Someone grumbled under his breath. I sent boosts everywhere in my body. The door closed. A figure came around the corner and reached for the light switch.

"I prefer the darkness," I said.

He spun around, arm already moving. I dodged to the left. A knife flew past my right ear and lodged in the wall. I lunged forward. Grabbing the captain by the shirt, I slammed him against the wall.

"Hello, Captain. I'm Beryl. We need to talk."

"I have nothing to say to you." He seized my wrist and twisted. That hurt! I released him, and he dropped down, kicking at my ankles. I tried to dodge, but hadn't been prepared for that one. I fell, half on top of the coffee table. My elbow smashed through it.

Captain Lime leaped to his feet, grabbed a lamp off the end table, and swung it down at me. I managed to get my arm up in time to keep it from hitting my face. Even so, I'd be feeling that bruised forearm for days. Any harder, and it might have broken the bone.

I boosted my legs and jumped up, but the captain rushed past me to the fireplace. He spun back around, holding a poker. Great. I backed up a few steps as he advanced.

A fifty-pound white cat smacked into Lime's side, knocking him into the couch. I leaped forward and caught hold of the poker. As he tried to push back at Glacier's jaws, I boosted my arm and yanked the poker away from him.

"Glacier! Come back!" Lainey stepped into the doorway, keeping her face hooded. The cat growled deeply, but took a step back from our prisoner. Captain Lime clutched his left forearm, which sported several gashes from Glacier's claws.

I aimed the poker at him. "Well, Captain. Turns out we do get to have that conversation."

He snorted. Lainey stepped forward and flipped the light switch.

I pulled the poker back and used it to prod the broken spot in the coffee table. "Obviously, you know who I am."

The captain didn't answer. His eyes darted between the three of us, but lingered on Glacier. She was an impressive sight, I'll admit. I never expected the cub to grow so fast. I guess when we found her, she must have been a month old, maybe two at the most. So she couldn't be over six months old now, and yet she was already much bigger and more powerful than any cat I'd ever seen (besides her mother).

I put a foot on the coffee table and gave an exaggerated sigh. "Fine. You are Rodney Lime," I said, pointing the poker at him again. "You're a long-time captain in the Viridian Guard. You've probably been hunting me for a while now, and yet I move freely through the city. The people are on my side."

"Not for long," he said.

I raised my eyebrows. "You must know something I don't know then. With the dragon dead, more and more people are following my way of thinking."

He stayed quiet.

"Hmm. The silent treatment again. Look, Lime, I don't want to fight you. We should be on the same side." I didn't have much hope, but I had to at least make the attempt to convert him. "We're both human. We should be fighting together against the dragons and draconics."

No answer.

"It's not right the way they've ruled over us," I went on. "They have no regard for human life. We're nothing to them. Why can't you see that?"

"They are gods," he said without emotion. "Why should they have regard for us at all? What regard they do bear us should be celebrated and embraced."

"Wow," Lainey said.

"Yeah, he's in pretty deep," I agreed. I shook my head and took my foot off the table. "Well, let's just get the information we need and leave him alone."

Glacier took a half-step toward the couch, but stopped again at a word from Lainey.

"The cat really wants to taste you," I said. "Just give me what I want, and we'll take it away. If not…" I shrugged. "She's hungry."

Captain Lime snorted, but kept his eyes on Glacier most of the time.

"You're doing that a lot," I observed. "Are you allergic to cats, maybe?"

He glared at me.

"Right, right. So tell me, great Captain of the mighty Viridian Guard… where is the Emerald Ascendancy's power generator?"

He blinked.

"Yes, I know it's separate from the rest of the city's power," I said. "And I wouldn't want to cause trouble for everyone else, anyway. The Ascendancy is the symbol of the dragon's oppression now, and I'm going to take it down."

He laughed without smiling.

"Who's going to stop me? You?"

"Viridia will stop you."

"Viridia is dead. I saw his head get ripped off right in front of me."

"Viridia lives on," he said in a cold undertone.

Hmm. Word of Troilus Green's claims must be spreading among the faithful already. That was interesting to know. But I saw no reason to let him know what I knew about it.

"Kind of hard to keep on living when your head's been separated from your body, but you go on believing that." I stepped closer to him. "Just tell me where the power generator is."

"Viridia will stop you," he repeated. "And after he's had his way with you, I'll be there to take what's left of you and your followers"—he glanced at Lainey—"away."

I laughed back at him. "And where are you going to take us? Those little prisons at your Guard stations? Please." I boosted my arms and bent the poker. "Those can't hold me." I tossed it back toward the fireplace.

"No." He shook his head, and for the first time, a bit of a smile crept on to his face. "But we wouldn't take you there."

“Where then?”
“To the Virescent Pit.”

19

I turned away so he wouldn't see the smile on my face at his words. Now we were getting somewhere!

"The Virescent Pit? What's that? A hole in the back of your station?"

"No one returns from the Pit," he declared. He seemed to be gaining confidence by speaking about it. Good. Let him.

"You've seen what I can do. You don't think I can escape from your little pit?" I erased my smile and turned back.

"No." He shook his head. "You would try. And you would fail. The twin draconics rule there. You do not stand a chance against them."

Twin draconics? I was learning all sorts of new things.

"This sounds like a fa—like a made-up story," Lainey said.

"Yeah. I've never heard of this pit," I agreed. "I've been all over this city. If there were a pit here, I'd know about it."

"It's not in the city, you moron," the captain said. "It's over near the mines. No one goes that way unless they have to."

Unbelievable. He gave me exactly what I wanted. I almost thanked him. But now I needed to find a reason to leave, even after threatening him. If we just walked out now, he might latch on to what we'd truly been after.

"Let me ask you something, Captain," I began, turning my back to him and walking a few steps away. "Have you heard of the explosion near Caesious? The one that left an enormous crater, destroying the rail line?"

"What of it?"

I rubbed the back of my neck. "I was there too, you know. We did that to stop it from destroying the city itself. The gold dragon was threatening all of the cities. Here's the thing, though." I turned back to look at him. "What if I told you we also got our hands on another of those devices, the one intended for Viridia? What would the Emerald Ascendancy look like if we set that off beneath it? In the dead dragon's lair?"

"You don't have that ability."

"What if I did? I don't want to use it, because too many humans would die." I held out both hands. "So just tell me where the power generator is. That's a much less violent target, wouldn't you agree?"

He didn't answer.

I rolled my eyes. "Not this again. Come on, man. The cat is getting hungry."

"If you're so reluctant to harm humans, why should I believe your threats?"

"I'm reluctant. The cat isn't."

He shook his head.

"All right." I turned to Lainey. "Watch him and I'll check the rest of the house. Maybe he has something we can use."

I walked back to the bedrooms and made a show of loudly searching through everything. I did find a few interesting items that I pocketed, but no documents from his work. In fact, his rooms were ridiculously clean and organized. It was sickening. I took delight in making a mess out of them.

I returned to the living room. "I think we've got all we need from here," I declared. "Let's leave the clean-up to him."

"The Guard will hunt you down," he answered.

"They can try. They've been trying." I pointed toward the kitchen. "We're going out the back way. Don't follow us, or the cat's set free. That's not a threat; it's a promise."

I turned my back on him and walked into the kitchen. There, I discovered Lainey had filled two enormous bags with food from the pantry and fridge. Good thinking. I grabbed one, and she grabbed the other as she joined me. Together, we left the house and disappeared into the darkness of the night.

"The Virescent Pit," I repeated, back at the shrine. "That's what we're looking for. Apparently, it's near the mines."

"Ohhh, the pit by the mines," Lovat said. "That place."

My mouth dropped open. "You know about it?"

He shrugged, then dropped onto the couch. "Don talked 'bout it. Said I should never go near it."

I put my fist on my forehead. "Next time, include Lovat in all the discussions," I said aloud.

"We didn't know it was a pit until the captain called it that," Lainey pointed out.

"No, Jaden called it a pit too. I just didn't think that part was important. Ugh. I didn't need this bruise on my arm after all."

"It wasn't a total loss." Lainey scratched Glacier's head behind the ears. "Glacier got a steak, and we picked up some more food."

"They dig for the green stuff there," Lovat offered. "Green rocks."

"You mean jade?" Carl asked.

Lovat shrugged. "Green rocks," he repeated.

"So it's like a mine, but they make the prisoners work it," I said. "Makes sense from their point of view, I guess."

"What's our next step?" Lainey asked.

"Find it, and see… what we can see." I stretched. "After we get some sleep. Lovat and I can check it out tomorrow."

He perked up. "I can go?"

"No one I'd trust better with this."

In the late morning, we set out. I knew how to get to the road that led to the mines, but nothing beyond. Lovat said he'd wandered down the road a couple of times, and knew of a side road that branched off before the mines themselves. It might be the direction we needed.

This time of day, the road to the mines was empty. As we walked along, I struggled to remember anything I knew about this region. The answer? Almost nothing. I couldn't even remember what was being mined. I think I heard the word coal at some point, but I wasn't sure. Kelly used to gripe at me for not paying attention during the Learning Years. And… she had a point. I didn't pay attention to things I didn't care about at the time.

We found the side road without much difficulty. It split off from the road perhaps a mile away from the edge of the mountains, and led somewhat northeast, staying parallel to the mountains themselves. At first, the road was level, but it soon began to rise. We entered a much rougher terrain. I saw a lot more trees, scrubby ones I didn't recognize. The road dipped down into a ravine at one point, for no particular reason, then rose back out and continued to climb.

The hills grew more and more turbulent, far different from the smooth and rolling hills we lived among out at the Asylum. Here, the road took abrupt turns to dodge sudden rock shelves towering over our heads, or crevasses that plunged several dozen feet down. If we met anyone along the road, it might be difficult to escape them. But the road stayed empty throughout our walk.

I had just begun to wonder if the road led anywhere when we crested a high point and look down into what had to be the Virescent Pit.

I'd never seen anything like it. The road turned to the left and circled down, down, following a sheer wall on its left and a sheer drop on its right. Lovat and I stared down an enormous slope of rubble. A few figures moved among the rocks near its base, scarcely the size of ants to our sight. Below them, we saw multiple rows of shelters covered in green tarps, followed by another rubble slope cascading down into a deeper pit area. When I zoomed in with my cybernetic eyes, I could see people working in that area, digging individual holes or moving along the walled edges. I spotted two of the large digger vehicles like Don had once stolen for us.

Pulling my vision back some, I examined the green tarp area. I could see a handful of people moving about. A pair of trucks were parked near what looked like the only solid structure in the place: a concrete building stationed near the road. The figures moving about there all looked green: Viridian Guard uniforms, I assumed.

I let my vision return to normal and looked around the outer edges again. Everywhere I looked, I saw rock and scrub and steep walls. The only way in or out of the pit appeared to be the road. No one would be able to sneak out of this place, with the Guard based right at the one exit. No wonder no one ever returned from here.

"Doesn't look like much fun," Lovat observed, tossing a rock down the slope in front of us.

"No. No, it doesn't." I scanned the walls some more, hoping to find just the slightest of advantages, maybe a place where we could mount a rope and climb down… I found nothing.

If any of our friends were down there… I didn't see any way to get them out.

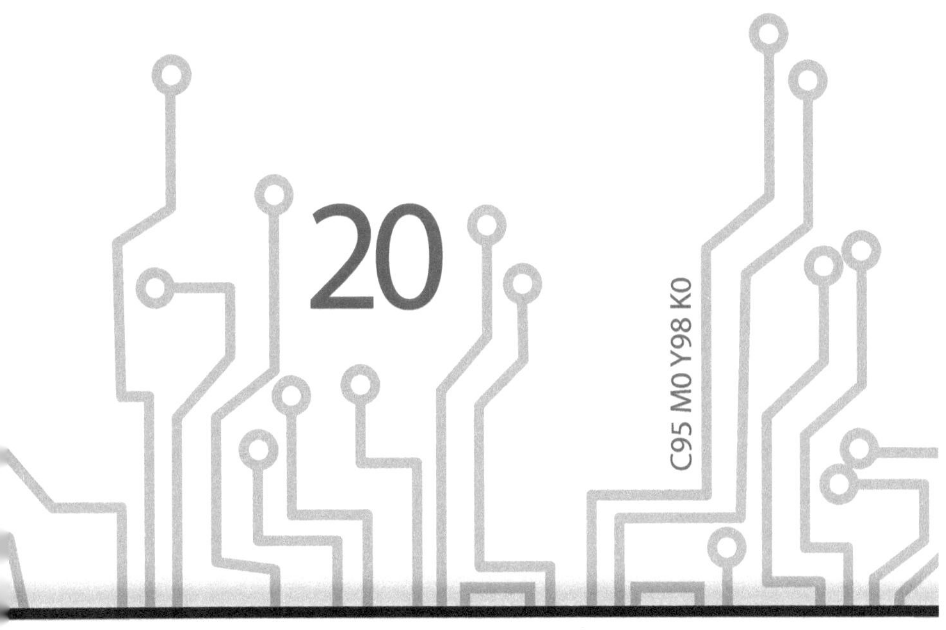

"Go down?" Lovat asked.

"No." I knelt on the edge and flicked a pebble down. I watched it bounce from rock to rock as it plunged deeper, until I lost track of it.

I needed a plan, an idea, something. I missed the Sky Claimer. I could have flown it straight down to the base of the pit without any trouble. But the smashed remains of my flying wings lay somewhere on the mountains miles and miles away. I doubt even Loden could have repaired it.

"The only way in is by the road," I said aloud.

"Yah." Lovat tossed a rock along the road, watching it bounce and skid. "Either walk or ride a truck."

"A truck," I repeated. If we stole a truck from the Guard, and maybe some uniforms… we could pretend to be delivering a prisoner.

And then what? Once we got down there, we wouldn't have long before getting noticed. Even from this distant vantage point, I'd spotted at least five or six Viridian Guard, and there had to be more further down among the prisoners. Plus, Captain Lime referred to twin draconics who ruled the place. They were probably inside that building. I couldn't think of any way our little band could take down that many. Maybe if we incited the prisoners to riot first…

All right. I had the beginnings of an idea, but I needed feedback. Time to head back home.

"You're insane," Stacy declared. I'd talked her and Jaden into joining us for a planning session at the shrine. Rather than crowd into Carl's cabin, we gathered in the sacellum itself.

"I've heard whispers of this pit," Stacy went on. "People go in, but they never come out."

"I can see why," I said. "It would be suicide to try to leave."

"Then why do you think you even have a chance?"

"We killed a dragon," I said. "We broke into the Flame. We saved Caesious. We keep doing impossible things. Why not this?"

"Because you don't have a plan yet," Carl said. "You have a way to get in, which isn't that far-fetched, but once you're discovered, then what? And you'll be discovered right away. You don't know the system for delivering a prisoner."

"And none of you have the right chromarks or even look like Guard members," Stacy pointed out, "except Jaden here, for obvious reasons."

"Thank you?" He raised his eyebrows.

"We start a riot," I said.

"The prisoners?" Stacy asked.

"Right. With all of them on our side, we can overwhelm the guards. Lainey, Glacier, and I can deal with the draconics…"

"Who starts the riot?" Jaden asked.

"That's the problem with the plan," I admitted.

"You would need someone down there with the prisoners," Carl said. "And that takes you back to your original idea of getting someone arrested and thrown in there." He shook his head. "I don't think you'll find a volunteer for that mission."

"Then we'll have to find another way in."

"How?" Jaden asked. "You already said no one can get down there except by the road."

I looked up at the afternoon sun shining through the open roof of the sacellum. "No ordinary person can get down there," I said.

"What are you thinking?" Lainey asked, her eyes narrowing at me.

"I think I can do it," I answered. "I can get down there. I'm the only one who can."

"Again: how?" Jaden demanded.

"Climbing, jumping, falling. Whatever it takes."

"Falling? You can't be serious!" Lainey argued. "You're not invincible!"

"I know. But I am constantly surviving things I have no right to survive." I gestured toward Carl. "And now we're starting to understand how I can do those things."

"I haven't seen what you've seen," Carl said slowly, "so you're in a better position to judge whether you could survive it. But even if you survive, can you be sure that you'll be in any condition to even talk, let alone survive a riot? You survived the crash in the mountains, but when we found you, you were almost dead. It took days before you could speak a single word."

"This won't be that bad."

"Are you absolutely positive about that?"

I opened my mouth to answer, but then stopped. I couldn't say it with complete honesty.

"It's not just a question of survival," Stacy said. "Do you really think the guards won't notice a man 'climbing, jumping, falling' down into their prison?"

"I was thinking of doing it at night," I muttered.

She laughed at me. I didn't blame her, I guess. The idea sounded more and more foolish as they kept pointing out all its flaws.

"All right. So does anyone have a better idea?"

No one answered. I looked around at each of them, and waited.

"How much could we mitigate the danger of your descent?" Carl asked at last. "How far could we lower you by rope?"

"Part of the way, for sure," I said. "But I wouldn't want to depend on it. There are so many sharp edges and ridges throughout, I couldn't trust a rope for long."

"Unless it was a really, really strong rope," Lainey said.

"Cable?" Carl asked. "Do you people have those?"

"Loden did," Lovat piped up. "In the workshop."

I did a quick mental inventory of the workshop I'd visited only a couple of days earlier. Yes, now that I thought about it: there was a big wooden roll of some kind of metal cable off to one side of the room. I'd always ignored it, because it wasn't a cool gadget.

"I guess I'll be making a trip back to the Asylum."

"You'll need a way to unroll it as you descend," Carl pointed out.

"Cable is not rope. The rest of us can't just hold on to it at the top."

I nodded. "I'll see if Caedan and his team have any ideas."

"Wait… did your insane plan suddenly become feasible?" Stacy asked. She sat back and shook her head. "You have no business getting as far as you have so far."

"Hey, at least I bounced it off the rest of you," I said. "Before I… bounced off the walls of the pit." I waited, but no one laughed. I guess I still wasn't as funny as I thought I was.

Jaden got to his feet. "Is that it, then?"

"No. While I'm gone, I want you and Stacy to both be exploring what it would take to steal one of the Viridian Guard's trucks. And some uniforms." I scratched the back of my neck. "And see if anyone's heard anything about these twin draconics. They don't worry me a whole lot, but anything we can find out ahead of time might help."

"And while I'm at it, I'll uncover the meaning of life," Stacy promised. "Any other impossible demands?"

"Oh, yeah, actually. Jaden, tell her about Olive."

"What about Olive?" Stacy's eyes shot from me to Jaden. Ha. Let him deal with that.

Lainey got up and approached me. "Do you want some company on this trip? I wouldn't mind seeing Caedan again."

"I'd love to have you along, but… I travel so much faster alone."

Her eyes seemed to grow larger. Was she doing that on purpose? "It's just… when you're gone, I have to sit around here with nothing to do." She gestured widely. "We can't go anywhere in this city because of our faces. My father doesn't mind, but… I'm bored out of my mind."

"I'm sorry." As often happened while talking with Lainey, my awkwardness grew with each sentence. I didn't know what to do with my hands while we stood there talking. "I guess I've never thought about what it's like for you."

"I've been spending time teaching Lovat," she admitted. "Did you know he couldn't read?"

I had a vague recollection of that, I think. "I'm glad you're helping him." I hesitated. "I guess you can come with me. Maybe we can use the four-wheeler on our way back."

"If Caedan hasn't already wrecked it." She smiled at her own joke.

"That's actually a distinct possibility," I said. "We'd better hurry. When can you be ready to go?"

"It's late afternoon. Do you want to go today or wait until morning?"

"Walking at night is cooler," I pointed out. Very pleasant, in fact. Winter wouldn't be here for a couple of weeks at least.

"Great. I'll be ready as soon as I can pack some things up."

"What about Glacier?" I asked as she turned toward her room.

"Glacier's a cat. She does what she wants," she answered over her shoulder. "If she wants to come, she's coming."

I couldn't decide whether that was a good thing or not.

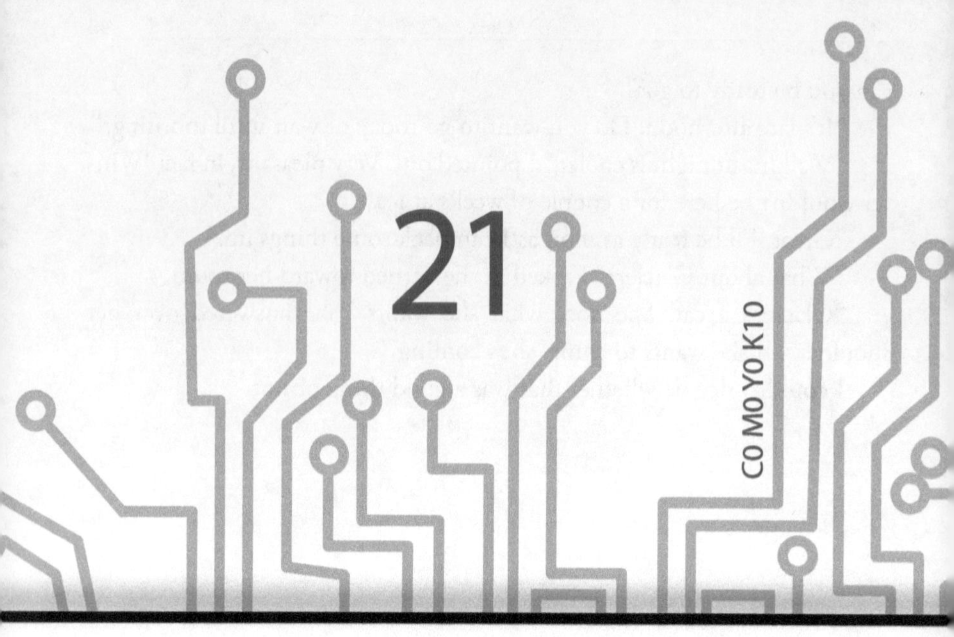

"Sometimes, I feel like I've spent half of my life walking back and forth to the Asylum," I said a few hours later.

Lainey laughed. "Didn't you spend the first seventeen years of your life inside that city, never going anywhere?"

"True," I acknowledged as Glacier bounded past me to chase a twilight shadow among a small copse of trees. "But ever since then…" I paused. "Wow. It hasn't even been a whole year since then. I guess I'm still seventeen."

"Youngster," Lainey teased. "All I do these days is hang out with little boys."

"Oh, yeah? How old are you, exactly?"

She grinned and arched her eyebrows. "I'm eighteen, I'll have you know."

"Oooo. No wonder we have to take things so slow, Grandma."

She laughed again. I liked her laugh. It had a child-like tone to it that didn't come across in her voice.

"Did you ever meet them?" she asked. "Your grandparents, I mean."

I cocked my head. I hadn't thought of other relatives beyond my parents and sister in so long. "I have some vague memories of some nice older people," I said, "from when I was a little child."

"So… last week?"

I aimed a pretend slap at her. She ducked and laughed some more.

"I remember my mother's parents," she said a few minutes later. "Grandma... I remember gray hair. And, uh..." She held out her arms in a circle. "Plumpness. Grandpa always smelled like cigars."

"What are cigars?"

She blinked. "You don't...? Wow. I guess I've never seen that in your society, either. Huh."

"So what are they?"

She tried to explain, but I couldn't grasp it. Something about leaves rolled up in paper and then set on fire in someone's mouth? Why?

Glacier trotted up behind us, and then pushed against my legs. I stumbled and almost fell. "Stupid cat."

"She likes you," Lainey said. "That's one of the ways she shows it."

"By trying to knock me off my feet?"

"She's demanding your attention. It's sort of like a human being yelling, 'Hey! Look at me!'"

I patted the white-furred beast on the head. "If she keeps growing, she'll knock us down without even trying."

"I know. I can't wait to see how big she gets!"

I shook my head. "It's going to make it harder and harder to keep her fed."

Lainey patted her rifle. "I'll take care of her."

A few minutes later, she turned back to the grandparents conversation. "Were the ones you remember your dad's parents, or your mom's?"

"I have no idea." I sighed. "It's hard to explain these things to people who haven't lived here." I grimaced, not wanting to say it, but... "Elderly people are of no use to the dragon."

"What are you saying?"

I pointed a thumb over my shoulder. "Have you seen a lot of old people in Viridia?"

She scrunched up her forehead. "No..."

"If you can't contribute to the dragon's purposes, you have no purpose," I tried to explain. "If you have no purpose, you aren't wanted. You consume too many resources that could be used for more productive members of society."

"I don't understand."

"Elderly people are encouraged to die, and stop being a drain on everyone else."

Her mouth opened in shock.

"I can't say whether they actually kill them," I conceded, "but they don't stick around long once they're past a working age. Some of them die of unexplained causes. Some of them just… disappear. Maybe they're sent to this Virescent Pit to do a little mining before they collapse. I don't know."

"That's horrible."

"Welcome to my world." I paused. "Um, not that I'm saying your life has been great, you know."

"I know." She walked on, unshaken. Sometimes, I really couldn't figure her out.

Despite my doubts, we made good time, walking well into the night before finding a place to sleep. As we spread our sleeping bags out in an open area not far from the rail line, I noticed a flash in the distant sky. Lightning? I surveyed the sky and noticed a lot more clouds than earlier in the evening.

"We might get rained on," I pointed out.

Lainey stopped and looked at the sky too. "Should we try to find shelter?"

"It would be better than getting soaked out in the open like this, I guess."

We picked our gear back up and resumed walking. Seeking shelter on a night like this created problems, especially since we had no light. The clouds obscured any moon, and we were far from the cities by now.

"Let's head back to the tracks," I suggested. "If I remember right, we aren't far from an old farming station. There's an overhang we can sleep under."

"Is that safe? You said they were running trains again."

"I think we can take our chances. I haven't seen another train since that one time. And why would they run it this late at night?"

She shrugged and followed me. The rain reached us before we reached the station. At first, we walked through a gentle mist. Then the drops started descending, intermittent at first, but growing ever more steady. In the distance, I spotted a small glow. "That's it!" We broke into a run just as the rain became a downpour. We dashed under the overhang, thoroughly soaked.

A single light bulb still shone from the ceiling above us, a lone hold-out among at least a dozen comrades who'd long since given up. The rain pounded on the metal roof, creating a cacophony of rapid noises. Glacier shook herself and complained loud enough to be heard over it.

"Sorry, girl. I can't control the weather," Lainey said. She stripped off her backpack and examined it. "Even the sleeping bag is wet. We won't be using these tonight."

I shivered. "We should get out of these clothes, though."

Lainey pulled things out of her pack. "I guess these other clothes are a little less wet?"

I followed her lead, pulling everything out of my pack. One pair of shorts were almost dry. I spread everything else out on a wooden docking ramp, then pulled off my soaked shirt to add to it.

"Don't look while I change," Lainey warned. I turned away. "Not that you would, anyway," she added.

"What does that mean?" I asked, studiously looking down the track.

"You're a good man. You've proven that. Why do you think my father trusts you?"

"He trusts me?" That was news to me.

"Of course. He lets me travel with you. Overnight." Her hand touched my back. "I'm done."

I turned around to see her wearing a new shirt and pants, both of which looked damp. I could see her shivering.

"My sleeping bag didn't get too wet," I pointed out. "Come on. We can wrap it around us."

We settled down next to the docking ramp. Lainey scooted up next to me, and I spread the sleeping bag over us, making sure to keep the dampest part on my side. The rain continued to pound on the overhang.

"I don't know if we're going to get much sleep," Lainey said.

"Not like this," I agreed. Besides the dampness, there was the awkwardness of the whole situation, the warmth of her right next to me… "Um, I've never been good at sleeping while sitting up."

"Why are you that way?"

"Not good at sleeping while sitting up?"

"No, silly." She started to shake her head, but stopped when her damp hair threw more water drops at me. "Why are you such a good man?" She turned her head to look at my face, so close. "Most guys in this kind of situation, at least the ones I've met, would be trying something. But not you."

"I'm terrified of the cat," I said, looking past her at Glacier licking herself. "If I tried something and you complained, she might eat me."

"What if I didn't complain?"

I looked into her green eyes and swallowed. "Lainey, I, uh…"

"It's okay," she said. "I understand."

"You do?"

She shrugged, her shoulder rubbing against mine. "You're worried about Kelly. You don't think you can have a relationship with anyone else until that's resolved."

"How are you so smart?" I asked.

"I actually paid attention in school—what you call the Learning Years."

"Ouch."

"Now put your arm around me. It doesn't have to mean anything, but this is awkward."

I complied and slid my arm back around her shoulders. She snuggled in against me a little closer. "That's better."

I agreed. I looked up and saw Glacier staring at me. "I'm not doing anything to her, cat!"

Lainey giggled. "Come here, Glacier."

The cat rose, stretched, and ever so slowly made her way to us. She curled up on Lainey's other side, but not until giving me another hard stare.

No one said anything after that. Lainey's breathing became more steady. My arm fell asleep, but I didn't want to move it. I considered what she'd said. Was I a good man? I didn't always feel good, but… some things were right, and some things were wrong. Bice had taught me a lot of that, actually. I wondered where he was right now. Was he sleeping under one of those green tarps in the pit?

"I'm coming, Bice," I whispered. "And Kelly. I'm coming for all of you."

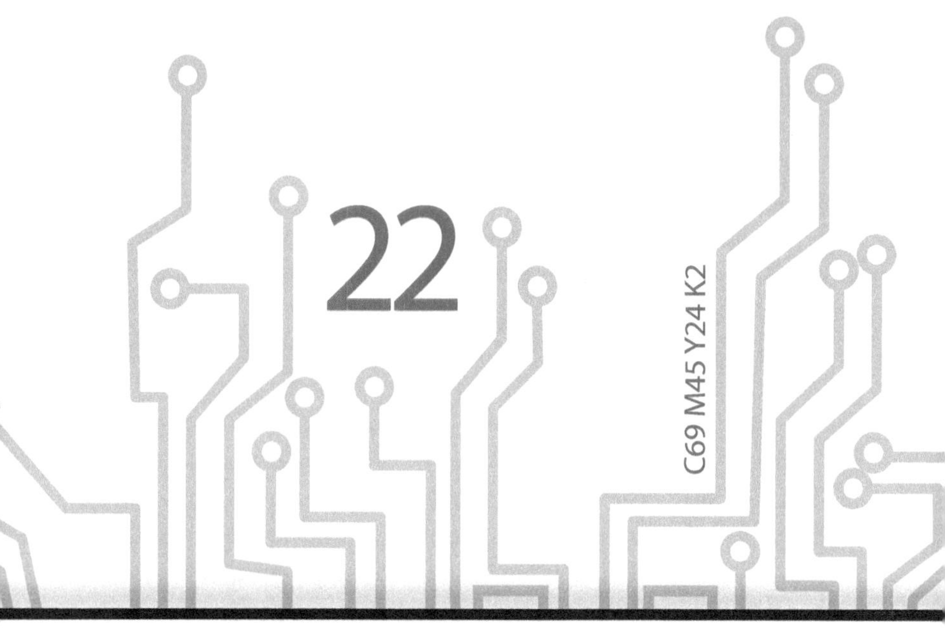

22

The rain stopped a few hours later. I may have dozed off a time or two. At some point, I did manage to get my arm out from behind Lainey. It took a while for it to return to normal. None of my cyb powers helped against loss of circulation. Glacier came and went several times. Where do cats wander off to, anyway?

When morning finally arrived, I slipped out from Lainey, letting her down onto the sleeping bag. I stretched achy muscles and jogged around for a while. A few boosts helped clear things up. I was learning to go without much sleep sometimes, but even with the boosts, I knew I'd be a bit fuzzy-headed until I could catch up.

Lainey woke soon after that, and it didn't take long before we set out again. Our progress became slower as we dodged muddy spots along the way. I had to admit the trip was much more pleasant with Lainey along, but I itched at the slowness. I could have made it by early morning at the latest, if I were alone. As it was, we didn't arrive at the ruined Asylum until mid-afternoon.

Two of Caedan's team—Saxe and… I forgot the other guy's name— were outside, relaxing by a small campfire. A few pieces of litter showed the remains of their lunch, or an afternoon snack. They scrambled to their feet as we approached.

"Mister Beryl, sir!" Saxe exclaimed. "We didn't expect to see you again so soon!"

"I'm here to pick up some stuff," I said. "Is Caedan around?"

The guys exchanged looks. "No," said the other one. "He and the others are gone to scout the Blasted Lands for you."

I should have known Caedan would take off on that mission right away. Well, we didn't really need him for this, I suppose. It would have been nice to get his feedback, though.

"This is Lainey," I said. "Caedan may have mentioned her. Oh, and Glacier."

The last time I'd been here, these guys looked at me like a big celebrity. Now that focus turned to Lainey, the girl without a chromark. They babbled incoherently to her, tried to ask questions about the world outside The Circle, and generally behaved completely awe-struck in her presence. She endured it with good humor, but Glacier looked annoyed. Then again, she looked annoyed most of the time.

We made our way into the workshop. Sure enough, we found the roll of cable shoved into a corner. I pulled the end loose and examined it: just as thick as a strong rope, but made of metal strands. This certainly wouldn't fray against rocks.

"What do you need that for?" Saxe asked.

"I need to get down into a very deep place," I told them. "You guys got any ideas on that?"

Again, they exchanged looks. "You might be able to rig a pulley system of some kind," the other guy said. Cobalt! That was his name.

"Would that work?" I asked. "I mean, no one can hold on to this while I descend. It would tear their hands apart."

"No, no," he said. "We could do it safely. I'm sure of it. Where is this deep place?"

"Viridia. A place called the Virescent Pit. It's a prison."

"Oh." Their excitement faded a bit. "How are you going to get this to Viridia?"

"Did Caedan take the four-wheeler?"

Cobalt laughed. "He really wanted to."

"But then Sapphire reminded him that it was a stealth mission," Saxe added.

"I can imagine," I said. Caedan probably whined and griped for a few minutes, but gave in to reason eventually.

"Wait, if you're using the four-wheeler, that will make lowering the cable even easier!" Cobalt exclaimed.

"Good. You're coming with us. Pack up your stuff."

"What?" His eyes almost exploded. "I can't go to Viridia! I have the wrong chromark!"

I pointed at my face with both hands. "Welcome to the club. Almost none of us do."

"I don't have one at all," Lainey added.

"Do you need me too?" Saxe asked.

I thought for a moment. "No, someone needs to be here when Caedan gets back, to let him know where we've gone. And also to keep an eye on the workshop. Can I trust you with that?"

"Absolutely, sir!"

"Did he show you how to shut the door from the inside?"

He walked to the door and reached for the lever hidden in a cleft to the right.

"You don't need to close it right now," I said in a hurry. "But if you think it might be discovered, do whatever you need to keep it a secret."

"Yes, sir!"

It felt weird to have people addressing me that way. Just yesterday, I'd pointed out to Lainey that I was still seventeen. These guys might be older than me, even if they did appear young. Now that I thought about it, they could almost be twins. They were both skinny, had brown hair, and big grins. Cobalt wore glasses, and Saxe had some fuzz around his chin, but otherwise...

"Are you two brothers?"

They looked at each other. They did that a lot. "Yeah, how'd you know?" Saxe answered.

"Lucky guess. All right, let's get moving."

Getting the cumbersome roll of cable out of the cave proved to be a bit more difficult than anticipated. But with four of us rolling and shifting it through the rubble, we eventually succeeded.

I fetched the four-wheeler from where I'd left it. It coughed and sputtered a bit when I first started it back up, but soon ran just as it always had. I made sure we had enough fuel, then loaded the cable on board. Then I realized my error: there was no way the three of us could ride on this thing with the cable... not to mention Glacier. Oops.

"Lainey, you can drive this, right?"

"I've watched you plenty of times, but never done it myself."

"I can," Cobalt offered. "I drove a few experimental vehicles back in Caesious."

"Hue. You drive. Lainey can ride. I'll run." I eyed the cat. "Can Glacier keep up with us?"

Lainey climbed on to the back of the four-wheeler with the cable. "She'll let us know when she gets tired. Then she can ride on top of the cable here."

Saxe stared at me. "You're going to run all the way to Viridia?"

I grinned. "Benefits of a cyb implant. Tell Caedan I'll be back." Without waiting for the others, I boosted my legs and took off. Cobalt got the four-wheeler running and soon caught up. Glacier trotted a little bit, then broke into a run with me when she realized we were going to keep moving.

We made good time for a couple of hours. The four-wheeler didn't care about puddles, and I could dodge the mud easier while boosted. About an hour before sunset, we stopped for a rest and considered the rest of the trip.

"We're not going to make it back tonight," Lainey pointed out. "You've avoided driving this thing in the dark."

"Yeah, we could all use the rest." I didn't want to admit how tired I was, but after hardly any sleep the night before, I didn't think I could make this entire run without more rest.

"Caedan taught us how to camp out," Cobalt offered with a grin.

"Good. 'Cause we're sleeping under the stars tonight." I looked up at the sky. "Hope it doesn't rain again."

Cobalt's grin faded.

Fortunately, the night sky stayed clear. We managed to find a dry spot on a short hill for our camp. Lainey's sleeping bag was still wet, so I gave her mine and slept on the ground myself. Over the past year, I'd done many things I never expected of myself. Who would have thought I'd learn how to sleep in so many different places and situations?

Despite his claim to learning from Caedan, Cobalt tossed and turned all night. If I had to guess, he'd only slept outside a couple of times on the way from Caesious to the Asylum, probably the only times in his life. But then, most city-dwellers were like that. I'd certainly never done it before starting our insurrection.

"Where are we taking the four-wheeler?" Lainey asked in the morning.

"We should probably stash it and the cable somewhere near the Pit," I suggested. "We can't take it into the city, and we may as well have it near our target."

Cobalt wandered back from relieving himself. He took off his glasses, wiped them with the tail of his shirt, then put them back on and squinted off in the distance.

"Were you aware someone is watching us?" he asked.

23

"What?" I whirled to look in the direction he indicated. A lone figure stood atop another hill some distance away, facing us. I zoomed in with my cybernetic eyes. I saw someone tall, clad in purple robes with green trim. The lower half of the robe fluttered from a slight breeze. A hood concealed his face.

"Anyone we know?" Lainey asked. She retrieved binoculars from the four-wheeler and joined me.

"No one I recognize." The robes reminded me of Troilus Green's, but the colors were reversed. And the shape looked more human than draconic. "Who wears purple?" I muttered.

"Lots of people," Lainey said, "Just… not in your cities."

"Who is it?" Cobalt asked.

I reset my eyes to normal. "I'll go ask him."

"Wait—" Lainey started to say.

I boosted my legs before she finished and raced toward the hill. The figure remained unmoving as I drew closer. But right as I reached the base of his hill, the figure rolled his head to one side. The robes swept up as if a stronger wind blew against them. He turned sideways, and… disappeared.

I came to a stop at the top of the hill and spun in a circle. I couldn't see where he could have gone. There was no cover for around a hundred yards in every direction. I continued to turn, trying to figure it out. No one just vanishes into thin air. Or thick air, actually, now that I considered it. I stopped turning. The air did feel thick. How odd.

Glacier caught up to me, then turned away, walking a few feet as if to pretend she hadn't been running. "Make yourself useful, cat," I said. "Find that guy." In response, Glacier stretched her front paws out and arched her back. She started licking herself.

The other two approached at a much slower pace. I noticed Lainey had brought along her rifle.

"Where did he go?" Cobalt asked.

"I don't know." I waved in a vague sweep. "He vanished."

"Why do you think it was a he?" Lainey asked.

"I also don't know that. I don't even know if it was human."

Lainey looked around at the empty land. "How bizarre." Her voice had an odd tone to it, but I agreed with her. Strange things seemed to follow me, but this one was truly perplexing. The watcher had clearly not been a member of the Viridian Guard in that outfit. A priest, maybe… but again, the colors were wrong.

"If we had a purple city, I'd say he came from there, but as it is…" I took one more look around. "I have no idea what to think."

"Creepy." Cobalt scratched his head. "Hey, did you guys bring anything for breakfast? I think I forgot to pack any food."

We returned to our hill, shared our meager fare with Cobalt, and resumed our journey. A few hours later, we parked the four-wheeler in the shadow of an eight-foot cliff, about a mile from the Virescent Pit. I used the talker to call for Lovat to meet us at the city's border. With his guidance, we made our way safely back to the shrine.

"How did it go?" Lainey's father asked, once we'd gathered in the sacellum and introduced Cobalt.

"We got the cable, the four wheeler, and Cobalt here to make it work," I said. "Anything from Stacy and Jaden?"

"No. You returned faster than I anticipated. I don't know if they've had time to scope anything out yet."

I paced the open area. "We're not technically under a deadline," I said, "but it feels like it. Caedan will be back in a few days from scouting the tower. I'd like to be done with this Pit job when he does, so we can move on with that mission."

"You seem pretty sure he'll find something there," Carl observed.

He leaned against one of the sacellum's pillars, arms crossed.

I spread my hands. "Where else could Onyx be hiding? He's got to be somewhere. This just feels right to me."

"You haven't told him the other part," Lainey said. "Dad, we saw someone in a purple robe watching us."

"And he disappeared when Beryl tried to catch him," Cobalt added.

Carl Roberts stiffened for a moment. I wouldn't have noticed if I hadn't already been looking directly at him. His body relaxed just as quickly. "Sound familiar?" I asked.

"Just out in the middle of nowhere?" he asked. "Sounds like one of your priests. Don't they wear robes sometimes?"

"None of them wear purple," I said, watching him intently. "This guy was on a hill, watching us. And he did disappear, with nowhere to hide."

"Strange." His body language gave nothing away now. Whatever it had been, he didn't want to share any more, at least not now. But I wasn't going to let it go.

Cobalt looked around at everything, eyes wide behind his glasses. "Isn't this, like, a dragon shrine?" he asked. "And you guys live here?"

"It used to be," I answered. "Lovat, why don't you show Cobalt around? He can sleep in the third room there, for now."

Lovat hopped up and led Cobalt out of the sacellum, chattering away about the shrine, what had happened here before, and how we lived now.

As soon as they disappeared, I turned back to Carl. "Okay, you're hiding something," I said. "The purple robes meant something to you. I could tell."

"I'm sure you're mistaken," he answered, not moving from his relaxed stance.

"No, you reacted." I pointed at him. "Cybernetic eyes, remember? I catch details." That wasn't necessarily true, but it made a good excuse.

Carl unfolded his arms and straightened. "Beryl, I'm going to say this once, and that's all. I have told you a number of things about life outside this valley. Lainey has told you some things about our family. But there are many, many things neither of us have told you, for a wide variety of reasons. And it's going to stay that way, until and unless there is good reason to tell you."

"Someone spying on us isn't good reason?" I clenched my fist. "Someone with the ability to disappear like that isn't a good reason?"

"No. It isn't."

I stared at him, unable to decide what to say. How dare he keep more secrets from me!

"Let it go, Beryl," Lainey said. "If he says it's not important right now, it's not."

"I've had too many people keeping secrets from me," I said, continuing to stare at Carl. "I'm not very tolerant of it any more."

"I'm not a dragon, if that's what you're wondering," Carl said. "Neither is Lainey. I can't be sure about the cat, though."

"You think this is funny?"

He rolled his eyes. "Beryl, relax. It has nothing to do with our present circumstances, all right? Let's move on with your plan."

I gritted my teeth, but turned away. I couldn't force him to tell me, but I didn't like it, either. Too many secrets. Too much trouble. I'd grown sick of it all.

I moped about the rest of the afternoon, debating over my next move. I had just decided to go find Jaden and determine his status, when he showed up with news.

"We know where to steal a truck," he announced as soon as he saw me.

"From the Viridian Guard?"

Lovat and Lainey joined us near the gate.

"Yes… and no."

I gave him my best "You're an idiot" look. He chuckled and explained, "It used to belong to the Guard. It's the same model they use now, but this one got old. So they traded it down to a shipping company, and got a new one."

"A shipping company?"

"Yes, and that's the best part. Since the trains aren't running, the shipping company can't ship anything." He waved an arm in excitement. "They would normally use the truck to haul stuff to the train station, but since they can't… it's just sitting around. It would be easy to steal!"

I nodded. "So far, so good. I don't remember, though. Are there any special markings on the truck we'll need to fix?"

"No, the Guard keep their trucks unmarked. I guess they don't want people to know when they're moving prisoners through the streets."

"Right." I had rescued Rick from one of those trucks once. What if I hadn't? Would he still be working in the Virescent Pit today? I doubted that. Then again, if Rick hadn't been with us, we might not have killed Caesious. Everything would have gone wrong in Incarnadine. I probably wouldn't be alive. And yet, even while helping me, he was working for his own purposes the whole time.

"I do have one important question," Jaden said. He licked his lips and glanced around.

"What's that?"

"Who's going to drive the truck?"

I opened my mouth to answer, then stopped. Who would? I might be able to do it, but I would be down in the pit. I'd planned for Lainey and Glacier to be in the back of the truck, where she could be ready with her rifle.

"Can you drive?" I asked Jaden.

"I mean…. Yeah. But that doesn't mean I'm willing to do it."

Stacy probably wouldn't do it, even if she could.

"Marcus?" Lovat suggested.

Marcus Vermeil drove a truck as part of his job, but… "There's no time to fetch him from Incarnadine," I said. "We have to handle this ourselves."

"I'll drive." Carl Roberts approached us from the cabin. "Just get me one of those uniforms. We need to take care of this situation and move on. I don't think it's safe for us in this city much longer."

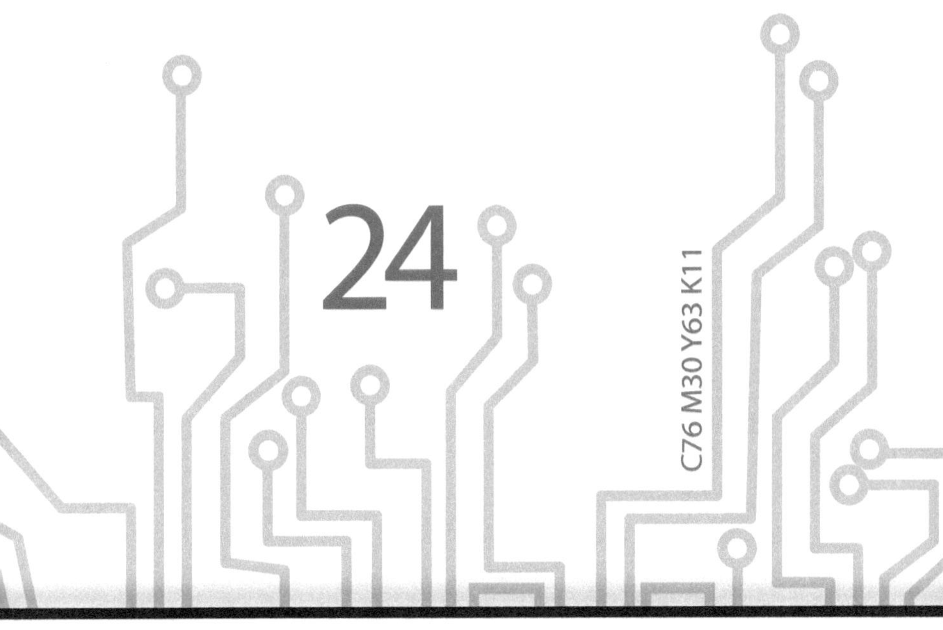

Carl wouldn't elaborate on why he thought the city was growing too dangerous. I guessed it had to do with Troilus Green, but I didn't pursue the issue. Why bother? He'd only keep more secrets.

Stealing the truck proved to be far easier than getting complete Viridian Guard uniforms. Jaden led Carl and myself to the shipping company's warehouse. We found the truck sitting in an empty lot behind it, with no one around.

"This is too easy," I said.

"Who's going to steal a vehicle when there are less than twenty of them in the entire city?" Jaden asked. "How long could someone keep something that big hidden after stealing it?"

"Where are we hiding it?" Carl asked.

"We're not." I opened the door and motioned him into the driver's seat. "We're just parking it somewhere near our base. But not too near."

"You're not worried they'll find it and bring it back?"

"In one day? I think we'll be all right." I got into the passenger's seat.

Carl shook his head as he climbed in. "You're playing fast and loose again, son."

"It's a temporary measure," I told him. "If you can think of another way, let me know."

Jaden scrambled into the seat beside me. "I really don't even think they'll notice for a while," he said. "They can't use it right now, so why would they check on it?"

"It's a great big motor vehicle," Carl said. He looked over the controls in front of him. "Why wouldn't they notice it was gone?" He found a lever and turned it. The engine roared to life.

"Half of what we do is a gamble," I argued. "It always will be."

"And that's why you'll always be in danger."

"No, I'll always be in danger because we have bleaking dragons and draconics ruling everything."

The truck started moving with a jerk. Carl guided it through the streets of Viridia as I directed him.

"I'm just saying you need to think things through."

"You sound like Bice."

"Bice must be a very intelligent man."

"He was. Is." I watched out the window for the next turn. In the time before Rick's betrayal, I'd relied on Bice a lot. But I didn't always listen to him, even when I knew he was right. Without his guidance, maybe I shouldn't be doing stuff like this. Maybe I should... but no. This was all about finding him, and my other lost friends. If it made a difference to the overall struggle at the same time, all the better.

We parked the truck in an alley a few blocks from the shrine, but miles away from the shipping company. Even with a detailed search, it would take them days to find it, or so I told myself. We regrouped at the shrine, where we found Stacy waiting.

"I have the cloth parts of the Guard uniforms," she reported, "but you're going to have to find helmets and gear on your own."

Jaden held up one of the uniforms. "This one looks like it would fit Carl. Where'd you get these, Stacy? Do you have someone inside one of the stations?"

She laughed. "You guys think too much like soldiers. I have someone on the inside, all right... the inside of the laundromat. Even oppressive police have to wash their uniforms from time to time."

"The helmets are kind of key," I said. "Unless we're going to disguise everyone's faces with fake chromarks again, we need them."

"I can't be seen," Jaden said. "Any one of the Guard might recognize me!"

Ugh. The plan called for Carl and Jaden to be in the front of the truck.

They would both need helmets.

"Fine. I'll go find some." I walked to our supply of tools and took out a crowbar.

"What are you going to do?" Lainey asked.

"Break into a Guard station and steal some helmets."

"That's insane," Stacy protested.

"They'll never expect it, and you react that way to all of my plans."

"I assume you'll at least wait until dark?" Carl asked.

"Yep. Lovat, you're the only one I trust to come with me on this mission. Are you busy?"

His face brightened at once. "Not busy!"

"Then let's go." Actually, I didn't trust myself to find my way around after dark. Lovat knew every street and alley in the city. And if I got in trouble, he could get back to the shrine faster than anyone.

With Lovat leading the way, we took our usual travel method, ducking in and out of alleys and shadows, avoiding people as much as possible. Part of me still wanted to be seen by people, to promote the movement, but Troilus Green had me shaken up. The last thing I wanted to do before this prison job was attract the attention of… whatever that thing was now.

We found the nearest Viridian Guard station, moved to the back, and waited for nightfall. It felt good to chat with just Lovat for a while. He admitted he enjoyed being back in the city, but would rather be out in the open again. I didn't blame him. I promised after the prison job, I'd take him back out to the Asylum again. We should probably all go, especially with Carl's confusing warnings.

Lovat also had interesting things to say about some of our friends. "Carl talks into a box sometimes," he said.

"He does what?"

"One of those metal boxes. He talks to it sometimes."

"What does he say?"

Lovat shrugged. "Can't hear him. Just saw through the window."

"You were spying on him through the window?"

He shrugged again.

I made a mental note to always check the windows while Lovat was around, before I did anything private.

Having staked out these stations multiple times, I knew that new patrols headed out right after sunset. We waited until they all left, and I walked right up to the back door. I didn't see the need to be subtle now.

A quick boost to my arms and the crowbar popped the door open with ease. I tried to lean more on my left hand, now that I knew its capabilities. It felt really odd.

"Stay here and watch," I told Lovat. He crouched just outside the door and nodded.

Inside the door, I found exactly what I'd hoped for: a locker room. And perched on top of many of the lockers were helmets. How easy. I could grab two and walk right out. Mission accomplished.

But… this was an opportunity. Maybe I could learn more about the Guard, or at least some of them, maybe even enough to convert one to our side. I listened for any sign that I'd been heard. In the distance, I could hear two people talking, but their tone indicated a casual conversation. They weren't getting any closer. I had time.

With the crowbar, I popped open the nearest locker. This Guard must be out on patrol, since it contained ordinary clothes, his wallet, and a candy bar. I took the candy for Lovat.

The next one greeted me with a large photo of a half-naked woman. I looked around, almost expecting to be discovered just because of that. I found nothing else of interest, and moved on… probably slower than I should have.

The third locker proved more interesting. This Guard kept a lot of personal items in his locker, from family photos to knick-knacks. A wrapped gift lay at the bottom of the locker, probably waiting for one of his children's birthdays. It was another reminder that the Viridian Guard, however misguided, were still human. Some of them had families, people they cared about.

In contrast, the fourth locker held a shrine to Viridia on the top shelf. I took the miniature statue of the dragon, intending to smash it later. Fewmets. Stupid dragon worshippers.

Were those voices getting closer? One more.

The last locker held ordinary clothes again, and little more. I was about to shut it and move on when a flash of unusual color caught my eye. I picked up a green shirt and a pair of jeans, knowing what I'd see before I saw the whole thing. Folded beneath the other clothes lay a purple robe. It had to be the same shade as the watcher we'd seen outside the city.

My mind raced. Was the figure we'd seen a member of the Viridian

Guard? Then how had he vanished? Were there more of them? Why purple if they worked for Viridia? I had the feeling that I was on the edge of discovering something much bigger than I'd anticipated. But I didn't have time for another mystery. I had too many of those in my life as it was!

The voices were definitely approaching the locker room. I tossed the clothes across the floor to make a mess, grabbed two helmets, and slipped outside. Lovat and I disappeared into the night. Tomorrow, we would stage a prison break.

"Are we lost?" Cobalt asked from behind me on the four-wheeler.

"What? No!" I looked around. "I'm just… I've never come at it from this direction. I don't want to drive right over the edge."

"Yeah, uh, please don't do that."

To be honest, I did feel a bit stressed. We had to get into position before nightfall. Cobalt needed to see what we were doing before it got dark. And I wasn't sure how much further to go, or what our current position was relative to the pit itself. All the rocks and ridges looked alike.

I brought the four-wheeler to a stop. "You know what? Wait here." I dismounted and pointed. "I'm going to run up to that ridge and see what I can see from up there."

Cobalt waited while I dashed up to a higher vantage point. Where was that pit? I looked in every direction. The rough terrain made it impossible. I could be three feet away from it, and I might not see it until I stepped over the edge, and… dust. A dust cloud! That had to be it. I marked the position in my head and scurried back down.

Only minutes later, we stopped the four-wheeler a few feet from the edge and dismounted. Cobalt took a few steps and stopped. "Wow. You told me how big it was, but… wow."

I let him study it for a few minutes. I did the same, only with my zooming eyes. Everything looked the same as it had a few days ago. I saw people working at various levels, Guard members moving here and there with shockspears, the tarp-covered shelters, and the one building. I watched a Guard walk up to the door and knock. The door opened, but he didn't enter. Instead, he pointed off somewhere, and then stepped away. I stiffened as another figure emerged from inside: a draconic!

I couldn't make out much about it from this distance, but it didn't wear a robe like Troilus Green. As I watched, a second draconic joined it. So the stories were true. These must be the twins. They seemed to be discussing something with the Guard who'd come to the door. They all pointed at various times in the conversation.

"Beryl? I think I know where to set up."

Cobalt's voice startled me. I zoomed my vision back to normal and turned to him. "What's that?"

He pointed, and then walked about a dozen yards to our left. "Over here. This is where we should set it up. This tree here"—he patted a scraggly-looking tree I didn't recognize—"will be just what we need."

"All right. Let's get to it."

I didn't fully understand what Cobalt was doing, but I pretended to listen as he babbled on about the way pulleys worked and such. I just moved the heavy cable roll when he asked.

"Did you bring the gloves?" he asked at one point.

"Yes, I—"

"Good. I mean, I'm counting on your cyb hand to be able to hold on to this, but I don't want you to tear off all your skin."

"Yes, that would be preferable."

I let him work and went back to check on the draconics. I couldn't see them anywhere, so I assumed they'd gone back inside. It bothered me that we knew so little about them. Protogonus Blue told me there was a limited number of draconics for each dragon, but he didn't say what that number might be. I knew of Troilus Green, Scamandrius or something like that, the other one I'd killed—Calchus or some such—and now these two. It seems like I'd seen one or two more at the Emerald Ascendancy at some point. Seven, maybe? That would go along with the seven dragons.

"Okay, I've got it ready," Cobalt said. "Let's hook you up while it's still light."

I turned around. "Already?"

He handed me a belt. "Put this on."

I obliged, noticing the small pulley attached to it by a short piece of rope. While I tightened the belt, Cobalt brought the end of the cable and ran it through the pulley. He took it back to the tree, ran it through several other spots, and did something I didn't see to secure it around the base of the trunk.

"Okay, so," he said as he returned, "you'll hold both parts of the cable in your cyb hand—left, isn't it?—and release it bit by bit to lower yourself. You'll have pretty good control, but I'll be up here, making sure it doesn't go crazy. If the cable starts moving way too fast, I'll put a stop to it."

"So if I lose my grip and start to fall, I won't fall too far. That's what you're saying?"

"Exactly." He pushed his glasses back up his nose. "Even so, I'd rather not have to do that. It won't be easy. And there's no way I can pull you back up. So, uh, take it easy."

I nodded and examined the system. "This is good, Cobalt. Great job." I looked up toward the setting sun. "Now we just wait for dark."

"I think it's crazy to try this in the dark," he said, "but I'm not you." He looked out over the pit. "And I guess you'd be noticed if you started descending right now."

"I might get as far as a third of the way before being noticed, but there's no way I'd make it to the bottom."

"Right, right." He laughed to himself. "This is so streak." He paused. "You know, I said I couldn't pull you up, but I think I could, if I attached the cable to the four-wheeler directly, and then drove it away at a fairly slow pace. I wouldn't be able to watch you, and you might slam into things on the way up, but…"

"Thanks, but no thanks. If I fall, I fall. Don't worry about trying to get me back up. I'll be riding the truck back out."

We settled in to wait. I wondered how the others were doing. They, at least, would be sleeping through the night. "I'm going to try to nap a while," I said aloud. "Since I won't be sleeping later."

"You won't? Oh, yeah, of course." He glanced down into the pit. "I guess it won't be easy to find a good spot down there."

"I'm going to be busy," I reminded him. "Finding people and getting them ready for the morning."

I tried to rest, but Cobalt kept moving around, checking everything over and over. I could hear him mumbling to himself about testing and tension and some other things I didn't catch. "Cobalt," I said after a few minutes, "the idea of napping generally requires some degree of silence."

"Oh! Sorry, sorry." He stumbled and walked back to the four-wheeler, giving me some space. Every once in a while, I could still faintly hear him, but I could tune him out now. Without Cobalt's noise, though, I began to hear other things, from a far distance. A clinking noise, irregular and inconsistent, intruded on my rest. After a few minutes, I realized I was hearing the sound of people at work mining the jade. None of them knew it yet, but this would be their last day at the job… assuming everything went according to plan tomorrow morning.

I rolled over, and something hard in my pocket pressed against my leg. I reached down and discovered the dragon statue I'd taken from the guard station. I'd mostly forgotten about it. I started to pull it out and throw it away, but changed my mind. I might find a use for it. With that thought, I finally dozed off for a while.

When I woke, I opened my eyes to stars and a half moon. That much encouraged me. Rain would make this whole thing even more of a nightmare. I got to my feet and found Cobalt sitting at the edge of the pit, watching down below.

"There are lights over there around the building," he pointed out, "but nothing shines over here. No one should be able to see you."

"Good. Let's get it moving." I pulled on the thick work gloves.

Cobalt moved back and forth, making sure everything was secure one more time. A single light shone from an electric lantern near the tree, but kept low enough so as not to silhouette us on the edge of the pit. "I wish we'd tested this somewhere first," he grumbled.

"Too late now."

"Right, right." He took a deep breath. "Okay. Ready when you are."

Sword on my back, talker on my belt, I stepped to the edge and turned around. One step back and I'd go over. I took hold of the two cables with my left hand.

"All of this depends on that hand," Cobalt said. "For it to work, you're going to have to maintain a strong grip almost the entire way down. You can do that, right?"

"Sure." I sounded more confident than I felt.

"Don't look down."

"What? Then how can I see where I'm going?"

"Um… I don't know. I just thought that's what I should say."

I shook my head. "I'm ready."

"Okay, lean back, but don't step off the edge yet."

It took faith in these preparations for me to let myself go even that much. Part of me fully expected to plunge over the side when I leaned back. Instead, I came to a halt at a sharp angle.

"Feel the tension?" Cobalt asked.

"Yeah." I swallowed and stepped back, letting off on my grip. With that, I fell into the Virescent Pit.

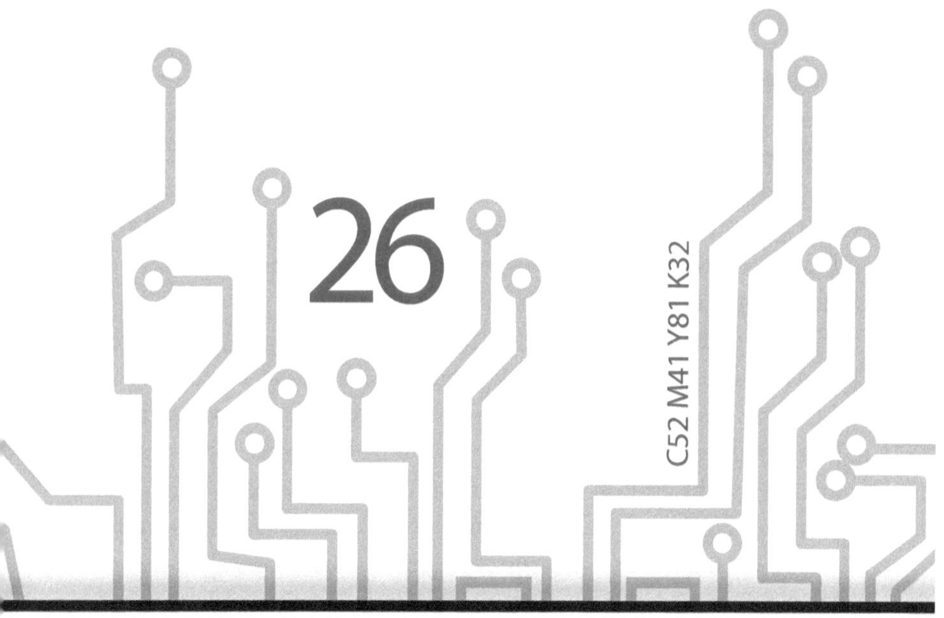

26

I fell four or five feet before I panicked and squeezed the cables together. It pulled at my glove before I remembered to boost my hand to strengthen the grip. I came to an abrupt halt, dangling beside the rocky wall.

"Are you all right?" Cobalt whispered loudly from above.

"Yeah, yeah. I just need to get used to this."

I found places to put my feet, then eased up on the grip ever so slightly. This time, I kept my feet moving as the cable slid through my glove at a reasonable pace. This I could do. It would take a while, but I could do it.

At least the darkness wasn't complete. The combination of moonlight and the distant glow of the draconics' building gave me just enough illumination to see some of where I was going. Once again, I mentally griped at Loden for not including night vision in my cybernetic eyes. Would it have been so hard? Then again, even if he had, how would I activate it? I only knew the one mental command for boosting, and that made my eyes zoom.

My feet landed on a large rock… and then it broke loose. I gripped the cables hard and held still as the rock tumbled down the wall below me. I'm certain I heard a muffled squeal from Cobalt above.

No lights swung in my direction. No loud voices. Falling rocks were probably a common occurrence here. I let out my breath and resumed my descent.

In some places, I could find solid spots to rest my feet. In others, I could go for yards without a foothold, having to put all my weight on my left hand's grip. I kept a steady boost going to it throughout the process. Every time I checked my progress, I fought negative thoughts. While my distance from the top steadily grew, the bottom seemed to grow no nearer. How deep was this place? What if the cable ran out?

I reminded myself of my purpose. Bice. Don. Even Hunter, whoever that was, could be waiting below. I had to keep going, for them.

Time passed as I made my way down. Slow progress was still progress, I kept telling myself. After about an hour, I found a solid ledge to rest my full weight against, the remains of one of the earliest mining levels, I assumed. I gave myself permission to relax and rest for a few minutes. I looked up and then down again. I might be almost halfway to the bottom. Maybe. It grew darker the further I descended, making it hard to tell.

I examined the glove on my left hand. The cable had worn it almost too thin to be of use. I should have brought a back-up pair. I pulled my right glove off with my teeth, and then wrapped it around my left palm, between the hand and the cables. It made the grip a little more awkward, but gave me more of a cushion. After a few more minutes of rest, I stepped back out into the air and continued my descent.

Though it didn't feel like it most of the time, the wall of the pit sloped inward. In a few places, the slope became so pronounced, I could almost walk, but most of the time, the angle was imperceptible. My cable, however, rubbed against more and more of the slope, more and more rocks, the further I went. No way any ordinary rope could have survived this.

I think I must have been three-quarters of the way down when things went wrong. My left hand, which had been doing so well, lost its grip. I don't know if I forgot to keep the boost flowing, or if something else happened. One moment, I was making steady process; the next, I was falling. The extra glove came loose and fell out of my grasp. I scrambled to get hold of the cable and re-establish my grip. My knee smashed against an outcropping and I spun out in a circle. I twirled three or four times, still falling, before the line abruptly halted, jerking me to a stop. The belt dug into my waist all the way around. It took another few moments to stop my spin. Once I did, I hung in the air, catching my breath.

Cobalt must have stopped the line. But now what? How would he know when to let me resume? I glanced down. It wasn't too much further to the first real mining area, but still too far for me to just drop. I checked my glove. It had torn completely open, and I could feel the wetness of blood on my palm. I hadn't even felt the pain.

I didn't have anything else I could use to protect my hand. I would rip my shirt off, but I couldn't get it off with my sword on my back. I removed the glove, then wrapped the back side across my palm, hoping I could keep it that way for the rest of the way down.

Just in time. Cobalt must have assumed I was okay again, because the tension on the cable lessened. I slid down a few feet, scrabbling with my toes for a grip. I found a few places to stabilize myself, then resumed the previous system of slow descent while boosting my hand.

After what seemed an eternity, I saw flat ground about a dozen feet below. I released the cable and let myself fall the rest of the way, boosting my legs against the impact of landing. Even so, I collapsed to the ground, breathing hard and trying to stop myself from shaking. My entire body, relieved of the stress, seemed to just give up. Every muscle suddenly ached. Once I recovered my breath, I sent a series of small boosts out to all of my limbs. I pulled myself up to my knees, and then got to my feet. I reached for the belt.

"Nice trick," said a voice out of the darkness. "Don't suppose you can get back out that way?"

I spun around. "Who's there?"

"Been watching you come down for about an hour. Pretty impressive work. Not sure why, though. This is where people come to die." A figure stepped out of the shadows: a tall, powerfully-built man. I couldn't tell much more about him in the darkness.

"I'm here to change that." I unbuckled the belt and pushed it aside, the cables still connected.

A short chuckle answered me. "You expecting everyone to climb out on your rope there?"

"No, we're going out the main road," I said. "Together. Everyone." I stepped a little closer. "Where do I find everyone else?"

"Same place you'll always find everyone at this time: asleep. After the way we work during the day, most folks just fall right out as soon as it gets dark." He shifted his weight. I tensed, reminding myself that not everyone down here was a hater of the dragon; some were just bad people.

"Why are you up, then?"

"I was thinkin' of going down, not up." He pointed past me. "Right over there." I glanced back, but couldn't see anything in the dark. "It's where we go when we're tired of it all."

"What do you mean?"

"There's a pit inside the pit, if you take my meaning." He took another step closer. "Sheer sides, can't see the bottom. Lots of Viridians have taken that way out. I was thinking of it tonight, but then I saw you."

I shuddered, finally understanding.

"Somethin' odd about your chromark."

"You can see that in the dark? I can't see yours at all."

A sudden light made me blink a few times. The prisoner held up an old-fashioned oil lamp of some kind. "Now c'n you see? I can see yours better. What is that?"

"My name is Beryl," I said. "My mark is different because I'm fighting for all humans, in all the cities. Two dragons are dead now, including Viridia, and we're just getting started. I'm here to get everyone out of here and end this place once and for all. Are you with me?"

He regarded me for a few moments. I returned the gaze. He appeared to be a rough man in every way, strong and thick, with wild, unruly hair on his head and face. His skin looked almost like leather from being exposed to the sun for far too long. Multiple scars were evident on his forearms. His clothing, ragged and thin, barely covered his body.

"I think you'd better talk with Sage," he said at last.

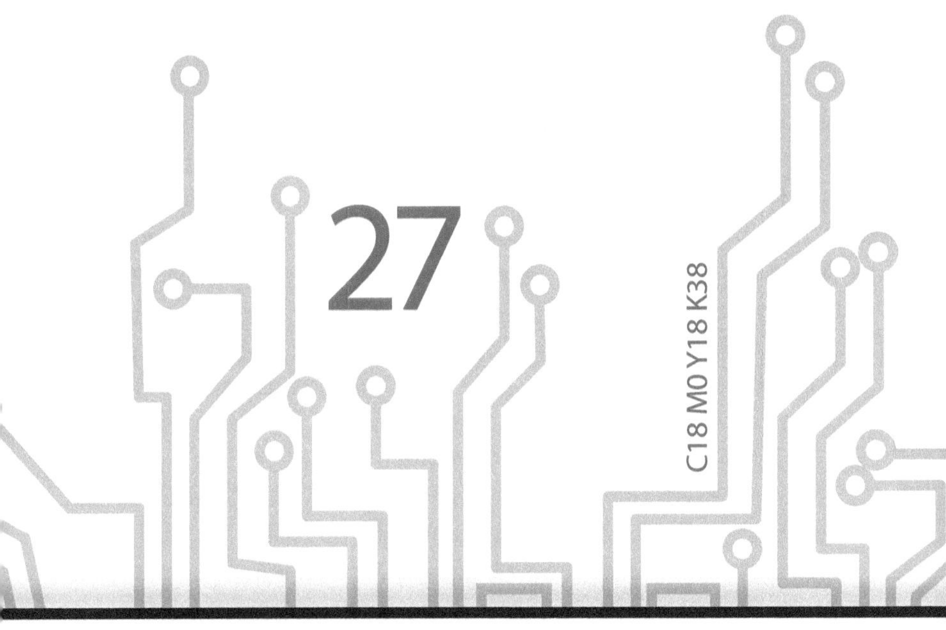

My nameless companion led me along a dark path. Everywhere I looked, I saw evidence of the mining work: abandoned tools left for the next day, uneven gashes and holes in the side of the rock, and chunks of boulders on the ground. A sudden thought occurred to me.

"Oh, wait just a moment," I said. Stopping, I pulled out the talker and flicked it on. "This is Beryl. I made it. Making contact now."

"It's about time," Lainey's voice responded, to the great astonishment of my companion. "We didn't expect it to take this long. I've been worried!"

"Is everything set up for the morning?"

"One hour after dawn. We'll be there."

"Good. I'll see you then. Shutting down now." I turned it off and returned the talker to my belt. "We can go now."

"What was that?" the prisoner asked, confusion in his voice.

"There's a lot of technology that the dragons have kept from us," I explained. "We've got our hands on some of it."

He shook his head. "Strange times," he muttered. Turning, he led me on.

I expected him to lead me up to the level with the green-tarp-covered shelters, but we didn't go that way. Instead, he took a turn into a narrow passage that crawled up at a slight angle while twisting back and forth between the rocks. It occurred to me that I had no idea where we were going, nor whether I could trust this man. I reached for my sword multiple times, but stopped myself. If I ran into danger, I could get it out fast enough. No need to invite trouble.

The passage abruptly opened up into a huge open area, about as big around as the entire shrine we used as our base. Tarps connected to overhangs created a makeshift roof over most of it, and numerous smaller caves surrounded it on every side. Everywhere I looked, I saw people stretched out on dilapidated bedrolls, strips of cloth, and sometimes only the rock itself. A couple of people grumbled at my guide for the light. He lowered a panel on the oil lamp, reducing it to a thin beam.

He motioned for me to continue following as he threaded his way through the sleepers. We moved through the open area, then off to the right to one of the small caves. He paused at the entrance, glanced at me, then leaned inside, letting the light beam play on the roof of the cave.

"Sage!" he called in a low voice. "Sage!" After waiting a few seconds, he called a third time.

A rustle came from inside the cave. "Sleep is one of the most valuable resources we possess here, Basil. Why do you wish to spend mine so recklessly this night?" The voice sounded… crackly.

"We have a visitor from outside. Says the dragon is dead."

Another rustle sounded, and a face peered out of the darkness. "Show me," Sage commanded.

Basil, my guide, opened the panel on his oil lamp and allowed it to shine on me. I blinked, but waited. If I were to get these people fighting, I had to win over these two first.

Sage emerged from the cave and walked a circle around me. A woman with a hunched back, she possessed the same leathery skin as Basil. Her hair, wild and white, seemed to almost explode out from her face. She stopped in front of me and stared at my face.

"Something's wrong with your eyes," she said at last.

"My chromark represents—"

"Not your mark. Your eyes. What's wrong with them?"

They widened, for one thing. No one had ever noticed anything strange about my eyes, not even me, until the day a red draconic ripped one out. "They're cybernetic," I said. "I have multiple… enhancements."

She looked me up and down. "I'll bet you do. What do you mean, coming here and telling stories about a dead dragon?"

"Two dead dragons," I corrected her. "Caesious and Viridia. And if I have my way, the others will follow."

"Dragons can't die. It's not possible."

"That's what I once thought. But the world is changing." I took a breath. "My name is Beryl. I'm here to lead you out of this place. One hour after dawn, we fight our way out."

"Ha!" Her laugh exploded from her parched lips. Multiple sleepers grumbled or rolled over around us. Sage waved a gnarled finger at me. "You want us all dead, do you? There are easier ways, you know. The pit within the pit would be far less trouble."

"I have friends attacking the front gates," I said. "We rise up at the same time. The Guard can't stop all of you." I gestured at all of the sleepers.

"And the twins? Have you considered them in this bout of insanity?"

This time, I drew my sword. The lantern's light gleamed from its polished steel. "I will take care of them."

Sage regarded me again. She didn't speak for a while.

"He has a box that talks," Basil offered.

I sheathed the sword and took out the talker. "It doesn't talk," I said. "I use it to talk to my friends outside. They hear me and answer. It's one of the dragon's technologies that has been kept from us."

"Show me."

I flicked the switch again. "Lainey? Do you hear me? Someone here would like to hear your voice?" I waited. "Lainey?"

The talker crackled. "Oh, sorry, Beryl. I was falling asleep. Who's there?"

"A woman named Sage. She's having trouble believing me. Would you tell her we have a plan?"

"Hello, Sage. I'm Lainey. Tomorrow morning, I'll be arriving in a truck. I hope to see you then."

Sage stared at the talker, then shot her eyes at mine. "Can you hear me?" she asked.

"I certainly can. Do you have any other questions?"

"Is... does..." Sage's voice shook. "Is the laundromat on Glorious Way still in business?"

I winced. Lainey wouldn't know anything about the city. Then Lovat's voice came across: "Lovat here. Yah, the laundromat still there."

Sage looked like she might collapse. I stepped forward, but Basil beat me there, catching her by the arm. "Are you all right?" he asked.

Sage closed her eyes and appeared to collect herself. She pulled free from Basil. "Against all that I ever believed," she murmured, "against all that I know, you come here tonight." She shook her head. "Somewhere, deep within, so deep I never thought it would see the light… a tiny, insignificant thing waited inside me. Waiting for you, Beryl of the cybernetic eyes. That insignificant thing was hope. And you… you bring it back to life. Can I trust this?"

Some more grumbles came from some nearby sleepers. Sage gestured, and Basil led the three of us back out into the narrow passage, where we could talk without disturbing others.

"What you are proposing will cost lives," Sage said. "I can ask them, but I cannot force them."

"I understand," I answered. "Can I speak to them myself, and explain what is happening?"

She nodded. "We will awaken everyone early, before dawn. But you have to understand: the tiny hope I mentioned: Most of these people lost that long ago, even more than I have. It will not be easy."

"Nothing I've done over the past year has been easy."

She studied me again with a steely gaze. "I imagine so. You are an interesting person, Beryl of the sword."

I kind of liked that one. Better than "godslayer," anyway.

"I'm also looking for three people," I explained. "Bice and Don—Celadan, his full name—would have arrived within the past three months." I gave their descriptions.

Sage shook her head slowly. "Many of us abandon our true names when we realize we are here to stay," she said. "I know of no one that matches your friends. But you said three?"

My heart sank at her words, but maybe she was wrong. Maybe they were here somewhere, and just hadn't made her acquaintance yet, or something. "The third one, I don't know personally. The name is Hunter. Probably been here for a year or maybe more. Scientist or doctor type."

"We have some of those," Basil confirmed. "People who worked for the dragon, but said something wrong, looked at something wrong, or told something wrong to somebody."

"Yes, but as I said, names changes," Sage said. "This person may be here, but with so little to go on, I couldn't say."

I didn't think it would be that easy, but I had to try.

A bright light illuminated our gathering. "You three! What are you doing out here?"

I squinted past the light and saw the unmistakable greens of the Viridian Guard.

I channeled boosts and rushed the guard. I slammed him against the wall, but he remained conscious enough to stab at me with his shockspear, connecting just enough to unleash its charge. As before, a solid boost to my nervous system helped me endure the electrical shock. I yanked the weapon from his hands. Before he could react again, I grabbed his head and knocked it against the stone. He crumpled to the ground.

I tossed the shockspear to Basil. "Here's the first weapon for the fight. Let's find a place to stash this guy."

"We can toss him down the pit," Basil suggested, stepping forward eagerly.

I shook my head. "No. We don't kill other humans unless we have to."

"You will have to in the morning," Sage said. "There will be no choice."

"Maybe. But I have a choice right now." I pointed at the unconscious guard. "Whatever his crimes, it's not right to just kill him like this. We just need to make sure he doesn't alert anyone."

After further discussion, Basil and I stripped him of his uniform, tied him with his own belt, and hid him in an unused side passage. "If he starts to yell in a few hours, we'll knock him out again," I said. I held up the uniform. "In the meantime, this might be useful, if we can find someone who can fit inside it."

We returned to Sage and discussed the plan. "How many guardsmen are there?" I asked.

"We've never tried to count them," she answered. "There are enough. Enough to keep the threat of a nearby shockspear throughout the day's work. At least twenty. Maybe more."

"What are those shelters for, up near the main building? The ones with the green tarps?"

"Those are for sorting the jade. Some of us work there instead of mining, when we're too weak to swing a tool."

I gathered a little more information from them. And then, over the next couple of hours, Sage and Basil asked me question after question about life in The Circle, the dragons, what I'd been doing, how I'd gotten into all this, and so on. I told them as much as I thought they should know, leaving out specific details, like the locations of our hideouts, or the truth about Carl and Lainey's place of origin.

Sage craned her head to look up at the sky. The sky looked a little less dark to the east. "It's time," she announced. She led the way back into the sleeping chamber. I stood in the center and watched as she and Basil moved among the rest of the people, waking them up and encouraging them to gather. While I waited, I considered my words. I had a fairly good idea of what I would say, but the reactions of Sage and Basil concerned me. I'd hoped to find people ready to rise up against their oppressors. Instead, I found people who'd given up. I needed to both convince them of hope, and motivate them to risk everything for that hope. No pressure.

The crowd began to gather around me, murmuring. I said nothing to anyone yet. It was still too dark to see much about them, but when anyone moved close, I saw similar conditions to what I'd already seen. Basil seemed to be the strongest-looking man among them, and he'd been ready to kill himself. Was this even going to work?

It had to. Even if Bice and Don weren't here, this place was evil. Shutting it down would go a long way to upsetting the status quo in Viridia, even with the dragon already dead and gone. If we managed to kill two more draconics, that would be two more who would never come back. One by one, we would rid The Circle of all of them.

Sage came beside me and looked out over the crowd. The sky had grown a little bit lighter, and a few of the prisoners brought one more oil lanterns and brought them near us. With Basil's help, Sage climbed on top of a large rock and lifted her hand. The crowd grew quiet.

How many people were here? I couldn't tell from this angle, but I guessed at least a couple of hundred. Were there other parts of the pit I hadn't seen, where more people slept? Sage hadn't implied it, but in a location this gigantic, anything could be possible.

"You all know me," Sage declared, in a voice that carried surprisingly well. "I would not awaken you all early without good cause. This morning… everything changes. For good or ill."

A murmur ran through the crowd. Even the concept of change disturbed many of them. They'd gotten so used to their slavery.

Sage pointed down at me. "We have a visitor from the city, a most… unique visitor. I have spoken with him over the past few hours. And now I want you to hear from him. Then you must make a decision. I will let him tell you about that." With assistance, she descended from the rock and left it to me.

I boosted my legs and leaped atop it with ease. My eyes ran over the crowd for a moment. Most of them were paying attention, waiting for my words. A few had already tuned out, going back to their blankets or getting ready for another day's work. Many whispered to each other about this strange man with the unusual chromark, and the sword on his back.

"My name is Beryl," I said as loud as I thought appropriate. "Like you, I grew up in the city of Viridia. Like you, I suffered under the rule of the dragon. For most of my life, I've dreamed of a day when the dragon would die, when we would be free of his tyranny." I paused. "That day has arrived! The dragon is dead!"

I would like to say the crowd erupted, but it was more like a sustained murmur.

"I saw it happen myself. And not just the green dragon, but the blue dragon, Caesious, is dead as well! With the help of a team of wonderful people, including a brilliant man named Loden, I've been a part of making this happen. And now we come to you." I threw Loden's name out, hoping to attract the attention of anyone who knew him.

With sudden inspiration, I dug into my pocket and pulled out the statue of Viridia I'd taken from the guard station. I held it up with my left hand. "The dragons are falling, one by one." I boosted my hand and squeezed. It hurt a little, but I crushed the statue, raining fragments and dust down.

I wiped the dust from my hands and pointed up. "One hour after dawn, my people will arrive at the front gate in a stolen truck. At the same time, those of us down here will attack the Viridian Guard. If we all do this together, you will all be free in a matter of hours!"

I saw eyes roll, and many turn away. "We can do this!" I cried out. I drew my sword and held it up. "I will lead the way. I've killed two draconics already, and I'm looking forward to killing two more today! Join me! We can do this!"

"We can fight," Basil shouted. "When we get our tools this morning, we can use them as weapons!"

"There are guards!" someone else cried.

"Then we take them down!" Basil pointed at me. "He took down one already. Look!" He held up the shockspear. "And the more we kill, the more weapons we'll have!"

The crowd erupted in discussion. I crouched down on the rock and looked to Sage. "What now? Should we just leave them to work it out? Or do we need to take more control here?"

She looked around at Basil and a few of the others. "Leaders are stepping up. Let them organize. But move among them. Answer questions. Tell them how you'll fight for them."

I nodded and hopped down. I sheathed my sword and started to walk through the crowd. People pressed up to me, asking about events outside, or my own activities. I answered what I could, trying to keep an eye on the approaching dawn. The hardest questions were those from people who asked about specific friends or family members they'd left behind. I couldn't answer those.

After a few minutes, Basil caught up with me. "You'll help us against the guards?" he asked.

"Of course. But like I said, if I can avoid killing other humans, I will."

He shrugged. "You can try. I need to show you the ladders. That's the biggest problem."

"Beryl?" someone called to me.

I turned to see a middle-aged woman, maybe not quite as worn down as some of the others. She wrung her hands together as she examined my face. "Yes, ma'am?"

"Your face is changed, but… it is you. I don't think you know me, but I know who you are. You… you worked at the bike shop… with my daughter. Kelly?"

29

I opened my mouth, but what could I say? Out of all the people I'd wondered about finding here, Kelly's mother was one of the last ones I expected.

"The Guard, the draconics…" she went on. "They asked so many questions about her, about rebellion against the dragon. And they asked about you. And other people. We didn't know anything." Her face tightened. "They killed my husband in front of me."

"I'm… so sorry," I managed.

"Tell me, please: is my little girl still alive?"

"Yes." I could say that much at least. "She… she's been with me since then, most of the time. She's in… some trouble right now. And as soon as we bust out of here, I'm going to help her."

Kelly's mom covered her nose and mouth with her hands. "Will you… will you take me to see her?"

I put my hand on my heart. "If we live through this morning, I promise I will take you with me. And tell you everything."

She nodded, still overcome.

I pointed toward the top. "I can't watch over you while we fight," I said. "So I want you to stay back from the main battle. But when you get to the top, look for me. I'll be with my friends and a truck. And hopefully a couple of dead draconics."

"Thank you," she whispered.

"I'm sorry," I said. "I only know you as Kelly's mom. What's your name?"

"Fern," she answered.

"I will not leave without you, Fern," I said. "I'll see you again in a couple of hours."

I turned back to Basil, who was waiting impatiently for me. He led the way through the passage, along with a large percentage of the crowd. Dawn had fully arrived. The others would be coming before long. By then, this riot should be in full swing.

"The ladders are our biggest problem," Basil said.

"Ladders?"

He pointed up. "There are only two ways to the next level: the elevator and the ladders. The elevator doesn't come down until we have a load of jade to take up. And the minute we start any trouble, the guards will pull the ladders up."

"Show me."

He led me apart from the crowd somewhat. Most of them stopped to see what we were doing. Basil pointed. "There's only one ladder down right now, the one the first guards used to come distribute the tools. They'll lower the others when they need to. And yank them back up if there's a problem."

I considered it for a moment. "Do you think you can handle the guards at the tools without me?" I asked. "If so, I can make sure the ladders are in place."

Basil tapped the shockspear onto his palm. "Yeah, I think so. People have talked about doing it before, but… what would we do then? No one had any hope of getting past this point. A couple of guys suggested splitting up and some of them holding the ladders, but… with guards at the top of the ladders, they can pick us off too easy."

"Right. I'll deal with them. As soon as I hear the disturbance, I'll go."

"What if they pull it up before you?"

"Then I'll jump up there."

He started to laugh, then cut himself off. "You're serious?"

I nodded. Without another word, I moved along the strip to a position in the shadows not far from the lone ladder. I watched the top of it while I waited. The cliff wall looked to be about ten feet high. A year ago, I would have balked at that. Now? Easy. Two of the Viridian Guard appeared near the ladder's top, talking with one another. They looked down, checking for any wayward prisoners, then resumed their conversation. They appeared casual: no helmets, shockspears strapped to their backs.

I took out the talker and called Lainey. I explained everything I knew about the situation as it stood now. "We're on our way," she promised.

It wouldn't be long now. If I understood correctly, only four or five guards would be present to distribute the tools. The crowd of prisoners could easily overcome them. But of course, as Basil said, without any other help, they'd never get far.

A shout echoed behind me somewhere. And then two more. A roar answered them.

The two guards at the next level jerked around, no longer casual. One grabbed the ladder and pulled. His companion stared off in the distance for a moment, then reached down to help him.

Using boost-enhanced speed, I shot out of the shadows. With the running start, the leap was even easier than I anticipated. I landed a few feet from the guards, hitting the ground with a palm strike to add to the drama and hopefully intimidate them.

These two were no slouches, though. For some reason, I always expected the Viridian Guard to be less competent than they actually were. One of them kept pulling the ladder up, while the other whipped out his shockspear and advanced on me.

"Nothing?" I asked. "The leap didn't surprise you at all?" I drew my sword.

"Sound the alarm," the nearest guard said over his shoulder. His friend yanked the ladder the rest of the way up and dropped it on the ground.

I took advantage of the slight distraction it created and charged. I whipped my sword up to parry a thrust from the shockspear, and punched the guard with my left hand. Now that I knew the insides were cybernetic, I didn't worry about injuring myself with those kind of strikes. His head snapped back and he collapsed.

I pointed the sword at the second guard. "Lower the ladder and I'll let you live," I told him.

He ran.

It took only a few seconds for me to catch him. I knocked him against a large boulder, then dragged his body out of the way. If I left it in the path, the prisoners would tear him apart. I did the same with the first guard and then lowered the ladder just as dozens of prisoners poured into the space below. I moved along the edge, lowering three more ladders. The prisoners swarmed up to join me, cheering and shouting.

"Which way now?" I yelled.

"Here!" one of the men shouted, waving a nasty-looking hammer. Together with the crowd, we moved along this level to a spot ahead where a ramp led up to the next one. A dozen guards gathered at the top of the ramp, scrambling to get themselves into an orderly line to block us.

"Get them!" someone yelled.

As we charged forward, the guards stepped up in unison and threw shockspears at the crowd. With my boosts, I managed to lunge forward and catch one, but many of the others struck home. Those who were hit collapsed, shaking from the electrical jolt. We'd have to check them for poison later. The crowd paused, giving the guards time to pick up another set of the spears. We couldn't let this continue.

I charged with a shout, throwing the shockspear at a guard in the middle. I wasn't as accurate in throwing, though I had more force behind it. He dodged, but that threw off his companion's attempt to throw another spear. The rest of the crowd followed me, even though a few more fell from the shockspears. But they couldn't stop us all. I grabbed one guard and slammed him to the ground before the others caught up to me and attacked the rest.

These guards were doomed, no matter what I did. There would be no stopping this crowd. I charged on to the next obstacle. By now, Carl would be driving the truck into the pit. I needed to be within sight of it soon.

We shoved some barriers aside and stormed up another ramp to the next level. A few more guards fled before us. On this level, we had to run several hundred yards to reach the next ramp. As I crested the top of it, I looked across the final level: the shelters for sorting the jade, the sole building, and the road leading out. A single truck sat beside the building, with a pair of guards talking to the driver.

The handful of guards we were chasing kept going, but one stopped. He turned back and laughed at us, pointing. I slowed my run, instantly wary. Why would he do that?

I didn't notice at first: the surface under our feet had changed. My shoes made a different sound. I looked down. Metal. We ran across an enormous metal surface. Why would they need such a thing, when every-thing else was rock?

The answer occurred to me a split second too late. A massive electrical shock struck me and dozens of others around me. Spasms seized my body. A few moments later, the shock stopped, and we all fell to the ground. I continued to shake uncontrollably, but my eyes locked on a single sight.

Two draconics led a crowd of Viridian Guard toward us. They were all laughing.

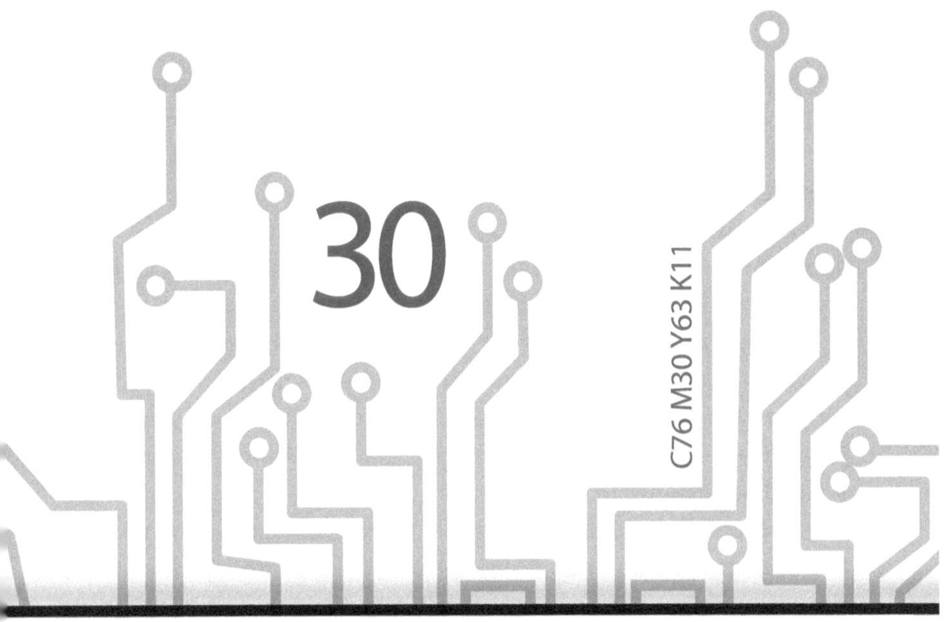

30

I could get out of this. I just needed to concentrate. I could see the enemies approaching. I could hear the moans of those who'd been electrocuted with me, and the murmurs of the rest of the crowd that hadn't reached the metal surface and now didn't know what to do. The truck was there, but the others couldn't act alone. It was on me.

I squeezed my eyes shut and tried to find my mental trigger. My body continued to shudder and tremble. Focus. Focus! Found it. A tiny pulse of boost energy flowed through my body, calming the shakes. At the same time, my mind cleared as well, letting me concentrate. I boosted everything, leaped to my feet, and jumped clear of the metal surface.

The draconics stopped and regarded me. "Ah, here we have the instigator," one of them said. They truly did look like twins, but how would we know? All of the draconics looked about the same to me.

"He's the one we've heard about," the other answered. "No wonder this uprising was different."

I lifted my sword. "You don't know the half of it," I said.

The draconics each raised a hand at the same time. The Viridian Guard responded by spreading out, forming a half-circle in front of me, restricting my options.

"You stand alone," the first draconic spoke again.

I caught a glimpse of motion in the distance and smiled. "Not alone,"

I answered. Sure, I probably could have come up with something better if I'd thought about it more, but I'm actually proud I said that much.

As a loud explosion echoed through the mine, the draconic on my left stumbled forward with a cry. Lainey's aim was superb. I launched myself forward with boosted speed, meeting it in the stumble and driving my sword up through its chest. The Viridian Guard whirled back and forth, trying to understand. They'd never experienced a rifle shot before.

"Follow me!" I yelled. "Avoid the metal! They can't stop all of us!"

The crowd roared and surged forward. Somewhere, a panicked guard activated the electricity again, catching more of the prisoners, but others found a way around or over it. Once you understood what was happening, it could be circumvented.

The second draconic charged me. I barely had time to yank my sword free from its brother's body. Claws connected with my chest. The draconic ripped my shirt apart and cut gashes across my skin. I used my boosted speed to dodge enough to prevent serious injury, but it still hurt like anything.

I stabbed in retaliation, cutting into its left side. But the monster twisted its body, using its own injury to wrench the sword out of my hand.

"I know who you are," it snarled. "Viridia will be pleased to hear of your death, regardless of what else happens here."

"Viridia is dead," I snapped back, dodging another swipe of the claws. I had plenty of room to maneuver, but no weapon now.

A second rifle shot rang out, and some of the draconic's shoulder scales exploded outward. It was only a glancing shot, not enough to affect the fight. Around me, the other prisoners engaged the remaining guards with shouts and grunts. I didn't expect any of them to get near the draconic. At least I didn't have to worry about guards attacking me while I fought the draconic. On the other hand, the crowd would make it almost impossible for Lainey to shoot again.

"Beryl!"

I risked a quick glance in time to see Basil toss a shockspear toward me. I managed to catch it while ducking under another sweep from the draconic.

The shockspear wasn't my favorite weapon, but at least I had one. My finger slid to the trigger action and turned it on before plunging it at the draconic. My boosted strength managed to thrust the spear point into the monster's right thigh. I looked up at its face, expecting some sort of reaction to the electrical charge, at least. Nothing. And if it the spear point was poisoned, I'm sure it was immune to that as well.

The draconic backhanded me with enough force to send me flying several feet. I rolled on the ground, bumped into a couple of people, and scrambled back to my feet. My opponent took the time to remove the shockspear, snap it in half, and toss it aside. When it reached for the sword still in its side to do the same thing, I charged.

I slammed into the draconic's arm, using it to push the sword deeper. It roared at me, as I managed to get one hand onto the sword's hilt. I yanked it free, but not before the draconic snapped at me. Its jaws caught on my left hand and tore skin and muscles. I screamed. Not the best look for a leader of men, but I couldn't remember experiencing that much pain.

Using all the boost energy I could, I thrust the sword up into its neck. The blade penetrated straight through, but the beast didn't stop. It hissed at me and clamped its arms around me in a crushing hug.

"I'll squeeze your bones to splinters," it wheezed, air escaping the hole around my sword's blade.

Even with my boosts, I didn't have the strength to break free. His arms squeezed tighter, driving the air from my lungs. I kept boosts flowing, trying to keep my body from being crushed, but it wouldn't last long.

I adjusted the grip on the sword hilt, released the boosts to the rest of my body, and at the same time put every single thing I could into my arm and wrist. In that split second before it could crumble my rib cage, I ripped the sword out through the side of its neck.

The draconic's arms lost their strength. Its eyes rolled back just before its entire head flopped to the opposite side of my cut, almost tearing off completely. The lifeless body collapsed as I stumbled back to keep from falling with it.

The crowd exploded in a cacophony of cheers and shouts. A dozen or so rushed to me, grabbing me and lifting me up over their heads. I held the sword aloft to keep from cutting anyone. I clamped my mouth shut to keep from screaming in pain again: the crowd wasn't careful enough with my ravaged left hand.

They carried me forward to the building and freedom. Carl, Jaden, Lainey, and Glacier waited beside the truck. It took me several minutes to convince the prisoners to let me down. By then, dozens of them were already running up the road to leave the pit forever.

"Looks like we didn't need to do much at all," Carl observed once I could hear him.

I shook my head. "If it hadn't been for Lainey's shooting," I gasped, "the outcome might have been very different."

Lainey stepped up and looked me over. "You don't look so good."

I held up my mangled hand. I could see the cybernetic interior for the first time, showing through the gaps torn by the draconic's jaws. Along with the gashes on my chest, I knew I'd be in pain for quite a while. But pain and I were starting to become better acquaintances. Or so I tried to convince myself.

A few minutes later, I sat on the back end of the truck while Lainey and her father worked to bandage my wounds. Basil and Sage found us there. Behind them, most of the prisoners continued to stream up the road. The city of Viridia was about to be in for a shock. The Viridian Guard would undoubtedly re-capture some of these escaped prisoners, but not all. They would return to their friends and family, tell their stories, and incite more anti-dragon thoughts. They would also tell about the man with the multi-colored chromark who helped free them. The legend would grow.

"This is truly a miracle," Sage declared. "Beryl of the sword, we cannot thank you enough."

"Freedom for all," I said, though it came out more like a painful gasp than a powerful statement of truth.

Basil's eyes looked over my companions. I could tell when he caught a glimpse of Lainey's face. The absence of a chromark shocked everyone. His gaze lingered there for a moment, then strayed down to Glacier, who sat calmly beside one of the truck's back tires.

"If you need help with your fight, I would like to join you," he said.

I nodded. "We can always use more fighters." I winced as Lainey tightened the bandage around my chest. "What about you, Sage?"

A smile split her leather face. "I… I have a laundromat to visit."

"Good luck to you then," I said. "I hope you find who you're looking for."

As Sage moved away, I scanned the passing crowd, watching for someone. Toward the end, as I'd instructed her, Kelly's mother approached the truck. I waved her over and introduced her to Lainey.

"Wow. We didn't know you were still alive!" Lainey exclaimed.

Fern gave a small smile. "I didn't know either."

I finally let myself relax. We'd done the job, even if we hadn't found the friends we sought. Bice and Don must be somewhere else... maybe prisoners in one of the other cities. Five more cities. Auric would be the next most likely, but they could be anywhere. Onyx might even have found them after they escaped the workshop. That was a depressing thought.

"Uh, young man? Beryl, was it?"

I looked up to see one of the prisoners standing in front of me. He appeared older than most of them, but still fit from long hours of work. His dark skin, still damaged in places from the sun, showed countless small scars from his years of work.

"You've been here a while," I said without thinking.

He nodded and wiped sweat from his forehead. "Over three years, if I've kept track accurately. I was sent here not long after I conducted major operations on a draconic... and a badly-injured young man." His eyes bored into me. "When I worked with a man named Loden."

31

I almost jumped to my feet in spite of my injuries. "You're Hunter?"

"That... that was my name, yes. You have heard it? Has... has Loden talked about me?"

Carl approached, eyes darting from me to the newcomer.

"We only found your name in his notes a few days ago," I said. "Finding you was one of the reasons I wanted to do this today." I winced as another wave of agony swept over me. Now that the adrenaline and boosts were wearing off, the pain from my chest and hand grew rapidly. And my boosts were having their usual aftereffect: exhaustion.

"His notes? Then..."

"He's dead," I said through gritted teeth. "I don't... I'd love to tell you everything, but I'm really... hurting here." I looked up at Carl. "Do we have any pain killers?"

"Your, uh, boosts should be able to help," Hunter said.

"Normally, yes, but I've been using them a lot over the past day, and..." My eyes almost fell shut. "I haven't slept at all."

"Right. We need to get out of here," Carl broke in. "Jaden! You and the big guy there—what's your name? Basil?—help Beryl into the back of the truck. Lainey! It's time to go!"

The two men climbed up, taking me by the arms and assisting me the rest of the way. I screamed when Jaden bumped my hand. While he apologized over and over, Lainey, Glacier, Fern, and Hunter climbed in with me.

"Where's Lovat?" I mumbled, feeling the fatigue overtaking the pain.

"He went to guide Cobalt back," Lainey answered. "Rest now."

I took her advice. The truck's vibrations as it turned around kept me conscious, but a few moments later, I was out.

When I woke, I felt much better. My chest still burned a little, especially when I moved, but I felt almost nothing from my hand. Once my brain grasped this, it finally realized that I lay in my own bed back at the shrine. I sat up, not without a wince and a gasp, and rubbed my face with my good hand. I examined my bandaged left hand, curious at the lack of sensation. The bandages were tighter and neater than what Carl and Lainey had done at the pit; someone else had been working on it.

As soon as I could stand, I walked out and found Lovat and Lainey playing with Glacier in the sacellum. Cobalt watched from a seat by the wall; I think the cat still intimidated him. From the sunlight, it looked like early morning. Had I slept for almost 24 hours?

"There you are," Lainey said, getting to her feet. "We've been wondering if you'd ever wake up."

"Guess I needed to sleep," I mumbled. "Where's everyone else?"

She pointed. "Father is talking with the new people. Jaden went home after we got back."

I nodded. "I'll go see them in a minute. I need to clean up."

I did the best I could with only one hand, and then walked to Bice's old cabin. Lainey joined me. She chatted a little about how they'd stashed the truck several blocks away to avoid drawing suspicion to the shrine.

Basil, wearing new clothes, emerged from the cabin as we approached. He stopped, glanced at me, and stared again at Lainey's face. He blinked and shook his head. "Good to see you up," he said to me.

"Starting to feel like myself again," I said. "Did they find a place for you here, Basil?"

He nodded, then gestured at the door behind him. "Did you want to see the others? They're talking above my head in there."

"What did you do before the pit, Basil?" Lainey asked.

He shrugged. "Worked odd jobs mostly. Did a stint in the regular mines."

"We'll talk more later," I told him. "I want you to feel a part of the group. We've got a really big job coming up soon, and you could help out."

"If it's against the dragons, I'm in." He nodded and walked away.

"He makes me just a little uncomfortable," Lainey said quietly.

I glanced back at him. "Why is that?"

"I'm not sure. Just an odd feeling. The way he looks at me. It may be nothing."

I frowned. "Sometimes feelings point to important things. I'll keep an eye on him. But honestly, it's probably because of your face."

"I've never had men stare at my face so much."

I wanted to respond with some kind of compliment, something about how I didn't blame guys for staring at her face, but I couldn't get the words right before they reached my tongue. Instead, I opened the door and stepped into the cabin. Carl sat at his desk. Fern and Hunter sat on the couch, also both in new clothes. Lovat must have "obtained" them somewhere. Fern had red eyes, like she'd been crying a little.

Hunter stood as we entered. "Beryl. I hope you're feeling better?"

I nodded. "Chest is iffy, but the hand isn't hurting."

Carl gestured with his chin. "Hunter is very experienced in the medical field. He took care of you when we got back. Knew exactly what to do."

"And we should change your bandages," he said, gesturing for me to sit down. I obeyed and awkwardly pulled my shirt off.

"Didn't you work at the bio-hospital, also?" I asked Fern.

She nodded. "Mostly, I just handed pills to people."

"Don't let her fool you," Hunter said, carefully unwrapping my chest. "She's a very skilled pharmacist."

To me, all that indicated was that she knew about pills. "So you've gotten to know each other?" I asked.

"We met in the pit," Hunter confirmed. "It was good to find someone who understood some of what I like to talk about." He paused. "Back when we still talked about real life." He took a deep breath. "It's hard. Hard to adjust to… being free again."

I winced as the last bandage came loose. "I understand. I think. I do have a lot of questions for you."

"But first, please…" Fern interceded. "Tell me about my daughter. You said she's in trouble."

"I haven't told her much of anything," Carl said. "All I know came from you, and I didn't want to share second-hand."

I nodded and closed my eyes. "This is going to be hard to hear," I began. "And I am so sorry about all of it. I take a lot of the responsibility."

"Start your story from the beginning," Lainey suggested. "They both need to hear it, and Kelly is there for most of it."

"Right. It all started when I ran into this guy on the street..." Beginning with my first encounter with Rick, I explained how we became insurrectionists. I told about Loden's death, killing the blue dragon, and what happened next. I talked a little bit about our trip to Incarnadine, but it didn't seem all that important now. I didn't elaborate much on my part in the story, emphasizing what Kelly did. I didn't even talk about my enhancements. Then came the hardest part: Onyx.

"I never saw it coming," I said. "If I had, maybe I could have stopped it from happening. Maybe I could have stopped him. Killed him. Whatever it took."

Fern's eyes were closed, and her head down. "You were deceived," she said. "We've all had to deal with that kind of thing at points in our life." She took a deep breath and raised her head. "I was taught to believe Viridia was a god, and never questioned it until I ended up in that pit."

"You don't know the worst," I said. I lifted my eyes to look at her, but couldn't keep them there. I looked down again. "Before Onyx disappeared with her, Kelly told me she was pregnant."

Fern gasped and put her hands to her mouth. "And... Rick is the father?"

"Onyx," I confirmed. "The dragon."

"How far along?" Hunter asked. He started applying the new bandages.

"I'm not sure," I admitted. "But it's been three months since they vanished, and she'd only discovered it shortly before."

They exchanged looks. "Draconic incubation is shorter than a human embryo's," Hunter said. "They grow very fast. We do not have much time."

That wasn't what I wanted to hear. I was counting on having a few months left. "Once we're all recovered, we'll go meet Caedan and find out about this tower." I explained what little we knew about it. "I'm counting on them being there. And then we'll get her back."

"It's a bit of a long shot," Hunter observed.

"But it's better now," I said. "Between the two of you… you'll know how to help her, right?"

Hunter hesitated. "I know how to surgically remove the embryo, if that is what you're asking. I just do not know what effect it will have on her."

"What do you mean?" Fern demanded.

He straightened. "Every woman who has ever given birth to a draconic has died. But if we remove it before it reaches full term… I think we can save her. I suspect it is the birth itself that has killed them."

Fern got to her feet. "Then let's leave today. Right now! We have to find her!"

"We will," I promised. "But I don't… um…"

"We need to give Beryl at least a day or two to recover," Carl interceded. "We can't do it without him."

Fern wrinkled her forehead. She looked so much like Kelly. "Why? What's so special about him?"

I looked at Hunter. "You want to explain that?"

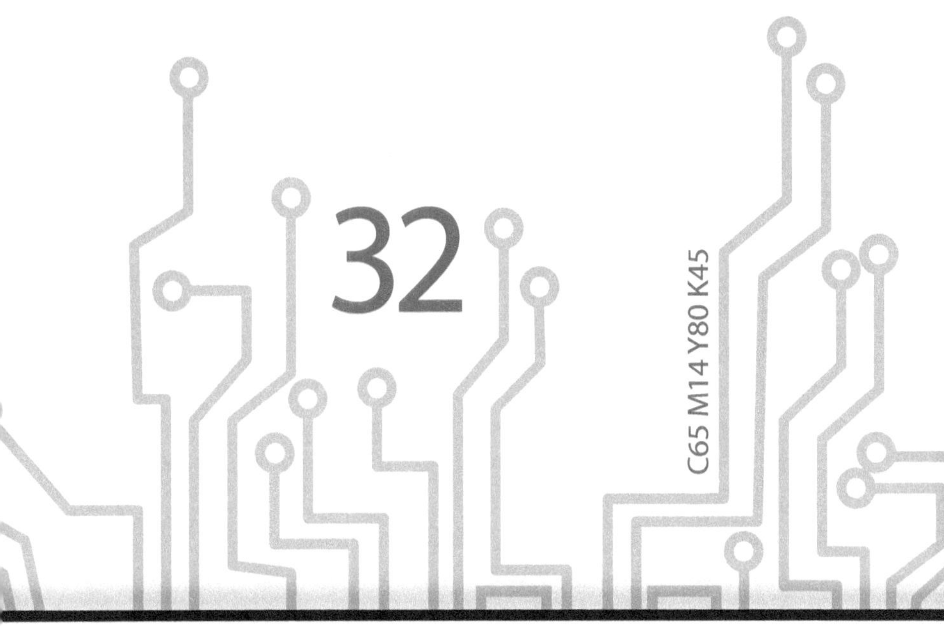

32

"Me?" Hunter's eyes widened.

"We know you assisted Loden in his operations," Carl said. "We'd like to hear more about that."

Hunter's eyes shifted. His thumb ran back and forth along the other fingers of his hand sitting on the arm of the couch.

"I'm not sure what I can tell you," he said. "Loden did the real work of creation. I just did the implantation."

Fern sat down. "What are we talking about?"

"My cybernetic implants," I told her. "I was in an accident that should have killed me, but Loden—and Hunter, apparently—saved my life. It's what let me get into the pit, fight the draconics, and so on."

"Oh."

Lainey sat on the arm of the couch next to Fern. I pulled up a stool and looked at it before sitting down. I tried to push away the memories of Bice sitting on this same stool so many times.

Hunter pursed his lips, then took a drink of water. He put the back of his hand to his mouth for a moment, then looked back up. "You have to understand. I have been… It is for this very reason that I ended up in the Virescent Pit. Even though I know you are the ones who rescued me… it is still hard for me to abandon three years of keeping my mouth shut about those events."

"Take your time," Carl said.

"We know some of the details," I added. "We have a few of Loden's notes, and I know what I can do. Mostly. I think."

"Do you?" He chuckled. "I would be very surprised if you had figured all of it out yet."

"Until a few months ago, I thought the implant was at the base of my spine, and I could only boost my legs. Just before he died, Loden finally told me it was in my brain. That's when I started being able to boost everything else."

"Do you know about the eyes?"

I nodded. "But again: I didn't know until a draconic ripped one of them out."

He snorted. "That must have been… traumatic."

"We understand that you basically gave Beryl an entirely new system within his body," Carl said. "We don't know how you were able to do that."

"It was the most complex thing I have ever done," Hunter answered. "Loden's designs were absolutely revolutionary. He needed my input and expertise to fully con-consolidate the cybernetic system within your biological systems."

"How extensive is this system?" Fern asked.

"It runs through virtually every muscle in his body, as well as a couple of other systems, I believe," Carl said.

Fern looked at Hunter. "How could you have possibly kept him alive while doing that? You're talking hundreds of operations!"

"Why?" I asked. "How many muscles are in the human body?"

"Over six hundred," she said. "Skeletal muscles, anyway."

Hunter held up a hand. "Let us be clear, though. We did not need connections to every muscle, only the ones that might be useful. The ones that move the bones, for example. It was far less than six hundred."

"What about his heart?" Lainey asked. "Isn't that a muscle?"

"Technically, yes," Hunter said. "The sole cardiac muscle of the body. And yes, the system connects to it." His eyes darted about again.

I almost put a hand to my chest before remembering my injuries. "What would happen if I sent a boost to my heart?"

Hunter raised his eyebrows. "I honestly do not know for certain. Perhaps it will allow you to stave off heart problems."

I didn't know what to think about that.

"Then why connect to the heart at all?" Fern asked.

Hunter shrugged and muttered something about Loden.

"You haven't answered the question," Carl pointed out. "How did he survive all of this?"

Hunter drank some more water and licked his lips. "We had to keep him in a coma, of course. But even that was not enough. His brain would not have been able to handle the trauma of so many operations."

We nodded and waited for him to continue.

"We—uh, I—disconnected his brain from his autonomic nerves, so that he could not experience pain during the procedures."

"That's possible?"

"No. It's not," Fern said, leaning forward. "Is it?"

Hunter looked down and mumbled something.

"What was that?"

"He created the process himself," Fern said. She sat back into the couch. "You're amazing, Hunter. All these months, you've been telling me how insignificant your medical work was." She shook her head. "That's absolutely groundbreaking. No one's ever even considered a way to do something like that!"

Hunter sighed and looked up. "Not only did I do it, I could do it again." He looked at me. "In order to finish all of the operations, I had to leave the mechanism in place. It is still there."

I put my hand up to the back of my head. "What are you saying? That you could push a button on my head and turn off my pain?"

"It is a little more complicated than that," he hedged. "But it is there all the same."

Fern continued to shake her head. "That's insane. I can't even grasp the possibilities."

If Fern couldn't, with her knowledge of medical stuff, that said a lot. All of this was way over my head.

"How long did this take?" Carl asked.

"It took weeks," he admitted. "We were working on the draconic at the same time, and kept delaying his recovery to give us more time."

"Was it just the two of you the whole time?"

"Other people came and went. I had a pair of interns who assisted with some of the procedures, but they never knew what all we were doing." He looked away. "I never saw them in the pit. Either they were able to convince the authorities of their ignorance, or they are dead, I suppose."

"But where are his scars?" Carl asked.

My what?

Before Hunter could answer, Carl went on: "He doesn't have a visible scar anywhere. Yet you say you cut into almost every part of his body. How is that possible?"

Hunter made a clicking sound, then sighed. "All right, yes. That's my doing, as well. The scar tissue is technically still there, most of it, but it's hidden under… well, under artificially-stimulated skin growth, I guess you could call it. I'm not sure the best way to explain it." He held up his own arms, covered in smalls scars. "Rather ironic, considering what happened to me."

I ran my right hand along my left arm. Scar tissue beneath the skin? This was getting too confusing.

"One more question," Carl said. "Where does the energy come from?"

"What?"

"The energy for Beryl's boosts. Where does it come from?"

Hunter blinked. "I… from the implant in his brain. Is that not so?"

"Energy has to come from somewhere," Carl explained. "The implant can't generate it all by itself."

"Then I do not know. Loden's notes do not explain this?"

"We only have half of them," I said. "The other half are in Incarnadine. I plan to get them back sometime, if Onyx doesn't beat us to it."

"Why does he want them?"

"He wants to have a similar procedure done to himself, I'm guessing." I flexed my hand. "Can you imagine a dragon with the abilities I have?"

Hunter scratched a spot beside his eye. "It would take many doctors to operate on a dragon."

"He would probably want to do it in his human form, and then transform back into a dragon." I thought about that. "Huh. It works for his cybernetic hand. I wonder…"

"It doesn't make sense," Carl said. "If that's his plan, he revealed himself far too soon. Even if he gets all of Loden's notes, he'll need people to perform the procedure, and he doesn't have them."

"That we know of," I corrected.

"Even so, he would need facilities," Hunter said. "It could not be done without all of the equipment we had available to us."

I hopped off the stool and strode around the room. "Could he have built such a thing inside the tower? Maybe we're all wrong here. Maybe he has allies in one of the cities after all."

"I'm sorry, but… what difference does any of this make?" Fern asked. "How does this help us rescue my daughter?"

"If Onyx is not in the tower, then Kelly isn't either," I explained. "They may be inside one of the other cities. I just… I can't imagine any of them helping him."

"Didn't you say that one of the red dragons was sympathetic to him at one point?" Lainey asked.

"Amaranth? She was on his side for a while, hundreds of years ago, according to the Books of Lore. But then she joined the other dragons in trying to destroy him. I don't see how she'd change now, especially with him killing two other dragons."

"What if he offered her the same procedure?"

I stopped walking and stared.

"Immortal life," Carl said. "Effectively. That would be a powerful tool of persuasion."

"Are you saying Beryl is immortal?" Fern asked.

"No," Hunter said. "In fact, I worry about the long-term consequences to his body from overuse of the boosts. But the dragons are already a thousand years old and looking for ways to extend that even further. With this procedure… I don't know what could stop them from living on for two or three times that long."

I opened my mouth to answer when a loud rumble erupted somewhere nearby.

Lovat burst through the door. "Out, out, out!" he yelled. "Get out! Drake coming!"

33

"Everyone out!" I snapped, knowing better than to question Lovat.

Carl grabbed the binder holding Loden's notes. Everyone else hurried out of the cabin into the open. Cobalt joined us, eyes wide. Another rumble came from nearby. I spun in a circle, seeing nothing.

"What's happening?"

Lovat pointed past the cabin. "Drake coming! Viridian Guard too!"

"What are you saying?" I caught hold of Lovat's shoulder. "A draconic is coming with the Guard? Here?" I assumed it must be Troilus Green.

He nodded, eyes wide. "Tearing things down!"

That explained the rumbles. But why? Some of the buildings around here were occupied. If Troilus Green knew we were here, why didn't it just surround it? Why destroy other buildings on its way here? Unless it were putting on a show of his power…

"Gather everything you can carry!" I yelled. "We're abandoning this place. Now! Move!"

The team scattered, except for Fern and Hunter, who had nothing to gather. I dashed into the sacellum, grabbed up my sword and stuffed my few belongings into a backpack. I gave my bed a final glance. I would miss it.

Back out in the open, I saw Carl emerge from the cabin, carrying some of his gear on his back. He handed a large bag to Hunter to carry. "How much time do we have?" he called. "I have more—"

Across the street, a two-story building—abandoned, I hoped—exploded outward. It fell, the top sections sliding off directly toward the cabin. "Run!" I shouted.

Carl and Hunter sprinted forward. Behind them, concrete, brick, and glass cascaded down on top of Bice's old cabin. It collapsed instantly under the weight of the debris. For a brief moment, I cringed at the thought of telling Bice about it… but then realized he wouldn't mind at all. He never cared for material things much.

As the dust from the collapse cleared, I could see through the fallen building. On the other side, Troilus Green, clad in its green robe, lowered its hand. A dozen or more Viridian Guard clustered behind it, and behind them I could make out other people watching. Something was very wrong here. How could the draconic be using that power? Hadn't it come from the same place as Viridia's source?

I grabbed Carl by the sleeve. "Get everyone to the truck!" I ordered. "Head north out of the city along the tracks. I'll catch up to you!"

"What are you going to do?" Lainey demanded.

I drew my sword. "Slow them down."

"Beryl! You're hurt already! You can't!"

"I can't defeat them all," I told her. "I know that. I won't be trying. I'm just going to give you all time to get out of here. Now go!"

Lainey looked like she wanted to argue some more, but Carl caught her arm and pulled her on. Lovat led them all through the gate and into the street.

I took a deep breath and walked forward into the fallen debris. Troilus Green watched me from a block away. It recognized me at once.

"Beryl! There you are! Come! Let us have words together."

"Sure. What do you want to talk about?" I called. I could now see a large crowd gathered behind the Viridian Guard. Maybe they were just curious about all the noise, or maybe the dragon/draconic had summoned them to witness its power.

"Behold, my children!" Troilus Green bellowed, confirming my suspicion. "The rebel: Beryl! The one who has wrought so much trouble over the past few months. He claims to fight for you, but he blasphemes against your god!"

"You're not a god, Troilus. Just a lizard who walks like a man." I stopped in the street outside the shrine, facing the crowd through the ruins of the building. I imagine I looked somewhat dramatic, between the devastation and the dust swirling around.

"I am Viridia!" the draconic shouted. It lifted its hand to the side and the wall of another building exploded inward. The power seemed significantly stronger than before the draconic's "death" on the train. Back then, it could knock me down, and maybe a bit more... but knocking down a building? That was new. "I am the dragon, born again into this form! My power is unquestioned!"

I boosted my legs and jumped high. I landed on a still-standing portion of the destroyed building's second floor. It shifted a little under my weight, but didn't fall. Thoughts raced through my head. If I could take Troilus Green down in front of this crowd, I could not only eliminate this threat, but swing public opinion in my favor. We could start a full-blown rebellion!

But could I defeat it? This power it wielded still confused me. I had no idea of its limits or capabilities. And Lainey was right: I wasn't in the best of shape myself. I could almost see Bice—or Carl—warning me against recklessness. Trying to kill Troilus Green right now would absolutely be reckless.

I couldn't just run away, either. Not only would it play into the draconic's hands with this crowd, it didn't do what I came to do: slow it down.

"If you're a god, why do you need all this help to come after one man?" I called.

"I don't need them." The draconic strode forward into the debris. Only a few feet separated us, both horizontally and vertically. At least I had the high ground.

"Are you sure you want this?" I taunted. "Why not tell them who jammed this sword down your throat once already? Or who watched while Viridia's head was torn from his body?" I held the sword high. "That was me! A nobody! Humans don't need dragons to rule them! We should be free!"

The crowd murmured. From here, I couldn't see them clearly. I wondered if any of the escaped prisoners were among them. That would certainly help.

Troilus Green lifted a hand and waited for the crowd to grow quiet. Fine by me. Every second here let the others get further away.

"If you are a nobody, as you say," the draconic said in a smooth voice, still loud enough to be heard by all, "if you are just a human like everyone else, how did you jump up there? How are you able to do these feats you claim? No ordinary human can do this."

"You know the answer to that." What was it playing at here? "I have a cyb implant. It helps me fight monsters like you!"

"You call for humans to rise up, yet you use enhancements to do it yourself," Troilus Green observed. It turned its back to me and lifted its arms before the crowd. "He is no more human than I! He only seeks to supplant your natural leader, the one who has cared for you for hundreds of years! He's had a taste of power and wants more for himself!"

"I don't want your power!" I shot back. "I just want you and all the dragons and draconics gone!"

"We all know you're in an alliance with the renegade dragon Onyx! Your words are full of lies!"

"If I can find Onyx, I'll kill him too!" I snarled. "The only—"

Before I could finish the sentence, Troilus Green lashed out, screaming something—I think I almost understood it that time—as it whipped its arm up. But I'd been waiting for this exact action. I leaped straight up as the ledge I'd been standing on was obliterated. I twisted in the air and dove toward the draconic, sword extended.

I stopped.

In mid-air, I stopped.

Troilus Green somehow managed to get its other hand up and shouted again. The power, whatever it was, stopped me. The air around me seemed to grow solid, freezing me in place. I could move my eyes, I could breathe... but that was about it.

Bice had done this to Troilus Green when the two of them fought with this magic. The draconic had been unable to escape; we left it hanging in the air at the time. I knew it got loose after we left, but I didn't know how long it took. How long could Troilus Green hold me here?

I sent boosts everywhere: arms, legs, brain, nervous system. Nothing made a difference.

"Behold the power of Viridia!" one of the Guard shouted. The rest of them cheered. A few cheers came from the crowd as well.

Troilus Green continued to hold one palm toward me, shaking ever so slightly from the effort. With the other hand, it swept a gesture to include all of the humans. "My loyal Viridian Guard!" The hand pointed at me. "There is the enemy of your god!" They murmured in response. "And your target!"

A dozen shockspears rose.

34

Only seconds separated me from death. With that many shockspears aimed at me, I had no questions about my survival. I had to do something, but nothing worked! I'd tried boosting every muscle in my body…

Except one. The one other big muscle connected to my boosting system. We'd just talked about it only a few minutes ago. It didn't make any sense for it to be connected. It made even less sense to try boosting it now. But I was desperate.

I concentrated and sent a boost to my heart.

Shockspears flew through the air at me.

Something exploded through my entire body and outward, a strange feeling like a rush of electricity. I snapped free of Troilus Green's magic. The shockspears behaved as if someone had stopped them all and thrown them aside like so many fallen sticks. They tumbled to the ground in all directions.

I fell straight down, but managed to land in a crouch right in front of the draconic. I swept my sword out and caught the beast just above the ankle. My blade cut a short gash across the iridescent scales and tore through the robe.

Troilus Green roared and stepped back. "What is this? This is impossible!"

"People keep saying that to me, and I keep proving them wrong,"

I answered. Actually, I didn't. I thought of that line much later. At the moment, I was too shocked myself to say anything.

"Get him!" one of the Guard shouted.

I boosted my legs hard and ran. I took an erratic path through the building debris and cut to the left as soon as I hit the road outside the shrine. Two or three more shockspears came near, but none hit me. The draconic continued to roar his outrage. The crowd, shocked silent at first, erupted in sound as I escaped. I think I heard one or two of them laughing.

Running through the streets of Viridia again. Nothing new to me. This time, at least, I could cut loose and run as fast as I could. Everyone else would be in the truck and maybe even outside the city by now. But I didn't want to lead the Viridian Guard straight to them. I would need to take a confusing route.

As I ran, I tried to understand what had happened. It made no sense. How could sending a boost into my heart do… that? Could I use the same power the draconics and priests and Bice were using? But when they used it, they needed to say something, some kind of magic words or something. Didn't they? I hadn't said anything. I couldn't say anything!

What I did shocked Troilus Green. I kept coming back to that. It was unexpected. Not only was it unexpected, Troilus Green hadn't been able to do the same thing when Bice had trapped it. I had done something the draconic couldn't do. While that brought a smile to my face as I ran, it also confused me to no end.

My escape was too effective. I'd outdistanced all the pursuers. That wouldn't work. I should lead them further away from the north side of the city. I stopped out in the middle of a street, sheathed my sword, and took a few moments to catch my breath. I waited, panting, until I finally heard a voice: "There he is!"

I took a quick glance and saw two of the Viridian Guard coming my way. I made sure they saw me turn right and run southward.

In this way, I led them on a ridiculous chase through the streets of Viridia. Dozens of people saw us. Some gave me surreptitious signs of encouragement, like a quick thumbs-up or half-wave. A couple of them yelled for the Guard. Most just watched, wide-eyed, at the unusual events.

After an hour, I decided I'd done enough. I double-backed, turned north, and left the pursuers far behind. I took quick rests in dark alleys, and so made my way to the train station. I left Viridia behind and set out into the wilds of The Circle, an area I'd come to know so much better over the past year.

A few miles down the track, I found the parked truck. The others had seen me coming with binoculars and were waiting. Lainey greeted me with a quick hug, which, I'll admit, felt good and hurt at the same time.

"What happened?" Carl asked.

"Did you kill the drake?" Lovat wanted to know.

I shook my head, and bent over, putting my hands on my knees. I let my body relax. When my legs started to tremble, I sat down in the grass. Once I recovered my breath, I gave a brief recap of what happened.

Carl looked to Hunter. "Does that make any kind of sense?" he asked.

Hunter shook his head. "I do not know anything specific related to resomancy," he said.

"Resomancy? That's what you call it?" I snorted. That's what those floors in the Flame had been all about. Why hadn't I figured that out?

"Reso… meaning sound?" Carl asked. "It has something to do with sound waves, then?"

"Um, is this the right place to discuss this?" Fern broke in. "Shouldn't we get further away?"

"She's right," I said. "We can debate it later. Let's get moving." I put out my hand, and Basil helped me stand up.

"Where are we going?" he asked.

"To the Achromatic Asylum," I told him with a grin. "Or what's left of it, anyway."

We drove the truck a few miles away from the tracks, aimed it toward the east, and abandoned it. It would have been nice to bring it along, but it was far too conspicuous and easily spotted. If a dragon happened to fly anywhere nearby, the sight of a truck so far outside the city would immediately arouse suspicion.

I dispatched Lovat and Cobalt to fetch the four-wheeler from where we'd left it. They promised to meet us back at the Asylum. Lainey and I led the rest of our growing band north, toward our former headquarters. A couple hours later, we stopped for the night. The former prisoners had no trouble sleeping outside. Compared to their time in the Virescent Pit, sleeping on grass was a luxury. As for me, I fell asleep immediately and slept later than I'd like. More consequences of using my boosts so much back in the city.

The next morning, we ate a cold breakfast and prepared for a new day of walking. I looked over the heavy packs of Carl's equipment. "Someday, you're going to have to explain all of this to me," I said.

"Not today," he answered with a chuckle. "Maybe when it's all set up again. This workshop you talk about has power, correct?"

"Electricity? Sure. But we, uh, don't know where it's coming from."

His eyebrows rose. "Interesting. Maybe we can track that down for you."

Lainey looked over from brushing Glacier's fur. "Don't give him another tech mystery to solve! He'll be at it for days!"

Glacier hissed and her fur stood on end. Lainey stopped and looked in the direction the cat stared. "Oh. Father…"

"What is it?"

I stepped around to get a better view and stopped. The purple robed figure was back, standing atop a short rise barely fifty yards away. But this time, there were two of them. I tried zooming in on them, but once again, their faces were completely obscured. I could make out more details on the robes themselves this time. The bottom half of each robe appeared frayed, split into dozens of strips waving in a stiff morning breeze. It looked almost like a hundred arms reached toward us.

"Blast it all," Carl muttered.

I spun on him, letting my eyes return to normal. "You do know something about them! I knew it. Who are they? Why are they watching us?"

He closed his eyes and bowed his head for a moment. Then he lifted it back up with a hard set to his features. He straightened and flexed his shoulders.

"They're here for me," he said.

35

"What do you mean?" I demanded. I took another quick look at the purple robes. They hadn't moved. "I saw one of those robes in the Viridian Guard station. If they're from Viridia, why would they be after you?"

Carl, his eyes fixed on the watchers, reached a hand out toward Lainey. She jumped to her feet and ran to his side. The three ex-prisoners joined us as well.

"What's going on?" Fern asked.

"They're definitely not from Viridia. Listen to me very carefully, Beryl," Carl said in a low voice. "I am going to go talk with them. Do not approach, no matter what happens."

"But—"

"Listen to me, boy! If you have any respect for me at all, if you value my daughter at all… do not approach! I will try to deal with them. It may go poorly. If so… I charge you with Lainey's protection. She will be your responsibility."

"Glacier and I can take care of ourselves!" Lainey insisted, fire in her eyes. "What are you thinking, Father?"

Carl tore his eyes from the watchers and looked at her. "I love you, baby girl. I'll be back. No matter what happens, do you hear? I'll be back." He embraced her.

"Roberts…" The voice seemed to drift to us on the breeze, undulating in broken tones that sounded decidedly inhuman.

"Fewmets," Basil murmured.

"Take my gear to the workshop," Carl said, apparently addressing me again. "Just leave it there for now." He hesitated. "Of course, it may be that I walk over there and then walk right back. I wouldn't count on it, though. They're not very forgiving."

"Who are they?" I demanded.

"They're like your priests… only much, much worse."

"They're from outside The Circle, then?"

"I've told you what I can, boy. Finish your work here before thinking too much about it."

"Carl…"

He gently pushed Lainey away from him. I stepped up and reached for his shoulder. He pulled away from me as well. "Don't. I told you. Stay here." He strode away from us with purposeful steps, heading toward the purple robes.

"I do not understand at all," Hunter said.

"Lainey?" I whispered. She reached out and grabbed my hand.

"Roberts…" came the unearthly voice again.

"I'm coming!" he called in return. "Don't you people still have eyes?"

Carl continued until he reached the base of the rise. He stopped, folded his arms across his chest, and stood before the robed watchers. A conversation started between them, but just out of my hearing range.

"What's happening?" Fern asked. "You said they're from outside The Circle?"

"That's crazy," Basil said. "No one lives out there."

"Lainey and Carl do," I answered. "Now hush. I want to try to hear them." I took a step forward, straining my ears. The voice of the purple robes had been strange enough when we could hear it. From a distance, I couldn't understand it at all. I could make out a word or two from Carl's answers: "report" and "late." But I couldn't hear much else.

"Wind's picking up," Basil noted.

He was right. How bizarre. I'd been out in the wilds for months and never experienced wind like this except during a big rainstorm. It didn't make sense.

The frayed lengths of the purple robes waved about in the sudden wind, curling and stretching out toward Carl. He slapped one away.

"…Chroma!" he yelled. "I told you already!"

A chill ran down my spine. Against his warning, I started forward. Lainey pulled back on my hand. "Beryl, don't!"

"He's in trouble! I can help him!"

"Don't!" she repeated. "I can't lose you too!" She maintained a death grip on my hand.

"What?" I glanced at her, then looked back to Carl.

The wind gusted hard, almost knocking us off our feet. Glacier growled.

Purple strands shot out to Carl and seemed to wrap around him at various points.

I yanked free of Lainey's hand and boosted my legs. I lunged forward.

The purple robes, including the strands wrapped around Carl, seemed to fold in on themselves. The air warped around them. I shot across the grass, reaching forward.

All three of them vanished.

I stumbled and slowed to a halt right where Carl had been standing.

The wind faded into the same slight breeze from before the watchers' appearance. They were gone.

Lainey cried, but she refused to talk about it. I managed to overhear a few things she said to herself: "He did what they asked. Why did they take him?" I wanted to ask more, but she was in no condition for questions.

I searched the area, but found nothing, just like the last time one of the strange watchers had appeared. The others knew even less than I did. Until now, Basil apparently hadn't grasped that Carl and Lainey came from outside The Circle. He'd skipped the longer conversations with Carl back at the shrine. He walked around muttering to himself about it for at least ten minutes.

We divided Carl's equipment up between us. I could follow those instructions, at least. For the next four hours, we walked in silence. The others followed me. What else could they do? Go back to Viridia? I'd promised them a safer place out here, and look what happened. Every time it seemed like things might be looking up, I got hammered down again by something else. I'd thought The Circle to be full of my enemies; I never expected more to come from outside it.

At a pause for lunch, I vented a bit in front of Lainey. "I can't believe we found Kelly's mother, only to lose your dad," I moaned, falling back in the dirt. "Why can't things go right for a few days?"

"He knew what he was doing," she answered, rubbing Glacier behind the ears. "All we can do is keep going."

"It's bad enough we have to deal with dragons and all their minions. Now we have magicians from outside coming after us? And why was one of them in the Viridian Guard? Was he spying on them? Or us? Both?"

"They won't bother us any more," she said in an odd tone. "They have what they wanted."

I rolled over onto my elbow to look at her. "You know more about it too. Why won't you tell me?"

"Focus on your enemies here, Beryl. That's what he wanted you to do."

"Right, right. And what I do here can impact the fight out there. That's what he told me. But he never said anything about magicians who can control the wind and disappear!"

"They're like your priests."

"What does that mean?"

"I don't know!" she snapped. "Okay? I just... I don't know!" She looked away. "He sheltered me from a lot of it. I've told you about my mom. After that... I didn't pay much attention to the rest of the world until he brought me here, to your world. And now everything is different. And what I do know... he's told me not to tell you yet. Don't make me break my word to him."

"I'm sorry," I said. "I didn't mean to upset you. I'm just frustrated. I don't want to lose anyone else."

Her eyes returned to mine. "Then don't leave us again."

I wrinkled my brow. "I can't promise we won't get separated."

"I know."

"And I may have to fight when others can't, like yesterday."

"I know all that. I meant: don't go off on these long journeys without us." She paused and shook her head. "When you would leave us in Viridia, we didn't know what to do with ourselves. I mean, my father was fine off by himself. But Lovat and me..." She pushed against Glacier, who'd settled on her foot. "There's only so much you can play with this cat before she gets annoyed."

"Lainey, I'm sorry. I'll do my best to include you from now on."

"Not just me."

"Right. No one left behind. But as our group grows, we have to pick the right people for different, uh, missions, you know?"

She cocked her head and frowned. "I feel like we're getting way off track here. We were talking about our emotions after losing people."

"We were?"

She shoved me then. Glacier jumped to her feet, sure something must be wrong. Lainey grabbed her and buried her face in the cat's fur, laughing.

"Are you two ready to move on yet?" Fern called.

I got to my feet and held my hand out to Lainey. "My lady?"

She smiled and let me pull her up. "Thank you, kind sir."

About an hour later, we heard the sound of an engine approaching. I swung up into a tree to get a look and saw the four-wheeler coming behind us. Cobalt and Lovat had caught up. They slowed to join us, but I told them to go on ahead. Our pace had been slower than normal, of necessity. Fern and Hunter, at least, weren't used to this much walking, even though they'd been worked hard in the pit.

We were less than a mile from the Asylum when the four-wheeler returned, this time with Caedan and Lovat. I guess he couldn't wait. Caedan leaped off and gave Lainey a big hug before turning to me. His iridescent blue eyes sparkled.

"They're in the tower, Beryl. I'm sure of it!"

"You saw them?" I demanded.

"Not exactly, but…"

"Who's this?" Basil asked.

Oh, right. I introduced Caedan to the newcomers, then quickly summarized our situation. "I'll explain more after you tell me about the bleaking tower!"

"Right, right."

We resumed walking, the others following. Out of the corner of my eye, I did notice that Lovat was alone on the four-wheeler. Caedan let him drive? He seemed to be doing fine, so I didn't object.

"It's a harsh trip, by the way," Caedan began. "We skirted around the outside of the Blasted Lands, and up to the base of the mountains."

"So you didn't actually get to the tower?"

He shook his head. "No, it would have taken too long. We got close enough to see it through the binoculars. I left Royal behind to keep an eye on things. He's stationed in a good hiding place, plenty of food and water… wish I had a talker for him, though."

"Yeah, we lost too many of them. Tell me what you saw, you bleaking idiot!"

He grinned. "At first, we saw nothing. We took turns watching for an hour or more, and didn't see anyone at all. I was thinking it was a dead end, you know? But that night, we saw lights. Someone's in the tower, all right!"

"Unless it has automated lighting," Hunter pointed out. I didn't even know he was close enough to hear us.

Caedan shook his head. "I saw shadows moving. People were there."

"But you didn't see anyone specifically?"

"I'm getting to that!" He was taking delight in this. I wanted to smack him. "The next morning, I was debating whether we should try to get closer, or just come back to you with this information. And then I took one last look for a while. While I was watching, someone came out on a balcony and I got a good look. You'll never guess who it was!"

"Kelly?"

"Nope. Mazarine! That double-crossing high holy priest who thinks he's found a new god."

I grabbed his arm. "You're sure it was him?"

"Positive. I could see the sun reflecting off his bald head and that stupid sapphire."

I clenched both fists. "Finally. Some good news! You ready for some action, Caedan?"

"Am I ever!"

We arrived at the ruins of the Achromatic Asylum. I guess they weren't really ruins, by the strict definition of the word. More like remains. Anyway, I pointed out where everything had been to the newcomers and then led the way down into Loden's workshop. There we found Cobalt, Sapphire, Turq, and Saxe. We made introductions all around.

Hunter stepped away from everyone and stared around at the workshop. I let him be. I understood how he felt. All of this, most of which we didn't understand yet, had been built by Loden. Just seeing it all again made me feel like he was here with us, encouraging us in the battle.

"So." Caedan rubbed his hands together. "We've got a mission. Everybody, find a seat and listen to Beryl."

I watched as this disparate and mostly new group settled in. There weren't enough chairs, but Caedan's young recruits didn't mind sitting on the floor. Lovat sat on a table. Glacier curled up right in front of the doorway and appeared to go to sleep.

"Thanks, everyone," I said. "This is… this is crazy. Even when we had all of our former friends here, it wasn't this crowded. I'm…" I swallowed back a lump in my throat. The movement was growing. No matter what disasters kept being thrown at us, we kept regrouping and growing. This wasn't even everyone. Stacy, Jaden, Marcus, Cerise… and our missing friends.

"I think you all know what we're talking about," I went on when I could. "Onyx kidnapped at least one of our friends, and we're going to rescue her."

"Kelly," Fern whispered.

I nodded. "We're going to get her back. And any of our other friends that might be there. From what we can tell, they're in a tower on the edge of the mountains overlooking the Blasted Lands. It won't be easy to get there."

"And it's going to get cold," Caedan added. "Also, the air is kind of… toxic, depending on how close to the Blasted Lands we get."

"Right. It's going to be rough. But I'm sure Fern will insist on coming."

"Try and stop me!" she said, eyes blazing.

"I don't want to. Kelly will be needing you." I turned to Hunter. "And you too, I'm sure. I'm counting on you to save her life."

"I will do my best," he said. "But I can not make any promises." He gave a wide gesture at the workshop. "Are there any medical supplies here?"

"Yes, a few," I recalled. "Bice had a stock. Lovat, do you—?"

He pointed under the table on which he sat.

"Oh, right there. Okay. Go through it and find what you need, Hunter. Now, the rest of the team will be myself, Caedan, and Lainey."

"And me!" Lovat interrupted.

I glanced at Lainey, and she gave me one of those little smiles of hers. "Right, I was about to name you. Basil, would it be all right if you stayed here and helped out Caedan's crew? They're going to be working at building this place back up. They could use your expertise."

Basil glanced around at Turq, Saxe, and Sapphire. "Sure," he said. "I don't really want to go near the Blasted Lands, anyway."

"I don't blame you." I looked around. "Let's spend the morning assembling any supplies we might need. Caedan, if I remember right, there's a chest of warm clothes somewhere, isn't there?"

"Yeah. We brought some blankets along too. Royal is probably wrapped up in three of them right now."

"Good. We'll need that, the medical supplies, our weapons, and the two talkers. We'll make specific plans when we get close. Any questions, anyone?"

Fern lifted her hand hesitantly, as if she were a student back in the Learning Years. "You didn't mention the dragon," she pointed out. "Is he at the tower?"

"Caedan didn't see him," I said, glancing at him for confirmation, "but that doesn't mean he's not there, or nearby."

"Then what will we do if he finds us?"

"You leave him to me, while the rest of you rescue Kelly."

"Forgive me, but… what can you do against a dragon?"

"I don't know," I said. "But Onyx is also Rick, who was my best friend. At the very least, I can get him talking. And maybe I can hurt him." I saw concerned looks on Lainey and Lovat's faces. "But maybe he won't be there at all. We just don't know right now. Any more questions?" No one spoke. "All right, then let's get ready!" I started to clap my hands before remembering the damage to my left. As the others got up, I helped Hunter drag out the box of medical supplies.

Caedan caught me and pulled me aside. "This feels really weird," he said, "but without Bice, or, or, um, anyone older and wiser, I feel like I need to be the one to point some things out to you."

"Somebody has to. I make tons of mistakes if they don't." I glanced around. "You're right, though. No Bice. Or Kelly. No one to calm me down and tell me think things through. Hunter might do it, I guess, if he knew us better and felt more comfortable. He seems that type of guy."

"That's kind of what I wanted to bring up," Caedan said. "We used to never let new people into the workshop, remember? Not until they proved themselves. And you brought these three in right away."

"You brought five!"

He held up his hands. "I know, I know. But I've been working with them for weeks before now. You just met these people."

"Look, I get it." I pointed at Fern. "But that's Kelly's mom. She was thrown in that pit because of us. And Hunter worked with Loden! I think we can trust them."

"And what about this third guy? The one you're leaving here with my kids?"

"Basil?" I started to answer, but stopped to think. What did I know about him? "He was about to kill himself in the pit when I showed up. He fought hard to get out. I guess… I guess I don't know much more about him. You have a point."

"We've been betrayed once already."

That hurt. He was right. "So… what do we do, then? Will your gang be enough to keep an eye on him?"

Caedan slipped his stun weapon from his belt. "I'll leave this with Turq. He's got a good head on his shoulders. I'll tell him what to do. Between the three of them, I think they'll be all right."

"Good." I looked at him and chuckled. "You go from action junkie to leader to wise counselor. What's next? You gonna build some tech here?"

He rolled his eyes. "Gods, no. I'd blow myself up."

I laughed. "Just as well. If you changed too much, I wouldn't know what to do."

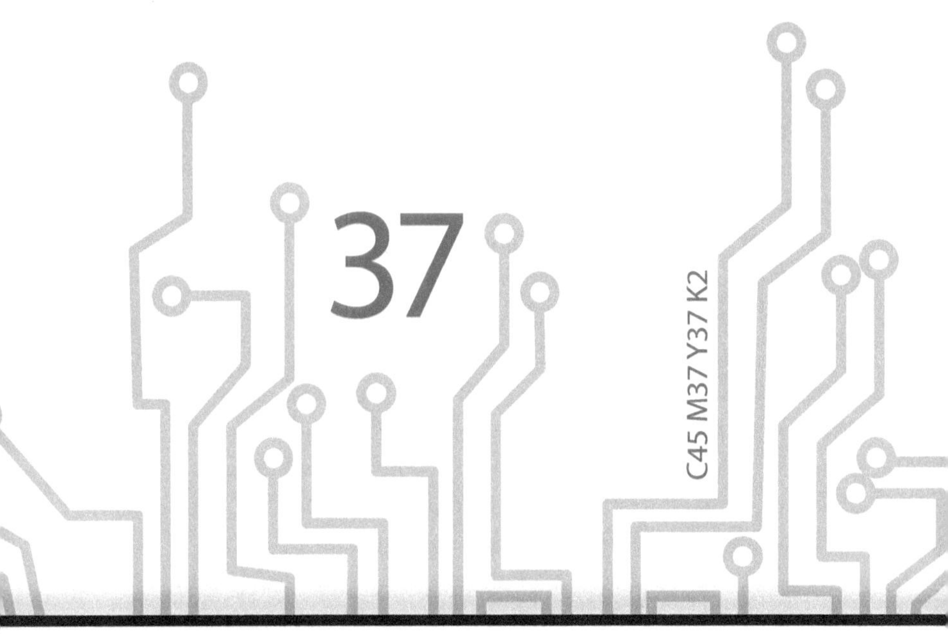

37

After lunch, we gathered everything together and prepared to leave. I regretted not being able to spend at least one night in the shelter of the workshop, but the longer we delayed, the more desperate Kelly's situation grew. We didn't know how much time she had.

I debated bringing the four-wheeler along. We couldn't drive it into the mountains, obviously, but maybe we could use it to bring more gear closer to our destination. And maybe Kelly would need a ride back? In the end, I gave up on it, because of the annoyance of driving it at walking speed.

The six of us set out, carrying all that we could imagine we might need. Caedan found a large coil of rope in the workshop, which he thought might come in handy. He looked a bit overburdened with that on top of his backpack, but he insisted he could handle it.

I glanced back at Basil as we left. Was Caedan right to be suspicious of him? It couldn't hurt to be cautious, I suppose. I kicked myself for not even asking Basil how he'd gotten thrown in the pit in the first place. I'd had my mind on other things ever since I met him.

We filled canteens and a number of extra bottles at the creek, then crossed it and headed east. The walk to the Blasted Lands would only take a couple of hours. Getting around the edges would take much longer. Based on what Caedan said, we wouldn't reach Royal's surveillance spot until late tomorrow. From there, we had no idea how long it would take to get to the tower. It depended on how difficult the climb proved to be. I was counting on Lainey to help out with that. She had more experience with the mountains than any of us.

After a while, we began to notice some changes. "What's that smell?" Fern asked.

"The Blasted Lands," Caedan answered. "It's not a pleasant place."

"It smells like… death." She wrinkled her nose. She must have had a stronger sense of smell. I didn't smell anything yet; in fact, I don't think I smelled anything the last time until I was right up on the edge.

"It is death," I said. "We don't know how many thousands of people died there. It used to infuriate me, thinking they did it as punishment for the humans rising up. But now we know the truth."

"What do you mean?" Hunter asked. "Did they not do it as punishment?"

"No. They were trying to kill Onyx." I picked up a rock and threw it. "In some ways, I guess that's worse. The people who died weren't even a concern. Less than nothing."

"And all this time, we were hanging out with the dragon they were after." Caedan shook his head. "Still blows my mind."

Right. I tried not to think about it too hard. These creatures that lived for hundreds of years… how could we even relate to them? Understand them? I wondered if that was part of why they didn't think much of us. What would I think of a creature that lived only eight or ten years? At that point, Glacier bounded past me. Did I think of her the same way the dragons thought of us? No. No, I didn't. I wouldn't treat Lainey's pet that way.

Dragons were just evil. And Onyx might be the worst.

When we did come in sight of the Blasted Lands, we stopped for a rest, and to let those who'd never seen it get a good look. Lainey sat down and just stared with a sadness in her eyes. Fern and Hunter remained standing, maybe in a little bit of shock. Unlike Lainey, they'd heard about this place all their lives.

"How close can we get?" Fern asked. "Safely, I mean."

"I stepped inside it," I told her. "But I wouldn't go far. The air gets bad after a bit. We'll shouldn't have any trouble walking around it."

"It feels… wrong," Hunter said.

"Yeah." That was it, of course. It felt wrong. The whole place was wrong, unnatural. It didn't belong in our world. The dragons had rained their fury on this place, poisoning it for generations… maybe forever! And the corruption it caused continued to spread, slowly for now, but someday, it might corrupt the whole Circle. Then what?

"Don went inside it," Lovat said.

"When?" I asked.

"He drove the digger into it and left it there." The boy pointed. "I think that's it."

I looked. Sure enough, I could see a dark shape parked not too far within the devastated land. I'd forgotten what had happened to the digger we used to tear out the blue dragon's throat. I triggered the zoom on my eyes and got a closer look. To my surprise, the digger was covered in rust. In some places, it had already eaten through the metal.

"Yikes."

"What is it?" Caedan asked.

I let my eyes return to normal and told him what I'd seen. "It's done that in only a few months. That's crazy."

"It is terrifying," Hunter said.

We watched in silence for a little while longer.

"All right, that's enough for me," Caedan said abruptly. "Let's move on."

Feeling like he'd snapped me out of some kind of trance, I agreed. The others shook their heads, pulled their eyes away, and joined us as we took a turn to the right. For now, we'd keep the Blasted Lands on our left as we circled around.

A sense of lethargy dragged at our feet until evening. I knew we had to go slower due to Fern and Hunter; neither were used to this kind of constant walking, and after yesterday, they were already tired. In addition, we were ascending now, though it would be a gradual rise until we got closer to the mountains. Even so, I thought we should have gotten further. We stopped early, before the sun fully set.

"How much further do we have to go?" Fern asked.

Caedan looked toward the mountains. "I'd guess about two to three hours tomorrow will get us to Royal. After that… we don't know. Depends on the terrain."

"So… get a good night's sleep," I advised. "We'll need it."

"My feet are killing me," Hunter said.

"I'll do whatever it takes to get my daughter back," Fern said. "Who needs feet, anyway?"

"Centipedes," Lovat answered.

The next morning, we felt the chill. If it was this cold already, the mountains would be frigid. We pulled on our warmer clothing and set out. Lainey and I had the clothes we wore in the mountains when I'd first met her. For the others, we had thick coats, but not much else. When it got colder, they would need to put on multiple layers.

Caedan led the way as we set out. I brought up the rear, to keep an eye on our slower walkers. After a few minutes, Hunter dropped back to walk beside me.

"Does the cold affect you?" he asked.

"Sure. Why wouldn't it?"

"Have you tried using boosts to stay warm?"

I hadn't. But I guess it made sense… somewhat. The boosts were energy, and they did often feel a little bit warm flowing into my muscles. But…

"The boosts don't reach all the way to my extremities," I pointed out. "And those get the coldest."

He nodded. "Right, right. I am just thinking it through."

We walked along without speaking a minute or more.

"You have to understand," he said at last. "This is absolutely thrilling for me."

"Walking in the cold air?"

"No, no. Watching you. Seeing the results of the work we did."

"That makes me feel… a bit awkward." What else could I say to that? Lainey, a few feet ahead, looked back at me and smiled. I smiled in return.

"I never got to see you leave the hospital," Hunter went on. "I did not even know if you could walk."

"Why is that?" I asked. "Why did they throw you in the pit? And not Loden?"

"It was not fair," he said. "I struggled with that for a long time. I spent a few months angry at Loden, thinking he betrayed me. But that was not it."

I waited for him to go on.

"Troilus Green was not happy with the work we did on him, not completely. He complained that something felt off. That was enough to send me away, for failing him."

"But not Loden?"

Hunter shook his head. "Loden's genius was too well known, and they wanted to keep him working for them. So I was blamed. I was just a doctor, after all, and they can find more of those."

"But you're not just a doctor. You did some amazing work! I don't understand it all myself, but Fern is sure impressed."

"It is not enough. They did not recognize it."

"Ugh." His story didn't surprise me, but I hated it. The dragons and their minions destroyed so many lives. How much good work could Hunter have done if he'd never been sent to the pit? How many lives might he have saved? Such a waste.

Something wet touched my cheek. I looked up. "Is that..?"

"It's snowing!" Lovat crowed.

38

While snow might delight our youngest friend, the rest of us did not greet it with pleasure. I hoped it wouldn't last long. The more snow that fell, the more difficult our travels would become.

As it turned out, Lovat wasn't the only one excited about the precipitation. Glacier bounded through the falling snow like a tiny kitten again. As it accumulated in small patches here and there, she rushed to them and stuck her face into each patch. She also became harder and harder to see against the white-speckled background. She blended in with this kind of environment.

We curved back to the left, following the boundary of the Blasted Lands. The terrain sloped steadily up, growing steeper and rockier the further we went.

Sometime in the late morning, I spotted someone waving at us from a pile of rocks. We climbed up and met Royal. As Caedan had predicted, he greeted us wrapped in two blankets.

"About time!" he said on our arrival. "It's freezing up here!"

Caedan removed a spare coat from his backpack and offered it to him. "Not sure it's your size, but it was the closest I could find."

Royal pulled it on without waiting. "Thanks. The tower's been pretty quiet while you were gone."

"Have you seen anyone at all?" I asked.

He nodded. "Every once in a while, someone will walk out in my view, either on the balcony, or the landing pad."

"The what?"

He glanced at Caedan. "He didn't tell you? It's what we call the spot on the back of the tower… Here, you'd better just look for yourself." He offered me his binoculars.

"I don't need them." I climbed on top of the rock pile and looked along the mountain range.

There it was, just as I'd seen it from the Sky Claimer that day: a tall, black tower overlooking the Blasted Lands. The distance and atmosphere had made it difficult to see back then, but our current position gave me a much better view. A full third of the tower appeared to be built directly into a sheer wall of the mountain itself; the remaining two-thirds stretched up into an open area. The mountains continued to climb much higher behind it.

I zoomed in for a closer look. The tower looked to be made of some type of black stone, though I think I saw some metal frames and joints in places. Mid-way up the side facing the Blasted Lands, I could see the balcony Caedan and Royal had mentioned. It curved around that whole side of the tower; I think I saw a single door leading inside. A dusting of snow lay on the balcony's outer wall. I didn't see anyone outside, but I wasn't surprised. It must be even colder up there.

I looked higher and then I understood. A different kind of balcony stretched out from the back of the tower, not far from the top: an enormous flat surface, now covered in snow, supported by thick beams reaching out at an angle from the tower below. An additional pair of support beams stretched in the opposite direction into the mountain. Royal called it a "landing pad," and I could think of no better name. It must have been built for a dragon to land on.

I let my vision return to normal and pondered this mystery. The tower must have been built after the destruction of Onyx's city. But how did he manage such a task? I reminded myself of the time factor. He'd had three hundred years to do this, and who knew how many people he'd converted to his cause during that time?

"How many different people have you seen?" I asked, hopping back down. Caedan offered his binoculars to Lainey, who took her turn examining the tower.

"It's hard to say," Royal admitted. "I know I've seen that priest guy a couple of times. His bald head is easy to spot. I've seen him on both the balcony and landing pad. But there's been at least two other people. At least I think it's two other people. One of them looked like a woman. The other I couldn't be sure."

"She's there," Fern said. "May I see?" Lainey helped her climb up and handed her the binoculars.

"What now?" Hunter asked.

"We rest here for a little while," I said. "Eat something. And then we head that way."

"You're going in?" Royal asked, eyes widening.

"Yes," Caedan said. "But I'm going to ask you to stay here and keep a watch." He pulled a talker from his pack. "I'll teach you how to use this. You keep an eye on things, and let us know if anything unusual happens."

"Like a dragon showing up," I added.

Royal's shoulders slumped just a little, but he nodded and took the talker.

I looked around at the others. "Does anyone want to stay here with him?" I asked.

"Not a chance," Fern said.

"You said she might need my help right away," Hunter pointed out. "We can do more for her there than we can down here in the open air."

"Yeah, neither is ideal, I suppose." I sighed and took another look at the tower. "Well… it won't be too long now."

"They're going to see us coming," Caedan pointed out, "if they look out a window at all."

"Let them."

We set out on the last leg of the journey. At first, we could walk as normal, though the ground continued to grow steeper, and we had to weave a meandering path through outcroppings. But that method soon gave way to a combination of walking and climbing. We might take ten or twelve steps along a ridge, then climb over a pile of rock slabs, then scramble up a steep slope. The snow stopped falling, at least, but it left treacherous wet spots almost everywhere. We moved much slower than I would have liked.

Glacier, however, rushed back and forth with visible pleasure. She never slipped once. During breaks, we would watch her agile movements in awe. She would bounce from one large rock onto a steep cliff, finding tiny spots for her feet to grasp, then bound over the top of the cliff and race along its edge. Even if I were boosting everything I had, I couldn't make those kind of moves. We were in her element.

Fern and Hunter looked miserable, but they kept moving. I had to admire their dedication, especially Hunter's. Fern I understood: she'd lost her husband and was desperate to find her daughter. Hunter… he came because I asked him to. I felt much better about Kelly's chances with him here. I'd been counting on Carl to help out, though he didn't have much medical training, or Bice, if we found him in time. But Hunter's medical expertise outshone anyone I knew.

"Can we take a break?" Lovat asked. He shivered beside me.

"Sure." I put an arm around him. If his boundless energy was flagging, the others must be truly exhausted. I'd been experimenting with small boosts to see if they warmed me much, so I hadn't noticed how tired everyone else had been getting.

We rested on one of the largest flat areas we'd encountered in the past couple of hours. Even so, we didn't all fit. Caedan perched on a nearby boulder, looking around. The others huddled together for warmth. I took off my backpack and considered our progress. Caedan motioned me closer.

"Have you seen how far we have to go?" he asked in a whisper.

I nodded. "We're not making good progress."

"We're not going to reach it before dark." He looked back the way we had come. "We may have to find a place to spend the night."

I hated the idea of waiting one more day, but we had other problems. "It's already cold," I said, looking back at the others. "How can we keep warm out here? A fire might be dangerous, but I don't think we have a choice."

"What would we burn?"

Another problem. I scanned the way ahead and spotted a thicket of pine trees, somewhat lower than our current position. But if we kept going higher, we would have no fuel, and also fewer options for shelter.

"We'll head down to those trees." I made the decision. "We lose some altitude, but we can start fresh in the morning. How long do you think it'll take from there?"

Caedan tried to gauge the distance we'd traveled so far and compare it with the distance from the thicket to the tower. "At the rate we've been going… five or six hours, at best. Maybe more, if it snows again."

Every hour was another hour endangering Kelly's life. Yet what choice did we have? I explained to the others what we'd determined. The promise of a fire awakened their resolve, and we moved faster in our descent to the thicket. I took one more look up at the tower and spotted a light in a window.

"I'm coming, Kelly," I whispered.

Gathering fuel for a fire proved to be more difficult than I'd expected. We had to wander further into the thicket to find branches that weren't too green or too damp. Hunter and Lovat dug a hole to get past the cold and wet surface earth. Caedan, Lainey, and I sought out the fuel. When we finally got a decent blaze going, I let the others stay with it while I made repeated trips to gather more wood. I kept myself going with small boosts. We needed enough for the entire night, and it would likely be coldest in the morning.

We positioned our sleeping bags to get us all within proximity of the fire's heat. Lainey had the best arrangement, with Glacier lying next to her, but we all stayed pretty close to each other.

I slept fitfully, my responsibilities for this group and worries about Kelly keeping me from enjoying deep rest. At least I was able to keep feeding the fire every so often. During one of these short trips outside my sleeping bag, something disturbed me.

I stopped in the act of breaking a stick in half. I scanned my sleeping friends. Nothing wrong there. The fire illuminated a very small circle around us. I could see little beyond it, but… something was there. I strained my eyes. I thought I could make out a dark figure standing outside the light… or was it a short tree trunk? I didn't remember any short trees around us. A breeze rustled my hair and changed the smoke direction. In that moment,

I was sure the figure shifted. I saw a flutter, like the frayed lengths of the purple robes. Or maybe just a branch moving in the wind.

Lainey mumbled something. I glanced at her, then turned back. Whatever I had seen was gone now. I couldn't make out anything. I took a step, but changed my mind. What could I do, anyway? I added the fuel to the fire and crawled back into my bag. This time, I slept a little better.

We woke to a new coating of snow on the ground and a deep chill in the air. Everyone pulled on as many layers of clothing as they could manage.

"We will feel warmer after we climb for a while," Hunter said. "Get our blood flowing." But his tone fell flat, and his face did not convey any confidence in his own words.

We set out, anyway. None of us were willing to give up now. The first hour of the ascent proved the easiest so far, a relief for our cold and weary bones. But soon after, we began to experience much more difficult passages. Several times, when I could see no way forward, Glacier romped past me and exposed a path I hadn't noticed. Without the cat, it would have taken much longer.

Even so, Caedan's estimate of five or six hours turned out to be too optimistic. It was late afternoon before we finally approached the tower at the one-third point where it met the slope.

Up close, it looked even more impressive. Its circumference had to be the size of a city block, at least. The enormous stones that made up its walls had to weigh tons. Again, I wondered how this structure could have been built. Three hundred years, I reminded myself. But that didn't explain everything. I don't care how much time someone has, they can't move stones that big without significant help. With the Blasted Lands just below, heavy machinery simply couldn't get here. The only way those stones could be here was… a dragon. But Onyx hadn't been able to access his dragon form until three months ago. I felt like I was missing something significant.

"How do we get in?" Lainey asked. "I don't see a door."

"You're kidding." I gave myself a boost and ran in an arc around the side of the tower nearest us. She was right. Not a door in sight. I circled all the way to the other side where the remaining half of the tower extended out away from the cliff. I looked down at the bottom third, built into the mountain itself. I couldn't see a door there, either. I returned and let the others know.

"Maybe it was built for dragon transport only?" Caedan suggested.

"But Onyx wasn't a dragon. I mean, he wasn't in dragon form," I countered. "It makes no sense."

"Maybe he didn't build it," Lainey said. "Maybe he took it from whoever did."

"Huh." I didn't like what that implied. Who else would have built a tower up here?

Lovat walked near the cliff's edge and pointed up the tower. "Up there!" he called. "Can you jump to it, Beryl?"

I moved to see what he meant: the balcony we had seen from a distance. From our vantage point, I estimated it was somewhere between two to three stories up.

Caedan joined me. "We've got the rope," he pointed out. "Can you throw that high?"

"I don't know. Do we have some kind of hook or something?"

He shook his head. "We can put something heavy on it," he suggested. "But…"

"But even if I got it up there, it probably wouldn't be able to hold our weight."

"Except…" I looked at Lovat.

Caedan wrinkled his brow. "You'd still have to throw something as heavy as he is."

"Yeah. What do you think? Sixty pounds?"

"We could get one of the backpacks that heavy, but… I know you're strong, but can you throw sixty pounds that high?" He raised his eyebrows.

"I won't know until I try it."

We gathered with the others and explained the concept.

"If anyone thinks they can't climb a rope, it might be helpful to have at least one person stay down here," Caedan suggested. He stuffed some things into a backpack and hefted it.

I nodded. "We don't know what we'll run into once we get up there. I mean, the fact that Kelly hasn't escaped on her own says there are guards of some sort, at the very least. We're going to have to fight."

"I can wait down here," Hunter volunteered. "I will not be much good in a fight. I did not do much in the pit escape."

"I can't fight either," Fern said, "but I'm still coming. You'll have to tie me down to keep me from trying it."

"We might be able to pull you up," Caedan said. He added a large rock into the backpack.

"It's the only way Glacier could get up there, if we want her to come," Lainey pointed out.

"Right. Well, let's find out if we can even get up there at all." I picked up the rope.

Caedan lifted the backpack, then lifted Lovat. "Close enough." He tied the rope to the pack.

"Why not just throw me?" Lovat asked.

"Because I'd rather not splatter your head against the rocks." I lifted the pack with the rope. Oof. Heavier than I'd anticipated. I boosted my arms and swung it around a few times.

"If you swing it like that several times before letting go, it should give you more momentum," Caedan suggested.

I practiced a couple of times, making sure I stepped over the rope with each swing, so as not to tangle myself up. That took boosts into my legs to be fast enough. Then I moved to what I thought would be the best spot from which to throw: near the cliff's edge, but not so near that I would accidentally step off.

I put heavy boosts into both arms, swung around twice, and released the weight upward toward the tower. It knocked into the side of the tower about ten feet too low and several feet wide.

"And that's why he didn't throw you," Caedan said to Lovat.

I pulled the rope back and tried again. I was further off the mark the second time.

"I'm thinking too hard about not getting my feet tangled," I said, pulling the rope back. "I need to try something different."

This time, I swung the pack only on one side, instead of circling me. I got the aim better, but still six feet or more too low.

"If anyone's home, they've heard us knocking by now," Lainey said. She trained her rifle on the balcony and sighted over the barrel.

"Maybe run and throw it?" Caedan said. "Or even run, jump, and then throw?"

"No." I shook my head, breathing hard. "To much to do at once. I'd never get the aim right. I can do this. Just let me keep trying."

Each of the next two attempts got closer. The third one hit the balcony's railing, but fell back on our side. So close. "Just a little harder,"

Lainey urged.

"Easy for you to say." I gasped for air. After a minute of rest, I picked up the rope again. I closed my eyes and concentrated. "Come on." I channeled boosts into my arms and swung the pack. Once. More boosts. Twice. More boosts. I lunged forward and released, boosting the entire time.

The backpack sailed up, bounced off the top of the balcony, then toppled over… inside. The others cheered, but not too loud. We walked to the tower's wall and looked up.

"Can you do it, Lovat?"

"No problem." He grasped the rope with both hands.

"When you get up there, find a way to tie the rope to something more solid," Caedan instructed.

He nodded, put his feet to the wall, and started up. I stood beneath him the entire time, ready to catch him if he fell. Unfortunately, to get to the balcony, he had to swing out over the cliff. If he fell now, I'd have to jump out into the open and then hope we could somehow both survive the rest of the fall. Not a good plan. Why did we let him do this?

Lovat reached the balcony, climbed over the railing, and disappeared.

"Lovat!" I called, while trying not to be too loud.

He waved over the top, and I breathed a sigh of relief.

"You'd better go next, in case anyone comes out to see what's going on," Caedan said.

Lovat appeared over the balcony, waving again. "All ready!"

I pulled at the rope. It seemed secure. Carrying only my sword on my back, I boosted arms and legs again and climbed. The gloves protected my hands in general, but even combined with the bandages, my left hand hurt with each grasp of the rope. I could feel the scabs ripping off. I didn't want to look at it after this was over. I'd rarely done much climbing like this, but I was surprised—and thankful—by how quickly I reached the top.

As we'd already observed, the balcony curved around this side of the tower. It was about three feet wide, made of the same black stone as the rest. Only the one door led inside. "Stay close to the door," I told Lovat. "Let me know if you hear anything inside."

After double-checking Lovat's knot-tying, I waved at the others. Then I watched anxiously as Lainey made her way up, far slower than Lovat or I had done. As soon as she was within reach, I caught hold of her coat and helped her scramble over.

"Fern is going to come next," she reported after catching her breath. "She volunteered to hold Glacier."

"Will the cat let her do that?"

Lainey shrugged. "I told her to. We'll see."

I watched below as Caedan fashioned a kind of sling for Fern to sit in, looping the rope around a couple of times and padding it with a blanket. A final loop went under her arms, as a fallback if she slipped out of the rest of it. Settled in, she called Glacier to her. The cat stared at her for a moment without moving. Then she looked up at us and saw Lainey waving. She jumped into Fern's lap, startling the woman. Caedan helped them adjust positions, then stepped back, hands up. I guess Glacier growled at him. He looked up and signaled for us to lift.

Lainey and I took hold of the rope and began to pull. I don't know how much Lainey did, since I kept boosting my arms the entire time. I gritted my teeth and didn't let on how much my hand hurt. I could feel more tearing of the skin. Things were getting slick inside the glove. When we got them near the top, I braced myself and held it alone while Lainey persuaded Glacier to jump over. The cat looked around, walked a few feet, and curled up next to the tower wall. With that weight gone, it was easy to get Fern over the top.

We threw the rope down again and Caedan clambered up in no time. He handed a pack with medical supplies to Fern, then took out the talker to inform Royal of our progress. He'd been able to watch us climb and reported no other visible movement. Caedan slid the talker back on his belt and looked to me. "Now what?"

"Now you let me rest a minute while you check out that door," I said, sitting with my back to the railing. Snow began to fall again, of course. Just when I wanted to relax. I was tempted to pull my glove off and put my hand into a small pile of snow next to the railing, but I didn't want to alarm anyone with the blood.

Caedan obligingly walked to the door and examined it. From where I sat, it looked solid, but had a metal latch like I'd seen on fancy houses back in Viridia.

"Surely they've heard us by now," Fern said. "Why hasn't anyone come out?"

"They're waiting for us," Caedan answered. "It's a trap."

"What do we do, then?"

He grinned. "We let Beryl walk into it and see what happens."

"I'm not indestructible," I grumbled, getting to my feet.

"I think we're the ones who've been telling you that," Lainey said. The snow fall picked up speed.

Caedan took out his baton. "We're right behind you, buddy."

I took a deep breath. "Well, it's either this or get buried by the snow out here."

"If you don't open it, I will. You know how much I hate the cold."

Lainey knelt and aimed her rifle at the door. Caedan stood to one side, waiting. Glacier got to her feet and stretched, then looked at me like everyone else.

I opened the door. A blast of warm air struck my face. I looked down a short hall that stretched ahead about a dozen feet, then made a ninety-degree turn to the left. A single electric light bulb glowed from the ceiling. I took a step inside. Glacier pushed past my leg and walked in ahead of me. She stopped just before the turn, her tail flipping back and forth. She crouched down, staring. I guess this cat did have its uses.

I leaned back. "Caedan," I whispered. "Hand me the rock you put in the backpack."

Taking the rock, I took a few more steps into the hall. Then I threw it as hard as I could at the corner. The rock shattered against the wall, making a tremendous noise. At the same instant, a crossbow bolt flew out from the other direction and bounced off the opposite wall.

Crossbows, huh? Even though I didn't know how many were waiting, I should act before that one could reload. I boosted my legs and shot past Glacier and around the corner, ducking low to provide a smaller target.

Two men in black clothing waited several feet down the new hall. One tried frantically to reload his crossbow, while the other fired as soon as I came around. The bolt struck the top of my head at an angle, tearing a gash, but ricocheting off. Must be the metal plates in my skull. Even so, the impact jerked my head sideways.

I charged them, threw an elbow at the first, and grabbed the second before he could reload. I slammed him against the wall, bouncing his head off the stone. As he fell, I spun back to the first, who'd recovered quickly from my elbow jab. He whipped out a knife and stabbed. With my boosts running, I dodged without difficulty. I disliked using the same tactic twice, but it worked so well to knock heads against walls. And I didn't have to kill them that way.

Caedan came around the corner behind me at a run. He slowed, seeing the two guards on the floor.

"I thought you were right behind me." I leaned against the wall, catching my breath.

"You moved too fast!" He stepped forward and looked down. "Rick always had an odd fashion sense." He picked up one of the crossbows and searched for bolts on both bodies.

I joined him in examining the guards. They wore black jackets with dark gray shirts underneath. Their jet black helmets included odd visors that covered the eyes and a spike down over the nose.

Glacier sauntered past us. The other three peered around the corner before coming to join us.

"You're bleeding," Lainey noted.

I started to reach for my head, but stopped before I touched it. No use getting more blood on my gloves. The gash burned a little, but my head already ached from the impact. My injuries were multiplying.

"No time to deal with it," I said. "They know we're here. We need to find Kelly fast."

"Only one door here," Caedan pointed out. He pushed it open without waiting for me. He leveled the crossbow at the interior, then stepped inside. "Just a big storage room," he announced.

"We can search those later, if we have time," I said. "Let's keep moving."

Lovat moved to the end of the hall. "Up or down?" he asked.

I joined him and saw a stairway following the arc of the tower's outer wall. We had no way of knowing where Kelly might be in here. I thought for a moment. "Up," I decided. "I'm going to guess that Onyx would want her near the landing pad for quick evacuation. Caedan, bring up the rear in case anyone comes up behind us."

I drew my sword, stepped into the stairs, and started up. The narrow passage couldn't be much more than three feet wide. Single file was the only way to go. I led the way with Lainey behind me, followed by Lovat, Fern, and Caedan. Glacier wandered between us, getting underfoot. Every six feet or so, a dim light shone from a sconce on the inner wall.

"That's far enough." The voice from above was deep and raspy. An enormous figure stepped into view, filling the stairway.

A red draconic.

My mind whirled. A red draconic. Red. Maybe Lainey's suggestion about Amaranth was more accurate than I'd thought. Had she been supporting Onyx all these years? It couldn't belong to Incarnadine, could it? Unless Rick had converted it while we were there months ago? More immediately, how did I fight it in these narrow confines?

"We have no quarrel with you," I said aloud. "We're here for our friend, and to fight against the traitor Onyx." Worth a try.

"I know who you are, Beryl," it answered, drawing out my name.

"Give the word," Lainey whispered behind me. I gave a short nod to let her know I heard.

"We all know who you are, and what you're about," the draconic went on. "This is where your little rebellion ends."

"You're going to stop me?"

"I am not alone," it declared.

"More coming up behind us," Caedan warned.

No time to waste them. As much as I enjoyed verbal sparring with these monsters, we needed to move. "Now," I told Lainey.

"Cover your ears."

I obeyed as quick as I could. An instant later, the staircase seemed to shake with the enormous blast of her rifle. I smelled sulfur and something a bit metallic. The draconic roared and staggered back. Blood gushed from a huge wound in its chest.

"Hit it again!" I urged, hearing the twang of the crossbow as Caedan fired at someone below us.

"Reloading!" Lainey snapped.

Too late. The draconic recovered enough to hiss, and fire erupted from its mouth, streaming toward us. I instinctively lifted my left hand to shield my face. As the flames struck my hand, I lunged forward. With another boost to my right arm, I stabbed up through the draconic's lower jaw. A guttural sound came from its throat, and it swiped at me, pushing me against the outer wall and re-opening at least one of the scratches on my chest.

"I can't shoot with you in the way!" Lainey yelled.

The pain from my left hand was excruciating. I yanked the sword free from the draconic's jaw, then spun around and stabbed it back through its gut. Still holding the hilt, I let myself fall onto the stairs. "Aim high!" I shouted.

Another boom reverberated through the narrow staircase, deafening me. The right side of the draconic's head exploded, and it toppled over me. I narrowly avoided twisting my wrist in pulling the sword free as it fell. The weight landed on my lower body, and I banged my knee against one of the steps.

I pulled myself free and staggered to my feet. "Come on!"

Glacier bounded past me and shot up the stairs. Lainey climbed over the fallen draconic, followed by Lovat. Fern took more time but also made it.

"Caedan!" Lainey shouted. "Come on!"

I heard a grunt from below, then Caedan came speeding up around the curve and vaulted over the draconic. Crossbow bolts ricocheted off the wall behind him. One caught in his coat sleeve.

"Two more of them behind us," he reported.

I hurried up the stairs until I found an opening into a new floor. I didn't know how high we had traveled, but a more open spot would be easier to defend against those guards. I didn't like the others being in that confined space with crossbows firing.

I stood beside the stairs and let the others get past me. I held my left hand against my stomach, but the pain kept getting worse. "Set up an ambush?" I asked Caedan through gritted teeth.

"Thought you'd never ask." He was breathing hard, but grinning. He ran into the new hallway, then slid onto the floor, where he reloaded his crossbow. He rolled over and aimed it at the opening to the stairs. The others, at a motion from me, all stood up against the wall.

"The draconic's already dead, as you can see," I called down. "Don't come after us if you don't want to end up the same way!"

"Will that work?" Fern asked.

"Depends on whether they're more afraid of us or Onyx," Caedan said from the floor.

We waited, and I listened. I heard some whispers down below. I somehow kept myself from groaning. "Leave us alone, and we'll leave you alone!" I added. "You don't have to die." How I wished Hunter could turn off my pain right then. I wasn't sure I could bear it much longer.

"Don't listen to him!" another voice insisted, then rose in a shout: "Beryl! Despite your enhancements, you have no chance here! You're up against the power of a god!"

My eyes met Caedan's. We knew that voice. Mazarine.

Fern inched past Caedan and came up behind me. "Let me see that hand!" she whispered. I held it out to her, but kept my eyes on the stairway. She gasped.

"Mazarine!" Caedan called. "We've missed you, man! Come on up so we can talk!"

"This is bad, Beryl," Fern said. "Very bad. It's a complete mess. Parts of your glove and the old bandages… we need to get all this out and debride the skin and—"

"No time," I hissed. "Just wrap it up for now."

I almost screamed as Fern began wrapping my hand in new bandages. She'd smeared some sort of cream on the interior, which felt cool to my burnt and torn skin, but just the pressure of the bandages made me see stars. Literally. I didn't know that was a real thing.

"I think not, Caedan Teal," Mazarine's voice answered. "Your doom is sealed as well, along with anyone else who allies themselves with the traitor Beryl."

"Priest!" I shouted, trying to ignore the pain. "If the dragons are gods, why are two of them dead?"

"Caesious and Viridia were unworthy! Onyx, the one true god, has slain them both. Only those who join with him can become gods themselves."

"You're going to be a god?" Caedan asked.

"If I serve him well, he has promised this to me. If you surrender now, perhaps you will have a chance yourself some day."

Onyx was offering godhood to his followers? How? I looked to Caedan and mouthed the question. He pointed at me and then the back of his head. My implant. Hunter and Carl called it near immortality for a dragon. Was Onyx promising the same to Mazarine? If he was able to do it for all his followers, it would be… impressive. An army of people with my abilities would be terrifying.

"We're at a standoff," Lainey said. "What can we do?"

"Is there anything helpful on this floor?" I asked, glancing down the hall. I saw two doors, one on either side. Fern finished bandaging my hand and stepped back.

Lovat yanked one of the doors open and looked inside. "Boxes," he reported.

"What's in them?" Caedan asked.

Lainey joined Lovat. "They're wooden crates," she said. "Nailed shut."

"Leave them," I said. "No! Wait. Bring one out here."

Between the two of them, they pushed a crate into the hall. It looked to be about two feet on every side. Perfect. I took a quick look down the staircase, then sheathed my sword. I came back and reached for the crate.

"Your hand," Lainey said, putting her own hand in my way.

"We've got to do something," I answered.

"Let me," Caedan said. He jumped to his feet and put both hands on the crate's sides. He strained and lifted it. "I got this. You get ready."

"When he throws it, we run up," I told the others, drawing my sword again.

Caedan took the crate to the stair, shifted his stance, and lifted it higher. He glanced at me and nodded. He stepped into the stairway and heaved it down the stairs.

"Let's go!" I led the way charging up the stairs again. The crash of the crate smashing down the stairs echoed behind us. It probably wouldn't hit anyone, but they would have to get out of its way, giving us plenty of time to move up.

I paused at the next floor, unsure. Down the short hall, I saw a single door at the end. A guard stood in front of it, and started forward when he saw me. That settled it. If he was guarding something, I wanted to know what it was. I charged, even as he tried to lower his crossbow to fire. I slashed upward with my sword, cutting into the crossbow and launching the bolt harmlessly at the ceiling. I lowered my shoulder and slammed into him, throwing him back against the door.

Lainey leveled her rifle at him. "Surrender and you can live," she said.

The guard looked from her rifle to my sword and at both of our faces. He lifted his hands. A promise of immortality from the dragon wouldn't do him much good if he died now, would it?

"Who's there?" a voice called from beyond the door. My head jerked up.

Kelly!

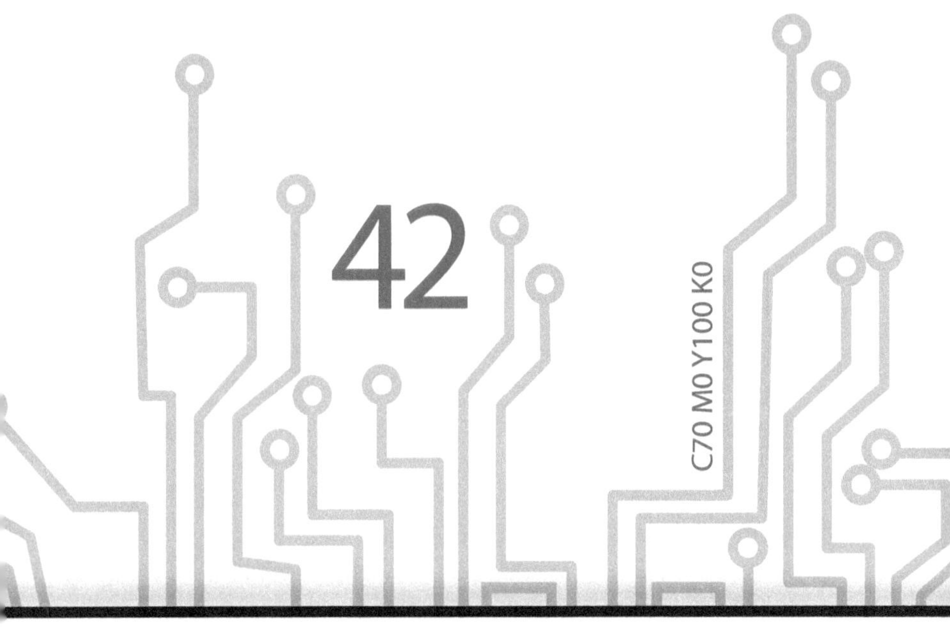

I pushed past the guard, trusting Caedan to watch the stairs. I tried the handle. Locked.

"Where's the key?" Lainey asked the guard.

"Don't bother." I boosted my hand and twisted the handle. It snapped off, but the door remained locked. Oh well. I stepped back, boosted my leg, and kicked it open.

I saw a sparse bedroom with a single window. Kelly stood in the middle of the room, eyes wide.

"Beryl! You—you're alive!"

"Sorry it took so long," I said, breathing hard. I'd been boosting myself a lot since the morning. I did have limits.

She flew into my arms, knocking my breath out of me again. I embraced her awkwardly with a sword in one hand and the other wrapped in a ton of bandages.

"Wow. You're… huge," I observed. The size of her belly really was amazing.

She stepped back and shoved me. "Idiot."

And then her eyes widened again. Behind me, Fern stepped into view. "M-mom?" Kelly put a hand to her mouth.

"Kelly…"

Where Kelly had slammed into me, her embrace with her mother took place almost in slow motion, but held so much more affection. They stood there, holding one another, tears falling. It might be the most joyful thing I'd ever seen.

I turned to check on the others. Lainey and Lovat stood just inside the door, both smiling. Glacier sauntered past, jumped up on Kelly's bed, and curled up. Caedan stood in the hall, crossbow still trained on the stairway. I moved back to him.

"What do you think?" I asked. "We found Kelly, but we'll have to go back down to get her out."

"Yeah. Not looking forward to that." He glanced at me. "Are you doing okay? You don't look good."

"I'll live." I couldn't think of anything else to say.

"Beryl!" Lovat called from Kelly's room.

I returned to see him looking out through the window he'd pushed open. I took a look. Snow continued to fall outside at a steady pace. We were much higher now, with the balcony almost directly below us. I might be able to survive that fall, but none of the others could. If we'd brought the rope with us... Ugh. None of us could think of everything.

"Can't get back that way," I said. "We'll have to fight our way down the stairs."

"Have you seen him yet?" Kelly asked, pulling away from her mother.

"Seen who?"

"Rick. Onyx."

"I don't think he's here," I said. "The landing pad was empty."

"No, you don't—Ohhh!" She doubled over in pain.

"Kelly!" Fern exclaimed.

"It keeps happening," Kelly said. "All night and this morning. I think this thing wants to be born... now!"

Fewmets. We should have brought Hunter up after all.

"We'll take care of it," Fern said. "We have a friend waiting down below. He's an expert surgeon. We'll get that out of you, and get rid of it!"

"Get rid of it?"

"Of course. We'll throw it over the cliff or something. You don't even have to see it."

"It's a draconic, Kelly," I said, as if she didn't know already.

"But..." Kelly put a hand on her enlarged belly. "It's not just his. It's mine too."

Did she want to keep it? But it was a draconic! Within a few years, its memories of its past lives in the service of Onyx would come rushing back to it. It would know precisely who it was: evil incarnate, like all draconics. Except… Protogonus Blue. He'd changed. Maybe…

"How are you even here, Mom?" Kelly asked. "I thought you were dead."

"Beryl rescued me, dear, but that doesn't matter right now. We need—"

"What about Dad? Is he here? Is he alive?"

"No." Fern shook her head slowly. "I'm sorry, dear. The draconics at the pit. They killed him."

Kelly closed her eyes. She'd already accepted her parents' deaths, but getting her mother back threw all her emotions off. Also pregnancy did that, or so I'd always been told.

"Beryl!" Caedan called. "You'd better get out here." He had an odd tone to his voice.

"Coming." I saw Kelly wince in pain again. Not good. I didn't know how long it took to give birth, let alone how long a draconic birth might take. The sooner we got her out of here and connected with Hunter, the better. I turned around and returned to the hallway. The disarmed guard and Caedan still stood in the same places, but someone else stood in the doorway, smiling at us.

Rick.

Onyx in his human form.

I did not expect this.

"Beryl! There you are!" he exclaimed. "What's taken you so long? I expected you weeks ago."

I glanced at Caedan, who kept his crossbow trained on Rick. His eyes did not move. "Why are you human?" I asked. "Did you lose the ability to turn back into a dragon again?"

Rick shrugged. He wore the same black leather jacket he'd always sported, same black gloves… he looked almost exactly how he did the day he first ran into me on the streets of Viridia. "No, not at all. There are just some things I can't do in dragon form, you know." He lowered his chin and smiled. This time it looked sinister. "Like check in on my child."

"I'm taking Kelly," I said, drawing my sword.

"That's not happening. She's carrying my child."

"Your draconic."

"Yes. It will be glorious to have him back. I've missed all my children. I'm so excited to find out which one this will be. I suspect Enlil, but it could be any of them, really."

I felt sick. This whole concept made me want to throw up.

Caedan shared my disgust. "Should I shoot him now?"

I almost said yes. He deserved it for sure. But the situation bothered and confused me. Rick was dangerous, yes, but not so much in human form. So why was he here like this? Did his arrogance force him to come down to confront us? "Not yet," I said at last.

Rick shook his head. "I was willing to let you go, Beryl. You helped me accomplish so much that I never could have done otherwise. So I left you alive. I left all of you alive. I didn't kill any of your friends or anything."

"You let Peri die," Caedan pointed out. "You could have stopped that bomb on your own."

"You killed Protogonus Blue," I added.

Rick cocked his head. "Did I? I hadn't realized that. Ah well. He was a traitor, anyway."

"He was a better man than you'll ever be."

"Man?" Rick laughed. "You can't even accept him as he was. You have to pretend he was one of you!" He pushed his hair back. "As I was saying, I was willing to let you go. I had the scientists in Viridia and Incarnadine working on what I needed to know. I had spies in both places, ready to give me what they discovered. You weren't important any more."

Kelly cried out behind us. I almost turned. Every second we wasted here took her one second closer to death, exactly what Rick wanted. Anger boiled within me, making my insides clench together like my grip around the sword hilt.

"It's almost time," Rick observed. "But you had to ruin everything, didn't you, Beryl? You interfered with the handoff in Viridia." He lowered his gaze and stared at me. "Where's Dusk?"

"Enjoying quality time with Troilus Green, I suspect," I said. "Telling him everything he wants to know about you."

"And that is why my patience with you is over," he declared. "You cost me a very valuable asset. Not only was she helpful on the tech side, but later she could have helped bring another of my children back into this world."

"Sick," Caedan muttered.

"I know the two of you have trouble finding girls, but why do you have to take mine?"

I wanted to give a snappy comeback to that. I really did. But nothing came to mind. Instead, the rage inside me threatened to spill over at any moment. The pain in my hand faded away, at least from my conscious mind. All I could think about was what this man—this dragon—had taken from me.

"Fire," I said through gritted teeth.

Caedan released the bolt in the same instant. Rick snatched it out of the air with his right hand, the cybernetic one, and threw it with tremendous force back. It struck the guard in the shoulder. He groaned and slid down the wall.

Rick drew a sword from his belt and beckoned to me.

"It ends here, Beryl."

For some reason, Rick's words cooled my rage enough for rational thought. I took a deep breath in through my nostrils.

"Once I get him out of the way, do whatever you have to," I whispered to Caedan. "Get Kelly to Hunter. Or get him to her. Whatever it takes."

He nodded, reloading the crossbow. I stepped past him and advanced on Rick.

"This is what you want, Onyx? A duel between the two of us?"

"Why not?" He switched his sword to his right hand. "I always won our practice duels."

Always? I didn't remember it that way, but maybe he was right. "I never used my full abilities in practice," I answered.

His eyes narrowed. "Then this should be fun."

I boosted both legs and lunged forward, swinging at an oblique angle. I didn't think I could actually hit him just yet, but I wanted to drive him back. He had to step back to dodge my reckless blow, countering it with a quick stab of his own. But with my legs boosted, I had the speed to dodge to the side. I boosted my right arm and delivered a succession of slashes as fast as I could. Rick backed into the stairwell.

Another cry of pain came from Kelly.

"My child is coming, Beryl," Rick taunted. "He'll be only the first, as I rebuild this Circle under my rule!"

"You're insane." I stabbed straight at his gut. He sidestepped down the stairs. Not where I wanted him to go.

I stepped out into the stairs, but held back. Rick stabbed and I stepped back and up. He'd have to follow me if he really wanted me.

"You think I don't see what you're trying to do?" he asked. "After we go up, Caedan tries to get Kelly down and out of the tower, right?" He took a step up. "Let him try. There's nowhere they can go where I can't catch them."

"Not if you're dead," I retorted, slashing overhand at him.

He had to step back down to dodge that one in the narrow stairway. "You'll have to do far better than that."

With a larger gap between us, I took the chance. I spun and raced up the stairs. I stopped at the next floor, surprised to see doors on either side. Oh right. The outside one must lead to the landing pad.

Rick caught up and nearly cut my feet from my ankles. I leaped up to avoid the strike. I landed off-balance and my shoulder slammed against the outer door. It flew open, and I staggered sideways outside, almost losing my footing on the icy surface.

I stood on the landing pad, surrounded by swirling snow. Drifts at least a foot high dotted the surface. I could hardly imagine a more treacherous location to fight.

Rick stepped through the door. "Oh, this will be fun. What's the endgame here, Beryl? Do you really think you can kill me?"

"In this form? Yes." I launched an attack, mindful of the slippery surface. We both moved unevenly, our strikes a little uncertain.

"Didn't you hear Mazarine? I'm a god! You're nothing. Your entire lifespan is the blink of an eye to me."

"Dragons. Are. Not. Gods." I spit each word out with a separate thrust or swing. Rick dodged, parried, and sidestepped, slowly circling me.

"You've been listening to that heretic Bice too much. Speaking of, where is he? I expected him to come with you. Instead, you bring a woman and an old man? Your recruiting drive must not be doing so well."

He didn't know about Bice. Then he and Don weren't here either. Unless he was just taunting me. Yet his comment earlier about not killing any of my friends made me wonder. He'd seemed genuinely surprised at the news about Protogonus Blue. What really had happened that day at the Asylum? And where were my friends?

I ignored his taunt and focused on my sword. I knew, if I kept my boosts going, I could fight harder and faster than he could. But I'd used so much already, my body didn't like it. Every new boost would give diminishing returns as the muscles grew tireder. My head still ached from the crossbow impact, and my left hand was all but useless. My chances were slimmer than I wanted to admit.

Rick's sword swept in from the left. I parried it down, then flicked my wrist and sword up with a quick boost. The tip of the sword caught Rick on the chin and cut a narrow scratch across his cheek.

He stepped back and put his hand to his face. "First blood to you, then." His eyes hardened. "But I'll take last."

I wanted to tell him he couldn't possibly hurt me more than he already had, but that would only encourage him. Instead, I sent another boost into my arm and drove Rick back with multiple swooping attacks. From right to left, and then left to right, I kept going, trying to find a weakness. To my frustration, Rick parried or dodged every blow.

"Your boosts give you an edge in speed and strength, but not skill," he pointed out. "All I have to do"—he switched his sword to his left hand—"is let you run out of boosts." He attacked with more strikes from his left hand, which were more difficult for me to counter.

"You always hated it when I fought left-handed," he said. "It's not so easy when your opponent's weapon is directly mirroring yours, is it?"

He was right, though I wouldn't admit it to him. I spent much more time focused on defense when he did this. It took so much concentration, I couldn't find time to make my own attacks. I stepped back and back. My foot slipped on the snow. I stumbled, and Rick took advantage. His sword cut through my upper coat sleeve and tagged my bicep, drawing blood. I regained my footing and stopped the follow-up thrust.

I brushed snow crystals away from my face with my left sleeve. The steady fall made our movements difficult and clouded our vision. Or at least it clouded mine; I had no idea what dragon-in-human-form eyes could do. Rick had never shown any superhuman abilities to my knowledge, aside from his cyb hand. But his deception ran so deep, there's no telling what else he concealed.

The blood on Rick's face appeared to have frozen already, though it had spread and run down his neck. That cut would definitely leave a scar. I wondered if it would show up when he turned back into a dragon.

"I don't expect you to understand what's at stake here, of course," Rick said. He had to raise his voice to be heard over the increasing wind. "Your human mind can't comprehend problems that are older than your civilization."

"I know what's outside The Circle," I told him. "I know why you won't go over the mountains."

"Did Lainey tell you then?" He laughed. "You did bring her too. That's very helpful. I can get all kinds of information from her. Not what she's told you, of course, but the real truth. I'm very curious to know how much it's changed."

I ducked under one of his wilder swings. It would have been the perfect opportunity to stab up under it, but the slippery surface kept me from gaining enough traction to step forward.

"And after I've gotten all that I need to know… well… I do need more incubators for my children." He licked the snow from his lips. "And she is pleasant to look at, as I'm sure you're very aware."

The rage overtook me again. I lunged forward, boosting everything. This time, Rick stumbled back, barely able to deflect or duck my blows. I sliced into his jacket at his right shoulder, but couldn't tell if I actually cut him. The slice again made him stumble.

I whipped my sword back and spun around in a complete circle, using my momentum to bring my sword down on top of him with as much strength as I could muster. He would not be able to dodge in time. I had him now.

My sword came to an abrupt halt, sending shockwaves through my arm. I stared. Rick caught the blade with his cybernetic hand. He wrapped his metal fingers around it and twisted it down and to his right. I held tight, twisting my wrist and arm with him. It was dangerous, but I couldn't let him wrench the sword out of my hand. My heavily-bandaged left hand was useless, unable to help. It was his cyb hand versus my normal one, and my boosts were running out.

Rick's sword in his left hand swung up. "It's the end, Beryl." The sword came down at my head.

I threw my left hand up to meet the sword. It slashed down between my forefinger and middle finger, cutting through bandages, skin, and muscle. And stopped when it hit the cybernetics inside.

"What's this?"

I strained against Rick, trying to pull my sword back while keeping his away. "Not the same as yours," I managed, "but it does the trick." In truth, I didn't even feel the cut of his sword. The flames earlier must have burned away too many of my nerve endings. Or I was just going numb from the cold.

"I knew I should have looked over those notes more throughly before giving them up," Rick muttered. We both held each other's sword blades. It might almost look comical, I suppose.

"I've learned more about myself than you can imagine," I gasped. Our faces were only about a foot apart. I could see him clearly for the first time since we'd made our way out here.

"Good. Everyone should know themselves," he answered. His face tightened. He was straining as hard as I was. As he'd told me himself, his cybernetic hand, while powerful, still had to be supported by the muscles of his arm. That was what I was fighting against. Could my boosted muscles win the day against his?

"Why… Kelly?" I asked, trying to distract him.

"What?"

"You had the look. You could have had almost any girl. Yet you chose Kelly, the girl you knew I loved. Why?"

"You said it was all right, remember?"

"I didn't know you wanted to implant her with a monster!" I was boosting both arms, but every boost seemed to do less. "I wanted happiness… for her and you!"

"I'm pretty happy now," he taunted.

"Why her?" I demanded.

"You just said it." He wrenched his sword free from my grasp, but the motion made him lose his balance in the snow. He fell back, but kept his grip on my sword's blade the entire time. I stumbled forward and fell to one knee, my right arm still twisted to the left. My sword bent in his cyb grip. If this kept up, he would break it soon.

He glared up at me. "Because you loved her!" He tried to bring his sword around for a weak strike from the left.

I screamed and punched his face with my mangled hand. That time I felt it. The punch derailed his attempted strike, and the sword only knocked against my right shoulder like a child striking me with a stick.

I could feel my knee slipping in the snow. My sword was breaking. I needed to do something.

I sent every bit of boost energy I could muster into my right arm and yanked. Rick held on to the bent sword, but I pulled it upward. As my knee slipped, I let go of the sword hilt. Because Rick was pulling so hard, he jerked it back. I let myself fall, but brought my right elbow down onto the inside of Rick's left elbow. He yelled and his sword fell out of his hand. I rolled over and snatched it up.

I came up on my knees, panting and staring back at him through the whirling snow. He rose up, holding my bent sword in his right hand now.

My boost energy was still cycling in my arm, so I tried to lunge forward again. It's not easy to lunge when you're on your knees in the snow. My stab missed him, but got me in close. I wrapped my left arm around his right arm and sword and held them.

"Now," I gasped, "we'll see… who gets last blood."

"One of us will," he answered.

And then he spit acid at my right eye.

I thought the pain of my burnt hand was the worst pain I could ever experience. I was wrong. The acid burned the flesh around my cybernetic eye with a fury and torment beyond anything I could imagine. I screamed into the storm and rolled away from Rick. I dropped the sword, grabbed handfuls of snow and shoved it against my face. The agony lanced through my face into my brain and down my spine.

"I'm a black dragon, Beryl." Rick's voice came from several feet away, but I could no longer see him, nor even care. "No matter what form I'm in, I retain my powers. Powers of seduction, deceit… and acid."

I heard the sword scrape against rock as he picked it back up. I knew I needed to do something. I needed to find the other sword. I needed to pay attention to his movements. But the pain—the burning—consumed everything.

"Really, I don't know how you never figured it out. How did you think I escaped that jail cell in Incarnadine before you got to me? Acid works wonders on locks." His voice grew nearer. "And cybernetics too, apparently."

I couldn't see a thing through my right eye. I could only hope the acid hadn't penetrated deeper than the removable cybernetic eye. With this pain, I would readily believe my entire head was burning away. The snow I kept packing against it gave me only slight relief.

"No more cyb tricks? I'm disappointed."

A sudden thump. Rick grunted. His sword struck the stone right next to me, throwing up sparks. Something threw off his aim.

"Beryl!"

Lovat's voice yanked me out of the pain momentarily. I jerked my head up. Through my one good eye, I saw Lovat struggling on Rick's back. His weight and movement threw the dragon-man off-balance. He tried to yank Lovat loose but slipped on the snow and fell. Lovat rolled free of him, scrambling across the freezing surface, but not fast enough.

Rick smacked the boy with his cybernetic hand. Lovat's head snapped back; he crumpled to the ground and lay still.

I don't know if anything else could have pulled me out of the pain. I gave a guttural roar and dove at Rick. I slammed against him, knocking his head against the rock. We rolled over through the snow drifts. Rick lost the sword somewhere in the struggle. He tried to grab at my neck with his cyb hand. I head-butted him.

We both rolled away from each other. My head, already aching, didn't take any new pain from the impact, but the acid continued to torture my face. I kept reminding myself of Lovat lying in the snow. I pushed off and stood, swaying in the wind.

Rick also stood, several feet away, holding a hand to his head. "I'm guessing your skull isn't just bone either," he said, spitting blood through a torn lip.

I glanced toward Lovat. "If he's dead, Onyx—"

"You'll what?" he interrupted. "Kill me? As if you weren't already trying. And failing."

Lovat needed me. Kelly needed me. Onyx was both the reason for their pain and the one stopping me from helping them. No more. This ended now.

I couldn't tell for certain, but it looked like the snow wasn't falling as thickly. I could see further. My one eye darted about, looking for either of the swords.

I spotted one half-covered in snow about five yards away, not far from the platform's edge. Rick saw it at the same time. We broke and ran for it simultaneously. Boosting my legs with what little I could gave me a slight edge over Rick. We dove, sliding through the ice and snow. My hand closed on the sword hilt first. A moment later, his cyb hand grabbed the blade. We slid together to the very edge of the landing pad.

I pulled. The sword slid an inch or two through his hand before he clamped down on it. Sparks flew.

I wanted to punch him again, but my left hand now hung loosely at the end of my arm. Somewhere in all the struggle, I'd damaged it beyond the cybernetic frame's ability to keep operating. I couldn't even boost it.

He had no such problems. Fortunately for me, the struggle over the sword kept him from making solid contact. His fist caught the tip of my chin. I barely felt it.

"No. More." I slammed my left forearm on top of his right arm. At the same time, I fed whatever boost energy I had left into my right arm and pulled with everything I could. The sword shrieked as it tore out of Rick's hand. I got to my feet, my knees shaking.

Rick also staggered up. "Beryl. You—"

I plunged the sword through his chest.

45

Rick stared at me, his ancient eyes full of disbelief.

How could a dragon be slain by a human with a sword? Like this.

I tore the sword back out of his body and stepped back. He put his hands over the wound, blood pouring out around them. And then he toppled back over the edge of the landing pad.

The wind must have concealed the sound of the wings. Either that, or I'd been too preoccupied with the battle and my own pain to notice.

An enormous red dragon swooped in and caught Rick as he fell. She rose up, wings beating through the snow and looked at me.

I stood on the landing pad, face-to-face with Amaranth. She looked nothing like Incarnadine. Her red scales had more of a rusty tint to them. Her horns curved in gentle spirals above a more rounded jawline... which made it no less terrifying.

One snort of flame. That's all it would take to destroy me. Or a quick lunge forward of the jaws. Nothing I could do would make a bit of difference. I fell to my knees, exhausted. The sword dropped into the snow again.

Amaranth's eyes narrowed as she continued to watch me. Then with a blast of warm air, she banked and flew away, still carrying Rick's body.

She couldn't save him, could she? I'd stabbed him straight through. He had to be dead, right? Right. Like Troilus Green was dead. My head slumped. I fell to my elbows and pounded my good fist against the un-yielding stone. Why couldn't these enemies die?

Lovat! I turned around and crawled to him, like a three-legged animal limping along. I brushed the snow away from him and pulled his head into my lap. Was he breathing? I couldn't tell out here.

I looked up and to the right. We were at least thirty or forty yards from the tower door. Even if I could pick him up, I didn't know if I could carry him that far. The snow, if it had slowed before, fell in dense waves now. If we didn't move, we'd be buried in short order. As my head drooped in exhaustion, I caught movement in my peripheral vision. I jerked my head to the left.

A dark figure stood not far away, watching me. I couldn't tell for certain through the falling snow, but I thought I could make out purple.

"You again?" I called hoarsely. "What do you want now?"

"Beryl Dragonslayer," the inhuman broken tones sounded. Despite the desperate situation, I had to admit: I liked that title a lot more than "godslayer." I should have been more concerned that this thing knew my name.

I didn't answer him. I put my hand on Lovat's chest, trying to tell if it were moving.

"You have come to our attention," the voice declared.

Once again, I found myself without anything to say. Even if I could think of something, I couldn't muster the necessary emotion to care. Instead, I pulled Lovat to me, cradling his body with my left arm and lifting him with my right. I managed to get my right knee up. I tried to boost it, but nothing happened. I was truly drained.

"We will be watching your subsequent actions with great interest."

"Whatever," I managed to grumble. I put my weight on my right foot and forced myself upright. I almost fell immediately, but got my left foot in front just in time. I took a step with my right foot, crunching through the snow. Another step with the left foot followed. Then the right. My eyes focused on the light shining through the tower door.

Two steps later, something eclipsed the light. Caedan burst out, yelling. "Beryl! Royal spotted a red dragon! Are you—?" He broke off when he saw us. I stopped and waited for him to come, slipping a few times himself. He carefully took Lovat from my arms.

"Gods, Beryl. What happened to you? You look horrible." He looked quickly around. "Rick?"

"Gone," I managed, and nearly fell.

"Let me get Lovat inside, and I'll be right back," he promised.

"Go."

Caedan moved with slow but steady steps back to the tower. I ordered my legs to follow him, but they didn't seem all that interested in obeying. In fact, they stopped altogether. How rude. I looked down, considering some harsh words for my disobedient legs. And then I toppled face-first into the snow. My eye closed. Sleep. That's what I needed.

"Mrow?"

I opened my eyes and turned my head. Glacier's face looked at my own. Her rough tongue licked my nose. Stupid cat. Where were you when I needed help?

Caedan reappeared then. "Come on, come on. Don't die on me now." He put his arms under mine and heaved. Again I ordered my legs to help him. Again they disobeyed me.

Somehow, Caedan pulled and half-carried me to the tower door. "You're heavier than you look," he complained. "Must be all that metal inside."

Once we got into the tower, he let me down on the floor so he could close the door. The lack of wind and snow hitting my face felt strange all of a sudden. I blinked and realized my clothes were completely drenched. A puddle formed underneath me. I shivered.

Caedan helped me roll over. Glacier moved near, and he pushed her out of the way. "What did he do to your face? It looks... terrible."

"Acid," I whispered.

"Ouch." He looked at the stairs. "All right. I need you to just... wait here, I guess. I'm going to get Hunter up here." He scrambled to his feet. "If he's not frozen already," he muttered.

"Kelly first," I managed to call.

"Kelly's okay right now, according to her mom. I'll be back as soon as I can, Beryl. Hang on." His footsteps echoed down the stairway.

Glacier shook herself, and a few drops hit my face. She then sat down and began to lick her fur. At least I wasn't alone. Wait. Lovat! Where was he? With a huge effort, I lifted myself enough to turn my head the other direction. Lovat lay on his back a couple of feet away. To my relief, I saw his chest moving with steady breaths.

Every time I hit exhaustion, I thought it was the tiredest I'd ever been in my life. This time… was worse. Exhausted and hurting. I shivered, soaked through to the skin. But as my body grew warmer, pain flooded back from my head, my hand, and my face.

Feet pounded up the stairs. Not Caedan's; they weren't as heavy.

"Beryl! Lovat!" Lainey fell to her knees between us. She checked on Lovat first. He moaned a little when she shifted him. Satisfied that his injuries weren't severe, she turned to me.

"Chroma, Beryl." She reached a hand out to me, then paused in mid-air. I'm guessing she had to figure out a safe place to touch me. She settled on my right forearm. "You did it," she whispered. "I don't know what happened, but I know you did what you had to do."

Had I? I stabbed Rick through the chest. I tried to kill him. But I think he still lived. At least he was gone. Kelly would be safe from him for now. But she still had that draconic inside her.

"Kelly," I whispered.

"Her pains have stopped," Lainey said. "Fern believes she still has some time. Hunter will check her out, but not until after he looks at you." She shifted and looked from Lovat back to me. "These wet clothes are going to be the death of both of you. I'll find some blankets."

She got to her feet and hurried back down the stairs. Glacier sauntered into the spot she'd left, yawned, and curled up to rest. I reached out and ran my hand through her fur. "You would have taken Rick down, wouldn't you? I could have used your help," I whispered.

Glacier yawned again. This time, I noticed what looked like blood on her two saber teeth. Oh. I guess she'd already been helping Caedan out. I wondered whose blood it was.

I may have lost consciousness for a while after that. The next thing I knew, Lainey was helping to remove my outer coat. When she removed the right sleeve, it tore open the cut on my bicep. I almost laughed at the insignificant pain it caused, compared to everything else. The left sleeve was another problem. Lainey considered my hand for a moment, then drew a knife and cut the sleeve off. My shirt followed in the same way. She patted me dry with a towel, then put a blanket over my shivering body.

"You're always taking my clothes off," I joked. Except I didn't. I wanted to, but my brain chose that moment to turn itself off for a while.

"I'm telling you: it's a full-scale blizzard out there now." The voice sounded familiar. I opened my eyes—sorry, eye—and looked up at the ceiling. I was on my back. My pants, socks, and boots had been removed as well, and I lay wrapped up in blankets from my neck down.

I turned my head, which sent a few spikes of pain into it, and saw Hunter beside me. Lainey and Caedan stood behind him, watching. Hunter was wrapping up my hand while he spoke to them.

"We are not going to be leaving this place any time in the next few days," he said. "We might be trapped here for weeks."

"Weeks?" Caedan exclaimed. "How?"

Hunter noticed me watching and patted my chest. "First of all, our fearless leader here will not be in any condition to travel for a few days, at least. And if we have to cut the infant out of Kelly, she will definitely be unable to do any kind of rigorous walking or climbing for quite some time." He reached into his pack and found a tube of something. "And finally, that blizzard out there may just be the beginning. If more snow falls, it will make traveling for anyone treacherous. Remember what we had to climb to get here?"

"Right, right." Caedan didn't look happy.

"What can you do about Beryl's face?" Lainey asked.

Hunter cocked his head to look at me. "You said it was acid? It must have been some powerful stuff. All of this skin is completely gone, and some of the muscles are badly damaged." He reached out and pushed some of my hair out of the way. "Nothing much I can do about the eye. We can hope the connections behind it are all right."

"We have replacement cyb eyes back in the workshop," Caedan said. "Loden left them there."

"Hands too," I said weakly.

Hunter raised an eyebrow. "It might be better, in the long run, to fully replace your left hand," he admitted. "I do not think I can reconstruct all that you have lost there the way it was before. But we might need a cybernetics expert to do a complete replacement."

We could find one. Eventually. After what happened in Viridia, more people would be interested in joining our cause. Except it sounded like we wouldn't be getting back to Viridia any time soon. The revolution was getting snowed in.

"Royal? Do you hear me?" Caedan spoke into the talker. "Yeah, we're going to be okay, I think. Beryl's hurt pretty bad, but he'll pull through. He always does. What? Yes, I know it's snowing. Listen…" Caedan walked a few steps back and forth as he talked. "I want you to head back to the workshop as soon as you can. Tell the others what's happened. Yes. We may be stuck here for a while because of the weather. No, I don't know how long. Hunter says weeks, maybe. Hey, calm down! Listen, do this: once a week, starting right now, you ride the four-wheeler back up to within range and call me on these things. I'll keep you updated on our progress. Sound good? Okay, right."

While he spoke, Hunter gently applied some kind of paste to the burned parts of my face. It felt cool, and the pain subsided a little. He took out a pair of scissors. "I am going to have to cut some of your hair away so I can clean up and bandage the gash on your head," he explained. "After that, I will bandage… well, about half your head." He started working on the hair. "When we have more time and equipment, I may be able to fix up the skin on your face at least. Just like I did the first time. But the muscle damage may be permanent. It might affect what kind of expressions you can make. Hopefully, you will not end up with a rictus."

"What's a rictus?" Caedan asked.

"A permanent grin." Hunter chuckled. "It is kind of creepy. But since he is not grinning now, I do not think that is likely."

"Good," I said, feeling a little stronger overall. "Don't want to scare the girls away too much."

"Instead, you'll just keep getting yourself burned and stabbed and stuff," Caedan said. "Good to hear your voice. Can you tell us what happened out there?"

"How's Lovat?"

"I think he will be all right," Hunter said. "He probably has a concussion, but with enough rest, he should make a full recovery. I gave him something to make him sleep, and we put him in one of the many bedrooms of this place."

"Give Beryl something to drink," Lainey interceded. She came around to my other side and lifted a pouch to my mouth. Liquid poured between my lips, and I swallowed greedily. I'm not sure what she gave me, but it felt warm going down my throat. Hunter also gave me some pills. For pain, I assumed.

In short sentences, I told them what happened in my fight with Rick. They were duly impressed, of course, or at least shocked at how I managed to survive another total disaster. I left out the part about the purple robe. I couldn't even be sure it happened. My imagination could have created the whole thing.

"You're going to need to sleep for days," Caedan said. "Or at least, that's usually what happens after you do something like this."

"He does this often?" Hunter's eyebrows went up.

"Overexerts himself? Yes. Fights a dragon-in-human-form with swords and gets acid spit in his face? Not so much."

"You're very funny," I said. Sleep pulled my eyelids down, but I resisted a little longer.

"We should get him into one of the beds," Lainey suggested.

"Wait…" I mumbled. "What about Mazarine? And the guards?"

"They're sort of locked up in the lowest level," Caedan said.

"Sort of?"

"Yeah. Sort of. I'll explain later. Hunter, is it safe to move him?"

"Should be. Just be gentle."

Caedan moved around behind me. "I'll get his big head, since it's the heaviest. You guys get his legs."

"But I… don't…" I tried to protest, but the words slurred in my mouth. They lifted me up and moved down the hall. I watched a light go by over my head… and lost myself after that.

I woke in a bizarre world of darkness. A dim lamp some distance away cast very little light, revealing only the vaguest details of the room. I lay in a bed, a very large bed with four tall posts at the corners. I half-expected it to have a canopy. Maybe it did. Everything was so… black, as if whoever did the decor only wanted to use the one color. Oh. This was the home of a black dragon. Of course. All of the dragons seemed to be obsessed with their own color. Did ego drive them to use it in everything? Or just lack of imagination?

In moving around as I slept, I'd pulled the blankets off my left shoulder. It felt almost frozen. If it were this cold inside, how cold was it outside the tower by now? I rubbed the shoulder to warm it up and pulled the blankets back up.

Only part of my face felt cold. The rest was still swathed in bandages. A dull ache came from both the right side of my face and from the gash on top of my head. I felt nothing at all from my left hand.

I needed to pee, but I didn't know where the bathroom might be, or even if there was one. I couldn't even see the door out of this room. Could Rick see in the dark? Was that one of his dragon abilities? He'd never demonstrated it before, that I could recall.

I didn't want to get out and pad around on these stone floors in my bare feet. But I couldn't stay much longer. Argh. I needed light. I needed a toilet.

I threw off the blankets and slid off the bed. As anticipated, the stone floor was icy. Goosebumps rose across my body as I ran on my tiptoes to the lamp. I tried to find some way to turn the light brighter, but failed. I hurried along the wall until I found a door. Next to it, a light switch. At last. I flicked it on.

Bright light filled the room and I blinked several times. It wasn't an enormous bedroom, necessarily, but it was larger than any I'd ever possessed myself. Even with the light, the blackness of it still felt wrong. Black bed, black blankets, black walls, black chair, black doors… Ah! One of them had to be a bathroom, right?

I scampered across the floor to the first door and found a closet. The second door opened to a bathroom about the size of my old apartment's living room. "Hue," I muttered.

After taking care of business, I returned to the bedroom. This time, I noticed the clothes lying folded on the chair. With my useless left hand, I struggled to get them on. I couldn't tie the boots, so I stuffed the strands in with my feet. With every step I took, I anticipated one of them falling off.

I opened the door and got tackled.

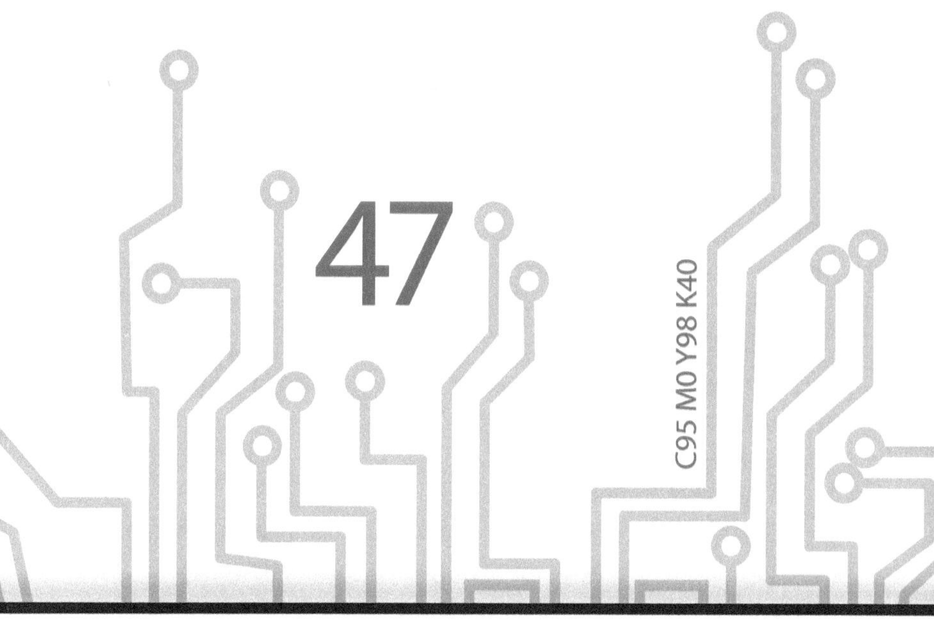

A ball of fur slammed into my chest and knocked me back. Instinctively, I grabbed the doorframe and boosted my hand to hold on. Good to know the boosts were still working.

Glacier slid to the floor and walked past me into the room, acting as if she hadn't done anything. "Stupid cat," I grumbled. But seeing her made me smile.

I followed the hall to the stairs and walked down, passing the door to the landing pad. I noticed someone had stuffed a blanket around the bottom of the door to keep the cold out. The ache in my head made the stairway descent a little dizzy, but I could handle it. I couldn't remember the layout of this place, but I was pretty sure we'd found Kelly on the floor just below. Maybe I could find her and the others there.

I turned into the hallway on the next floor and found Lovat walking out of one of the rooms with a yawn. He spotted me, and his eyes widened. The next moment, I was getting tackled again in a fierce hug. I hugged him back with my right arm, at least.

"Good to see you, buddy. You feeling all right?" I tousled his hair. It looked shorter. One of the others must have given him a haircut while I slept.

"Little headache," he said. "Not bad."

"Good." I put my hand on his shoulder. "Listen. You saved my life out there. Thank you. I'm just sorry you got hurt."

His face lit up. "I'm good."

"Yeah, you are. Where do I find the others?"

"Right behind you," Caedan said over my shoulder. I turned to see him grinning. "About time you woke up."

"How long?" I asked, stifling a yawn.

"It's been three days. How do you feel?"

"Tired. Sore. Cold."

"Yeah." He nodded. "This tower has some heat running, but it's not enough, especially in these upper floors."

"How bad is it outside?"

"Snow hasn't stopped," Lovat said.

"It really hasn't," Caedan confirmed. "It's piled high out there and still coming down. We're not going anywhere for quite a while."

"Beryl?"

I turned and saw her. Kelly stood in the doorway to her room. Still very, very pregnant, but also… beautiful. I'd always thought so. I swallowed. "Hi."

"Why are you all standing around in the hall?" she asked. "Come in my room. It's warmer."

"Go ahead," Caedan said. "I just came to get Lovat. It's his turn to watch the prisoners down below."

"Aww," Lovat complained. "That's boring. Almost everything here is boring."

"Sorry, but we made a deal, remember?"

Lovat nodded. He and Caedan headed toward the stairs while I followed Kelly into her room. It looked the same as… three days ago, I guess, except someone had hung two blankets over the one window. Another reminder of the cold.

"You'd better sit down," Kelly said. "You still look awful."

I settled into one of two wooden chairs. "And you still look… pregnant."

She giggled. "Yeah." She sat down facing me. Neither of us spoke for a few moments. "I guess… we never saw things ending up like this, while we made our plans back in Viridia," she said at last.

"No, nothing like this," I agreed. "I never imagined my—one of my best friends would end up my worst enemy, and my other best friend would end up… pregnant from him."

"What happened, Beryl?" she asked. "Lainey's told me some of it, but I need to hear from you. How did Rick… how did all of it happen?"

I took a deep breath, and told her about the day it all went wrong, the day Rick regained his power as Onyx, with my help, the day he killed the green dragon and flew away. Throughout the story, she sat still, but tears filled her eyes.

"We came back to the Asylum as fast as we could," I told her. "But he'd already been there. Everything was destroyed. You were gone. Bice and Don were gone. I found Protogonus Blue dying."

Kelly put a hand over her mouth and then wiped her eyes. "Did he?"

I nodded. "He… showed me draconics could be different. Could change. I never expected that."

Kelly sniffed and wiped her eyes again. "I don't even… that day was such a blur. A black dragon came swooping out of the sky. It tore the roof of the Asylum apart. We ran for the workshop, but then Mazarine grabbed me from behind and stopped me." She swallowed and looked down. "Bice started to come after me, but Protogonus pushed him into the cave, just in time. The dragon landed between us. At first, I thought Mazarine had saved me from getting crushed, but then he called out to it. He called it his god and said he'd captured me for it."

I clenched my fist. Mazarine would answer to me at some point soon.

"The dragon picked us up," she went on. "I couldn't breathe. The air rushed around us. I think I passed out. The next thing I knew, we were on the platform outside this tower. The dragon looked down at us… and then he spoke." She looked up. "I didn't… I couldn't believe him. I thought it was Atramentous. But he knew everything Rick knew. He said… he said you were all dead—that he'd killed you. And he'd brought me here to bear our child. It took me a little while to grasp what that meant."

I shuddered.

"Mazarine's job would be to take care of me, along with the guards."

"Did they hurt you?" I asked. They'd been here over three months. Anything could have happened.

"Physically?" She shook her head. "They never laid a hand on me. I could go anywhere I wanted in the tower." She lifted her hands. "But there's no way out without jumping thirty feet or more." She lowered her hands and twisted them in her lap. "I thought about it… more than once."

I winced. But I might have considered the same thing in her shoes. She thought we were all dead. What hope did she have?

"So, um… Bice and Don?"

"We'll find them," I said. "It's my next priority, when we leave here, whenever that is."

"Mom thinks we'll be here for weeks. Do you think it's safe?"

"I don't know. I mean, Onyx is not coming back any time soon. Even if he heals really fast." I glanced toward the covered window. "My big fear is that Amaranth returns and tears this place down around us."

"I don't know if she can." Kelly stamped her foot on the floor. "Rick told me he had this place built to withstand a dragon attack."

"So he did come and talk with you? As a human, I mean?"

"Yeah. He showed up about… I don't know. Two weeks ago, I think." She closed her eyes. "For one brief moment, I thought he was the real Rick, and the dragon had been lying all along." She opened them again. "He made sure I knew the truth right away. He was so excited about… about this." She put her hands on her swollen abdomen.

I reached up to rub my eye, which turned out to be really awkward. I wasn't used to rubbing my left eye with my right hand. "So… that's the big question now, isn't it?"

Kelly kept her eyes down. "I don't know. I just don't know."

"Kelly, every woman who's given birth to one of those things has died."

"I know that. I know it has to come out, but… what then?"

"You want it to live?"

"I… I think so. I mean, it's not the baby's fault its father is a dragon, right?"

"But it's a draconic. Once it's old enough, it will recover all the memories of its past, uh, lives. It'll remember serving Onyx down there,"—I pointed toward the window—"when there used to be a city. It'll remember how it treated humans and what it did to enforce the dragon's rule. So no matter how you raise it at first, now matter how much you teach it to care about humans… you can't stop that."

"Protogonus Blue had all his memories."

I nodded. "Yeah. He was special. But every other draconic we've encountered—every one!—has been wholly dedicated to their dragon, even after the dragon died. Bleaking Troilus Green thinks it is Viridia now!" This time I dropped my head and closed my eye. "I just… I just don't know if it's worth the risk. I've been betrayed by someone I thought was the best friend I ever had. I don't want to risk that happening again."

"I understand. But Beryl… what if? What if we can help this draconic overcome its programming? Those memories. What if we can turn him against the dragons? To fight for us?"

"I don't know," I repeated.

"This is what I know," Kelly said. "If you had come three months ago, even two months ago, and told me all this… I probably would have insisted on getting rid of it. But now? I've felt this life grow inside me. I don't know… if I can let it die now."

I guess I kind of understood what Kelly was saying… from her point of view, anyway. From mine, it didn't make any sense. If we were to try to raise this thing, and if I were to put odds on our success… I'd say we had about a ten percent chance of it being on our side in the end. Which gave us a ninety percent chance it would be an evil, ferocious enemy we'd have to fight. The rewards didn't outweigh the risks, in my opinion.

But it wasn't my decision, was it? Kelly was my friend, and I could give her my opinion, but that was it. I had no say in this. Or so I thought.

We talked a little longer, about Fern and the prison break, and what I'd been doing with the others in Viridia. A few minutes later, Lainey came in. "Beryl! You're up!"

"Yeah, no thanks to your cat. She tried to knock me down again."

"I was wondering where she wandered off to. She got bored, I guess."

"Why?" I asked. "What have you been up to?"

She looked to Kelly. "You didn't tell him yet?"

"Tell me what?"

"About the top of the tower?"

"What about the top of the tower?"

"Show him," Kelly said. "I don't feel like hauling myself up those stairs again. I've barely left this floor in the last couple of weeks."

"Except to come see you while you slept," Lainey confided.

"I needed to know he was all right!" Kelly protested.

I smiled. She'd checked on me in my sleep. Nice.

"Lainey's the one who was in your room every day," Kelly added under her breath.

Oh. Well, this was awkward. "So what's at the top of the tower?" I got to my feet.

"You are not going to believe this!" Lainey led the way.

I glanced back at Kelly. She smiled and motioned for us to go. I followed Lainey up the stairs. We passed the door to the landing pad, and the floor where I'd been sleeping. The next flight of stairs seemed to be longer than the other floors. But then we emerged into a small room I assumed to be the top of the tower. I stopped and stared.

A single large padded chair sat in the middle of the room, facing the opposite wall from the stairs. On the wall hung six… boxes of some kind. The front of each box consisted of some kind of glass lit up by internal light, or rather, five of them did. The first box, on the left, was dark. The other five, though, were not only lit up, they each showed an image, like an illuminated photograph. It took me a few moments to realize what I was looking at.

"They're the cities!" I exclaimed.

"Yes!" Lainey walked to the one on the right. "This is Auric. I can see the building we visited." She pointed.

"That's amazing." I walked closer.

"I know. I think they're what the cities look like right now. Look, it's cloudy over Caesious."

"How is this possible?" I wondered. "How can we see what's happening somewhere else?"

"It's like television."

"What's television?"

"Right. You don't have that here." She frowned. "Rich families have them where I'm from. They're like… um… You know about the talkers. You know how people can send sounds over distance. This is kind of the same thing, except it's pictures, not sound."

"Pictures that move," I said. I put my hand near the glass surface of the Caesious image. Those clouds were moving.

"It's called video," Lainey explained. "And yeah, I guess moving pictures is one way to describe it."

"So there's some kind of device, some kind of camera aimed at each city, then?"

"Right."

"Where?"

"What do you mean?"

"Where are those cameras? These images are all from high above the cities! Are there cameras in the sky?"

Lainey cocked her head. "I don't know. There must be, somehow."

"The skies belong to the dragons," I repeated. "How would they allow this?"

"Maybe the cameras are even higher than the dragons fly?"

I looked from image to image. "Why is Viridia dark?"

"Because that dragon is dead, maybe?"

"No." I pointed. "We still have a view of Caesious."

"You're right. I don't know, then."

I sat down in the chair, which was surprisingly comfortable, and considered. "The power source," I said. "We destroyed Viridia's power source, but not Caesious's."

Lainey brightened. "That must be it!"

I gestured to all of it. "But why? What good does this do?"

Lainey pointed at the Incarnadine image. "They all seem to be centered on the dragons' lairs. So we can see if they leave their city."

I checked the others. Sure enough, I saw the pit of Atramentous, the broken tower of Caesious... "So Rick wanted to keep track of the other dragons? Monitor their comings and goings? What good would that do him?"

"You're not thinking," Lainey scolded me.

I shrugged one shoulder. "I've been asleep for three days. And I have a head injury."

"Excuses." Lainey pointed back at the Viridian box. "You recognized it. The power source is the key. Isn't he trying to find their power sources?"

"Oh, sure. Makes sense." I leaned back in the chair and discovered it reclined, bringing up a foot rest. Nice. But as I leaned back, the boxes on the wall moved with me, keeping within my forward view. "Whoa."

"Yeah, look on the arm of the chair."

I checked the side of the right arm of the chair and found six buttons. I pressed the third one. The box with the image of Incarnadine moved forward until it was right in front of me. I could reach out and touch it. I stared down into the Flame, remembering the dragon emerging from it and chasing me.

Lainey stepped beside me and pushed the button again to send the box back to join the others. "They all do the same thing. It's interesting, but not very creative."

"A nice, lazy way to spy on the other dragons." I frowned. "But it just doesn't feel like Rick. He's not a tech guy. He couldn't have built this himself."

"Dusk?"

"I don't think so. This doesn't seem like her kind of thing, either. Even Loden didn't do stuff quite like this." I gestured at the boxes. "But you've seen this kind of thing before? Outside The Circle?"

She nodded. "Rich people have these type of screens in their houses. They can watch stuff."

"What kind of stuff?"

She shrugged. "Entertainment. News. You know about newspapers, right? Imagine someone on one of those screens"—she pointed—"reading the news to you."

"Oh." I still didn't understand, but it didn't seem very important. I brought the chair upright again. "So this tech exists outside, and now Onyx has it." I paused, then told her: "And one of those purple-robed priests appeared after Onyx escaped."

Her eyes widened. "What?"

"Your dad said they were only interested in him." I looked at her. "This one said I had come to their attention, and they would be watching me."

Lainey pulled on some of her hair. "No, that can't be right. You must have imagined it."

"I wondered if I had," I admitted, "which is why I didn't mention it before. But now that my thoughts are clearing up, I remember everything that happened. Right after Amaranth flew away, one of them showed up. It was hard to see through the snow, but it was there. And it talked to me."

Lainey turned her back to me and paced away.

"Will you tell me who they are now? Do you think Rick got this tech from them?"

"No, no. They can't be working with him. That would make no sense at all."

I closed my eyes, trying to remember something. "In the Books of Lore, the dragons discussed sending someone outside The Circle. I think Onyx was the one in favor of it."

"That was hundreds of years ago," Lainey said. "It can't have anything to do with right now."

I got out of the chair. "It shows that he's always been interested in outside. Maybe he's made contact since then. Maybe they even helped build this tower!"

Lainey spun around. "I'm telling you: it makes no sense!"

"Why?" I spread my hands out. "I don't understand. You haven't told me enough."

She rubbed her face. "I can't. I can't tell you." She took a deep breath and looked me in the eye. "But as soon as I can, I will. I promise."

"What's stopping you now?" I couldn't understand.

Feet pounded up the stairs. Caedan emerged. "Hey! Hunter says the time to save Kelly is right now!"

Lainey and I rushed down the stairs with Caedan to Kelly's floor. Hunter met us in the hallway, sorting through blankets.

"What's happening?" I demanded.

"It has to be now," he answered. "She is on the verge of delivery. If we do not cut it out in the next few hours, the birth process will begin, and I cannot guarantee she will survive." He paused. "I should say I cannot guarantee she will survive at all. But I will do everything I can."

I started past him, but he put a hand on my chest. I winced. Still had some sore spots there.

"Fern is in there with her," he said. "I will be starting in a few minutes. It will take some time to calm her and get her unconscious before we begin." He paused. "Are your boosts working again? Do you have your strength?"

"Yes. What do you need?"

He nodded. "When the time comes, I may need you to hold her down. I am not completely confident in our anesthesia."

"You mean she might feel it when you cut her open?" Lainey exclaimed.

"I am confident she will not feel pain," Hunter said. "But I am not confident she will feel nothing. And I will need her to stay still."

"Whatever you need," I said. "Just tell me."

"Good. Like I said, it is going to be a while yet. Maybe an hour. You should get something to eat." He stopped. "On second thought, do not get something to eat. I cannot have you throwing up in my operating room." He left us in the hallway.

We looked at each other. "Now what?" Caedan asked.

I bit my lip. "I'll go nuts if I have to just stay out here waiting." A thought occurred to me. "I want to talk to Mazarine."

"Take him down there, Caedan," Lainey suggested. "I'll come running if Hunter needs you before you get back."

"We won't be too long." I wouldn't want to leave anything to chance.

"He said an hour," Caedan muttered, leading the way down the stairs.

"It's Kelly," I said. "I'm not risking it."

"Sure. Of course."

We walked down multiple flights of stairs. I think it might have been four, but I wasn't keeping track. My thoughts were all jumbled. The city images. Kelly. The purple robes. Baby draconic.

"Almost there," Caedan said.

"How did they end up trapped, anyway?" I asked.

"Lainey and I fought the guards," he explained. "Or, well, I fought them, and she scared them with her rifle. Mazarine ran down this way like a coward. The guards followed. We chased them but not too close. They got down here, ran into this room, and slammed the door. I, uh, may have smashed the lock with my baton."

"So the door won't open?"

"I don't know. Haven't tried. We just make sure someone's always watching. They seem to have food & water in there, so we just leave them alone."

We reached the final floor and found Lovat sitting on the bottom step. He jumped up. "Is my turn over already?"

"Nope, sorry, man," Caedan said. "Beryl just wants to talk to them."

"Awww."

I walked to the lone door, noting the broken lock and handle. Light shone from a small rectangular window in the top of the door. I moved toward it.

"Careful," Caedan warned. "Crossbows."

Right. I came to a stop next to the window. "Mazarine!" I called. "Mazarine Chal-eb-whatever! I want to talk to you!"

I heard a scuffling inside, and then: "I have nothing to say to you, Beryl, blasphemer of my god."

"Oh, come on. Onyx is not your god."

"He has slain two of the lesser gods. How else to prove his dread majesty?"

Great. He'd reverted back to his fancy priest language. "I stabbed your god through the chest and he fell from the landing pad. In the snow."

"Even if you told the truth, which I doubt, it matters not. The might of all six other dragons combined was not enough to slay him. You are nothing compared to them. He will return for me… and for his child!"

"Yeah, well, that child is about to be cut out of Kelly. After that…"

"Should the child die, his wrath will be unspeakable. Unstoppable. Unyielding."

"Uneven?" Caedan suggested.

"Undone?" I said. "Nah, that doesn't work. I'll probably think of a good one in a few minutes."

Caedan grinned. "I understand that."

"Mazarine, what do you know about the room at the top of the tower?" I asked.

"It is forbidden to enter it, or to look upon its wonders."

"You mean, in the months you've been here, even when your god wasn't present, you never climbed the steps to the top?"

"Never. I am a loyal and obedient servant. My reward will be great."

"Uh-huh." I thought for a moment. "Have you ever seen anyone hanging around here in purple robes?"

"No one visits here save for those who serve the almighty Onyx."

"And us," Caedan added.

I rolled my eyes. "Fine. Have any servants of the almighty Onyx shown up in purple robes?"

"His followers wear black, in honor of his—"

"Yeah, yeah. Whatever." I leaned closer to Caedan. "Is it me, or is he avoiding the question?"

"It's hard to tell through his blathering."

I tried again: "Mazarine, does Onyx have contact with people outside The Circle?"

"No one lives outside The Circle!"

Argh. This was pointless. I turned away from the door. Then I thought of something else. "Why is Amaranth working with Onyx?"

"Amaranth recognizes the greatness of Onyx. She will be spared while the other false gods fall. She will rule as queen of all, beneath the rule of the magnificent Onyx himself."

Really? Interesting. Then why was he spying on her from the tower, just like the other dragons? Onyx betrayed me. I suspected he would have no qualms about betraying Amaranth either. In fact, I wouldn't count on his loyalty to anyone he called an ally.

"Okay. Well, let us know if you need anything in there, Mazzy. It looks like we're all going to be trapped in this tower for a while. Winter is here, you know."

"Excellent. Then my lord Onyx will have no trouble finding you again when he decides to return."

"You keep on believing that." I shook my head and followed Caedan back up the stairs.

"Can you believe that guy?" Caedan asked. "I can't believe I used to work for him. What was wrong with me?"

"Same thing that's wrong with most people. Everyone's been trained from birth to believe the dragons are gods." I pointed my thumb over my shoulder. "Mazarine back there was deeper into it than most. It was his job, his whole purpose in life. Then we killed Caesious, and he didn't know what to do."

"So he came to us."

"Protogonus Blue apparently talked him into that," I said. "If I had to guess, I'd say he came hoping to find a new cause to worship. Maybe he thought he was seeing the birth of a new god, since we killed his. Maybe he thought one of us was a god or something."

"It's clearly me."

"Haha. No, think about it. We tore away the foundation of his beliefs. He was flailing about, looking for something else to believe in." I stopped on one of the landings. "Then Rick went to him and revealed his identity. He latched on to that, desperate for something, anything."

"Because he can't believe in nothing."

"Yeah." Is that what we were? Did we believe in nothing? No, of course not. We believed in freedom for humans. That was surely a cause worth fighting for, something to live by... but I had to admit: not having someone to look up to, at the very least, was a problem. I missed Bice. He would know what to say to Mazarine now.

"Undying!" Caedan exclaimed.

"What?"

"Undying wrath. That works."

I laughed and started up the stairs.

We found Lainey waiting outside Kelly's room, sitting against the wall. "Anything?" I asked.

"No, they've been in there since you left. I haven't heard a sound." She got to her feet. "Learn anything from the priest?"

"Nothing much. He's too busy proclaiming his loyalty to Onyx."

"It's like he believes Onyx is listening to him all the time," Caedan added.

"That's a scary thought." I looked at Lainey. "Do you think Onyx could have some kind of tech in the tower so he could listen to what's going on?"

"It's not impossible. We can look around some more and see. I mean, we're going to be here a while."

"Even so, let's not talk about our plans much in the open, until we've done that search. I don't want to give anything away."

The door opened and Hunter stuck his head out.

"Beryl? Lainey? It is time."

50

Kelly lay fast asleep on her bed, her swollen belly exposed to the air. They'd pulled the bed out from the wall, leaving room to walk around it on all sides. As I stepped closer, I saw markings on her skin where Hunter planned to cut. I swallowed.

"You sure you need me in here?" I didn't like the idea of watching this.

"I have given her the anesthesia I possess," Hunter answered, "but that will not prevent all movement. If we were in a hospital, I could give her more effective anesthesia, or she could be strapped in place. But since we do not have sufficient supplies, I need you here, in case she starts to regain consciousness. You will need to hold her down if that happens."

"I only have one good hand," I pointed out.

"Then use it. If she flails about, Fern will hold her other hand, and I will depend more on Lainey to assist me."

"So just hold her hand?" I could do that.

"Everyone must wash their hands thoroughly," Hunter instructed. "The greatest risk from this kind of operation comes from infection. Let us minimize that risk as much as possible."

We all obeyed him. I walked around to Kelly's right side and took her hand. It felt cool, so I massaged it a little. "How long will this take?"

"Under ideal circumstances, no more than an hour," Hunter said, moving next to Kelly on the other side. He pulled a chair next to him, covered in his tools. "Fern, if you will be ready to soak up the blood, I will begin the incision."

My eyes widened, and I turned away. I'd help out and hold Kelly's hand, but no way would I watch him actually cut her body open.

"Don't like the sight of blood?" Lainey teased as she walked around me to get to the other side.

"I don't like the sight of my friend's blood," I answered.

"All right. I am beginning," Hunter announced.

To my distress, Hunter talked while he worked, describing his process. I didn't need to know this information. I didn't want to know this information. Big words tumbled from his lips at a rate beyond my understanding, but the words I did understand I didn't like. I understood that he had to cut Kelly open, and then cut open her uterus to remove the infant. It sounded horrible.

I held her hand and whispered to her from time to time. "You're going to make it through this, Kelly," I told her. "You're strong. I know you've got this."

Hunter kept working and talking. He suggested a theory on why the mothers of draconics always died. "These creatures are toxic in many ways," he pointed out. "The black ones, like this, spit acid, do they not? So they have some strange form of biological process that creates that. Perhaps that process releases a toxin in the mother at the time of birth, and it is what kills them."

"It doesn't matter what kills them," Fern said. "We're preventing it from happening. She's going to live."

"I am cutting into the uterus now," Hunter said. "I will have to double suture this when I am done and—oh, my."

"What is it?" Lainey asked. I almost turned to look.

"I was not prepared. I mean, I knew it would look different, but… it is so black."

"Get it out of her!" Fern insisted.

"I am working on it. We are getting there. Not too much longer now."

Had it almost been an hour already? It didn't seem like it. I felt a wave of relief. Maybe this wouldn't be so bad after all.

"There is too much blood," Hunter mumbled. "And a black liquid mixed in. This is not good."

"What do you need?" Lainey asked.

Hunter talked to her about tools and things. I concentrated on Kelly's hand and face.

"Almost there…" Hunter said.

Kelly's eyes flew open. "She's awake!" I exclaimed.

"Hold her!"

"Beryl…" Kelly's voice slurred, but she gripped my hand tight. "Is the baby…? I don't know now."

"Shhhh. It's all right. It's almost over. You're going to be all right."

Fern joined me next to her head. "I'm here, baby girl. You're going to be fine. We're getting it out. Almost done."

"I don't know," she repeated. "Should it… live? Beryl…"

Her eyes rolled back. Her hand went limp in mine.

"She's unconscious again!" Fern reported.

"Lainey, put pressure right here!" Hunter ordered. "Fern, I need you to stay right where you are in case she wakes again. Beryl, come here!"

"What?"

"I am taking the fetus out, and I can't hold it. Come here!"

I let go of Kelly's hand and stepped down, across from Hunter. I tried not to look down at Kelly.

"Put out your hands! Yes, I know one is bandaged. I am the one who did it!"

I held my hands out, still trying not to look down. Hunter placed something surprisingly heavy in my hands. "Now get out of the way!"

I staggered back several steps. A cough and a whine came from my arms and I looked down.

I held a baby draconic.

Tiny black scales covered the creature, slick from blood and whatever other liquid was involved in birth. It couldn't be longer than my hand and forearm. It waved its limbs and coughed, causing a whitish liquid to leak from its mouth. Its snout was far shorter than I expected, giving it an almost human-shaped face… until it opened its eyes. The eyes were huge and stared up at me. It coughed again.

I was not expecting it to be cute.

Only then did I notice Hunter's feverish activities. "Hold it here!" he snapped at Lainey. "Here!"

"What's happening?" Fern asked.

"She's lost too much blood. I need to get the placenta out as fast as I can."

"Too much?" I asked. "What does that mean?"

"If you cannot help, get out of the room!" Hunter snarled.

"And get rid of that thing!" Fern added.

"That's Kelly's decision," I said, but headed for the door.

I left the room and found Caedan still waiting, sitting in the hall. Glacier had shown up and lay beside him, tail twitching. Both looked up as I came out.

"Is that… it?" Caedan got to his feet.

"Yeah. Is there another blanket? We should wrap it up."

"You're not going to… get rid of it?"

"Kelly didn't want to kill it, but she wasn't sure, either. I'll let her decide."

He raised an eyebrow, but went to find a blanket.

The infant didn't complain at all, which also surprised me. Weren't babies supposed to cry a lot? I mean, I knew this one wasn't human, but I expected something more than coughs and staring. With Caedan's help, I wiped it off and wrapped it in a blanket.

"Hard to believe the huge draconics we've fought once looked like this," Caedan observed.

"Yeah." I continued to stare back at it. "It looks so… innocent."

"You know it won't be. It's a dragon's child, Beryl."

"Yeah…"

Glacier rubbed at my legs, curious about the odd-smelling thing I held. I stumbled and scowled at the cat.

Caedan looked at the door to Kelly's room. "What's happening in there?"

I blinked and looked away from the infant. "I don't know. I think… I think Kelly's in trouble."

Caedan turned to me, concern in his eyes. "Do you want to go back in?"

I opened my mouth, then paused. "No," I said at last. "I'm responsible for this thing until Kelly's awake enough to decide." But the longer I held it, the more difficult it became. Could I really kill something so tiny, so harmless?

We waited. The draconic's eyes closed, and it slept, or at least I think it did. I couldn't tell for sure. And what would we feed it, if it stayed around? Surely it couldn't nurse like a human baby. I grimaced at the thought.

About fifteen minutes later, Lainey emerged from the room. She'd washed her hands, but I could see blood spatters on her clothes and face.

"Is Kelly all right?" I demanded.

"I think she will be," she answered, "but it's not good. Oh, can I see the baby?"

I let her look, but held on to it. I don't know why.

Hunter and Fern exited Kelly's room about ten minutes later. To our anxious looks, Hunter lifted a tired hand.

"She will live," he said. "At least, I am fairly sure she will. It was a very near thing."

"What happened?"

"As I suspected, the fetus released some form of toxin when we removed it. Fortunately, most of it remained within the placenta and came out. But not all. Combined with the loss of blood, she very nearly died right then." He wiped his forehead. "I have done everything I can now. It is up to her body to fight off the chance of infection now."

"Can we… see her?"

"Yes, but she will not be waking up." He gestured back at the bedroom. "In essence, I have had to place her into a coma to let her body heal."

"Why do you still have that thing?" Fern exclaimed, finally noticing the infant in my arm.

"It's Kelly's," I said. "She wanted it."

"She didn't understand. It's a monster. Throw it out of a window."

"I can't do that."

"Then I will." Fern stepped toward me and reached for the blanket. I pulled it away.

"Only Kelly can make that decision."

Hunter shook his head. "She will not be making any decisions for quite some time."

"Then we'll wait." I looked down at the infant.

"The longer you wait…" Hunter sighed. "The harder the decision will become. You need to decide now. Do you let it live or not?"

"No!" Fern insisted.

"But it's a baby," Lainey protested.

"Think of it as Troilus Green," Caedan suggested. "What would you do if you held his life in your hands?"

But what if it were Protogonus Blue?

"Beryl?" Hunter bent his head to look at my face. "You must decide."

The draconic opened its eyes and stared at me again.

"Beryl? What will you do?"

Beryl's story continues in

Amaranth

For more information on the Dragontek Lore series,
and other upcoming books,
visit timfrankovich.com

Joining the mailing list is the best way to stay informed,
plus you get free stories!
(including Rick's story before he arrived in Viridia!)

If you enjoyed this book, please post a review
on Amazon, B&N, Goodreads, etc.
There's no better way to spread the word.

Author's Notes & Acknowledgements

The Dragontek Lore series is like nothing I've ever written in my life... except maybe some stuff I wrote in elementary school. I've said before that I'm writing this series for the boy I was back then, riding my bike to the library and looking for things to read. I didn't want just anything, though. I wanted "cool" books - with dragons or weird technology... or both. When the idea for cybernetically-enhanced dragons popped into my head, I knew I needed to write it. Too much fun.

But as it progressed, the stories got a little deeper, exploring more... "human" things. Beryl is a young man with a young man's desires and curiosity about the world around him. I'm enjoying seeing where that takes him, and what answers he finds.

As always, I am greatly indebted to my beta readers, Stephen Tallman and Allen Perkins, who give me different perspectives and encourage me in excellence (Sorry I ran so behind on this one!). Special thanks again to the Apex Science Fiction & Fantasy Writing Group. Our weekly meetings are inspiring and motivational.

If you want to keep track of my progress on all my writing, you can connect on timfrankovich.com, my Facebook author page, Twitter, etc. But the best way, which keeps you informed and gives you exclusive previews, is to join the mailing list. Sign up on the website. (You'll get free stories too!)

Tim Frankovich has been exploring fantastic worlds since third grade, when he cut up a grocery sack and drew a Godzilla-meets-superheroes story. Since then, he's gotten a little bit better at the writing part (not so much with the drawing).

His goal as a writer is to transport readers to another world, make them care deeply about characters in dire situations, and guide them deeply into life itself.

At the moment, he is probably suitably conscious somewhere in Texas with his beloved wife, awesome four kids, and a fool of a pup named Pippin.